The Dark Mermaid

Cursed Water Series Book One

Christina L. Barr

Table of Contents

Chapter One

I was born with a serious defect. On the surface world, they call it "kindness." My father first noticed it when I was a child. When we turn thirteen, we swim out of our territory with nothing but a small blade. I watched my king's eyes dig into mine as violently as the knife that bled my arm numb. He always told me that he had a lot of faith in me. It's funny how faith only felt like heavy expectations on my tiny shoulders. And when I could feel the vibrations in the water from an oncoming threat, he made sure to leave me in the darkness, surrounded by a cloud of my blood.

I heard tales from my sisters of their glorious fights against the monsters of the deep. They only had to face one and return home with the corpse. They spoke of their fear boiling and bursting out of their hearts like a geyser rushing out uncontrollably, but they had a thirst for battle that was born as soon as they saw their vicious opponents in the water. The victory shifted their terror into a satisfying thrill, but I was not as fierce as my sisters, and I was surrounded by three fish, three times my size.

I swam up fast and avoided two of them, but the third nearly took my bloodied arm off with its sharp and jagged teeth. I did manage to stab its eye as it swam past me, which was the only easy meat to get to. The rest of its body was covered in scales as hard as stone.

Taking on all three was impossible, and my little body was pumped full of fear. The adrenaline helped me swim faster, but they were made to chase and kill. They couldn't hide their nature, and I couldn't run from mine.

When I had about a thousand feet on them, I turned around and braced myself. I had little hope in my blade, but I gripped it firmly and told myself that I could defeat those monsters if I truly believed in myself. My father would not accept me if I needed to be rescued. The rumors were that he'd rather have me dead than be a disgrace. I could not fail!

I closed my eyes and swung my blade forward. I put all my strength into that swipe, and I felt my energy leave my body and expand forward like a giant fin. I opened my eyes just in time to see their bodies disintegrate into ash and glitter from the fading light that I somehow produced.

I was too stunned to move for a great while. I never had such an incredible power on my own, so I looked at the blue and red crystals embedded in the golden blade. It was an ancient weapon forged by my ancestors, but I had no idea that it could do so much damage. My sisters never mentioned it, and I'm certain they would have boasted about their exploits.

Even though I had rightly fought for my survival and won, I was rattled. I was certain that I could do it again—in extreme circumstances—but I wasn't changed like my sisters. They were reborn as warriors, and I still felt like a child. Worst of all, I didn't have any remains. I would have to find another creature to kill, but I needed to tend to my wounds.

I returned home, struggling not to break down from fear of what my father would do to me. When I entered the walls of our crystal palace, my people were my enemy. They once revered me like a princess, and now they sneered at my repulsive presence. I could feel their eyes whispering tales of my cowardice, and they were not as subtle as they believed. And when I entered my father's throne room, so I could properly explain, I was met with his trident pinning my arm against the wall.

I couldn't afford to lose any more blood, and he had severely cut me again. I tried pulling the trident away, but I couldn't even get it to budge. I took my eyes off my bloodied arm, and by the time I looked up, his coal eyes were peering into mine. "Father—"

"Silence!" His hand clasped tightly around my neck. "Do you think I'll grant mercy to a failure? You are my blood, and you've disgraced me!" It was insane to me at the time, but beyond the intensity of his rage, I remember sensing that my failure wounded him.

I whimpered as he freed me from the trident's grasp. His disappointment overwhelmed me with unbearable guilt. The only reason it didn't crush me was that I saw my demise reflected in the golden trident my father raised to strike me down. "Do you have any last words?"

"I did kill!"

"Then where is the body?" He glared with a hatred I thought he only reserved for his enemies. I didn't understand how his disappointment could transform into such violence. When I was smaller, he would often tell me that I was his favorite. What good did his favor do?

I held up the blade that he had given me, and out of my desperation, I was able to make it glow a radiant blue with speckles of golden dust. "I used this blade to kill them, Father. Their bodies were completely blown apart. I swear!"

His eyes moved to the blade. Then, he looked at me in awe. "You do hold the power." He smiled and cradled my face. "You are my true successor."

My sisters gathered around. They were mildly jealous before. They would have ripped the flesh from my bones if not for their fear of our father.

My father was never affectionate toward me, but he'd always gaze upon me with a curious eye. When I trained with my sisters, I thought he was testing me and assessing my potential as a warrior. It was no secret that he wanted a son, but Fate gave him six daughters instead. He made us twice as fierce to make up the difference. I couldn't have known that he was expecting me to have such great power. "I want to see what you can do."

"Sire." One of his warriors came into the throne room and bowed. "Humans are sailing in our waters. What are your orders?"

He looked down at me and smirked. "My daughters and I will handle this ourselves."

My sisters all cheered. They apparently had enchanting voices, but I had never heard them, nor had I ever opened my mouth to speak. I suspected that I shared a similar gift, but I didn't want to use my voice to lead unsuspecting sailors to their deaths.

"Keep the blade," my father instructed. "I want to see you in action."

I looked at the dagger in my hands. I heard such terrible things about the humans. Everything they touched, they laid waste to.

Father said we had to kill humans to keep their dark nature from destroying us, but I didn't see how we could be any better than them. I didn't know if my life served any purpose beyond hunting and defending my home.

"Come, my children."

He must have been in a good mood because he let my eldest sister bind my wounds before we followed him into battle. Each stroke of my tail made my heart pound faster. I had never been to the surface before. My sisters told me that humans didn't have tails. They had legs to stand upon, and they loved to watch them run for their lives as they tried to save their ships from sinking. It was one of their favorite games.

The water illuminated the higher we rose. I saw something large and round far up into the sky, but it glowed and brightened up the world. And when I breached the surface, the light gently rested on my skin as I whipped my hair back.

There were hundreds—thousands—of lights far up into the sky, and the biggest one radiated a foggy white. I took in air, and it filled my lungs with an odd sensation. I wanted to finally hear my own voice, but for some reason, I was afraid to speak.

"Scout the area," my father encouraged. My sisters waded just a few feet below the surface and waited for my report.

I gulped and slowly swam to a boat not too far away. I had seen ships before, but they were sunken treasures abandoned by humans and eroded over time. I don't know why the mystery of humans intrigued me so much. I heard they were an evil menace that threatened our way of life. I had also heard they were cowardly weaklings that we could easily destroy. I didn't know how to imagine weaklings with such power. Some of the stories must have been false or highly exaggerated.

But when I finally snuck close enough to see the faces of the terrible creatures, I saw they were just like us.

A boy was running along the deck with some sort of white animal. His smile was infectious. He was making noises with his mouth that I didn't quite understand. Spoken words were very different than thought. There were also other sounds coming from some sort of box that an older human male controlled. He sat beside a beautiful woman with golden hair.

The sounds coming from the box were magical, like the melody that the whales would sing to each other, except there were so many different noises to make it complete. It was fast, and his human feet moved along with it. It was incredibly strange but so intriguing. The boy could have been from my world if he weren't having the time of his life on those legs. I moved my tail along with the sounds, but it wasn't the same as his clumsy and wonderful feet.

When the boy smiled, the right side of his mouth curved just a little higher than the left, and it made his eyes shrink, just a smidgen. They were as vibrant as the blue lights flickering in the sky. His short but bountiful hair bounced with the rhythm of his body, and even though it was as dark as the deepest of the ocean's depths, the white glow of the night reflected onto his locks so brilliantly, I wouldn't have questioned if he held some sort of power over the night sky. His skin wasn't too different than mine, but he had a glow that made him look as if life itself had kissed him. I know this sounds silly, but I found myself wishing that I could keep him as a treasure to gaze upon.

He had a pretty face. His arms were frail and easily breakable, but threats could come from even the tiniest of creatures, so I closed my eyes and listened to his thoughts. I tried to connect his mind to the words he was speaking, and it wasn't long before I could understand his conversation.

"It's good to know that those expensive hip-hop lessons haven't paid off," the older man teased.

He stumbled from the insult, and his bushy brows furrowed against his sparkling eyes. "Aw, I'm not that bad," the boy said.

"I think he's wonderful," the woman encouraged. "But stop dancing around on the boat. You're gonna make the whole thing tip over."

"How old do you think I am? Five? I can't tip over this huge thing."

"Maybe," the man said. "We're in the Bermuda Triangle. All sorts of weird things happen here."

The boy rolled his eyes. "Those things aren't true."

"We're here to explore the mysteries of the Atlantic."

"Really? Because I thought we were sailing to Puerto Rico, so Mom could buy shoes."

"And other things," she laughed. "You'll love Puerto Rico. It's gorgeous. You might even meet a little summer girlfriend."

"What makes you think I don't already have a girlfriend?" he teased with a dashing smile.

"You better not!" She got up from the comfort of her husband to tackle her son. He fought her off viciously, but he was laughing as if he enjoyed it. It was odd. I had never seen a family interact in such a way. A family was supposed to be a pack you could hunt with. They were supposed to look out for you while you slept, and you did the same for them when they needed to rest. What the humans were doing was completely different than anything I had ever experienced. They were enjoying each other's company. They were…happy? I think that's the word I'm looking for.

"What are you doing?" My father's voice rang in my head. He wouldn't understand what I was seeing. I hardly did, but I yearned for it so badly. Why couldn't he hold me in his arms like the human father did to his son? The boy didn't fear his father as I did. He would probably never intentionally hurt him, yet I still ached from the wounds my father inflicted upon me. Any lessons the boy learned were probably for his benefit, and not because of some war that I didn't understand.

"I'm observing."

"You've done enough observing," he said. "It's time we attack."

"No!" Out of desperation, my words entered through my mind and out of my mouth. My voice was still weak, but I had finally heard it, and I thought it was beautiful.

"Did you hear that?" the boy asked.

"Ian, don't!"

He didn't listen and ran over to the edge of the boat. I quickly dunked under the water to escape his eyes, but I felt like such a fool. It was forbidden for humans to know of our existence. Anyone who saw us had to die.

I thought I had gone down far enough, but I felt a light shine on me. "Who's there?"

I heard him speak to me, and I was at a loss for ideas. If only I could have convinced him that I was a human! It was either that, or I had to make him and his parents leave immediately. I slowly breached the surface so he could see my face.

There was a slight pause as he laid eyes on me for the first time. My sisters enchanted humans with their beauty before they dragged them into the ocean's dark waters to drown. Perhaps I was doing that to Ian. I should have grabbed him by the back of the neck to finish him off. That was our way.

"You're beautiful…" he mumbled very quietly, but in complete awe. I suppose I was right about him being enchanted.

But—for some mysterious reason—I found that I felt the same. My world was incredibly vast. It didn't matter how far I ventured out in the water; there was always so much more to explore. Suddenly, my world was rapidly shrinking until it was small enough to fit into a speck of light inside his eyes. "Ian…" My voice wasn't strong enough. I tried reaching out to him through my mind, but he wasn't ready to listen. "You have to—"

"How did you get out here? Are you hurt?"

I shook my head, hoping that was a sufficient answer.

"Mom! Dad!" he called.

"No." My protest was only a whisper. "They can't see—"

"Where did you come from?" his mother asked in a panic.

"Give me your hand." His father got on his stomach to reach me better. He didn't know me. He should have assumed I was dangerous. In my world, we didn't tolerate any threats. He was probably three times my age, so how could he have lived for so long being that naïve?

I wanted to know why they were being such fools, but I felt the vibrations in the water from my family fast approaching. "I'm sorry…" I dove back into the water and waited for the worst to be over.

They called out to me, and I knew that if I didn't come back up, they would dive back in to get me. They must have at least feared sharks. It boggled my mind as to why they would risk their lives for mine.

I heard Ian's parents scream, and then, there was a splash in the water. I backed away and prepared to strike them—if I needed to—but it was young Ian who bravely came to my rescue. And when he saw that I did not need to be saved, he yelled something in the water and lost his air.

Was he afraid of what I was? Did I disgust him? I wasn't sure. All I sensed from him was confusion at the herd of mermaids coming to rip him into pieces. His father dove into the water next. I knew my sisters would attack him. We always tackled the biggest prey first.

I'm not sure why I did what I did, even to this day, but I grabbed Ian by his waist and swam as fast as I could. He reached out to his father, but I couldn't stop if I was going to save Ian.

He screamed, and I knew he would not have enough breath to survive the journey to safety. I had no choice and pressed my lips against his. His eyes bucked, but he soon relaxed enough to close them, and he allowed me to breathe life into his weak and pitiful body.

Through that moment, his mind was open to me. I could feel his desperation to be reunited with his father and mother. What he felt for them was deeper than anything I had experienced my entire life. His father wanted to protect him because he loved his son, and he loved his son because he was his. There was nothing more to it than that. It was their bond of blood and a covenant they forged together from the first time his father held his newborn son in his arms. I didn't understand how something so simple could be so definite and infinite. My father only wanted to protect his legacy. If it weren't for my strange power, I would be dead, and he would have been glad to be rid of his weakling daughter.

I wanted to leave. I wanted to go with Ian and be with his family. If all the humans loved like he did, then that's what I wanted to experience. If only I were born into their world…if only I had a pair of legs to stand upon—to dance! What a glorious life I would have.

Ian tried to swim back to his father, but my sisters already grabbed him, and they used daggers to slash him apart. I grabbed Ian to keep him from leaving, and we were compelled to watch as his father's flesh was ripped into pieces.

My eldest sister jumped into the air and over the boat, returning with Ian's frightened mother in her arms. Ian's struggle to get away from me intensified, but I held him tighter. I was much stronger than him, and there was no escaping their fate.

My father enjoyed watching his daughters kill. It made him proud to know he had raised such ruthless warriors. But he couldn't rest while his daughters did all the work. He was also a warrior, and he needed to destroy to feel powerful. "Stand aside."

My sisters quickly separated and waited with glee. My father was king because he could control the most powerful of weapons that my ancestors left for us: a trident. He didn't use its powers too often. He much preferred to kill with his bare hands. But when he outstretched his hand toward his victim and summoned the might of the trident, it was a glorious sight to behold.

Ian's mother began to swim toward her son, and he reached out his hands for her. But they were too far apart to ever touch again, even after she exploded in golden and red streams of light.

His father was a bloodied corpse. His mother was eradicated from existence. Only Ian was left, and I had a serious choice to make. I could feel his broken mind. His tears were lost in the immensity of the ocean. He was screaming, so he was surely about to suffocate. It would have been a service to put him out of his misery. He couldn't take care of himself. His mother and father were his entire world. It was only right to let him die like all the other humans my family had destroyed.

I still don't understand why I swam away. I even rose to the surface for a jump, so Ian could catch a breath.

"What are you doing?" my father yelled. "Kill him."

His furious command echoed in my head. When and if I returned home, he was probably going to kill me. My sisters chased me for a good while, but they eventually let up when I started approaching the shore.

I found a rock large enough to place Ian on. Someone was sure to find him. I only hoped he could salvage what was left of his life and find people who loved him as much as his mother and father did.

"Ian?" The dawn was beginning to break. I didn't want him to become crispy in the sun, but I couldn't stay with him. "Ian?" I shook him, but he would not open his eyes.

I pressed my ear against his chest. His heart was still beating. "I think you'll be alright, Ian."

I brushed some hair off his face. Ian certainly was a handsome creature. I was desperate for him to open his eyes, and I think it was more than wanting a mental memory of his sea glass gems. I saw that my fingers were trembling as I stroked his cheek, and I realized that if he never opened them again, I would be lost without a world. His heart was pulling tightly onto mine, and I was being ripped into pieces. "Please, be alright."

I pressed my forehead against his and looked inside Ian's mind again. He was at peace in his mother's arms as she hummed a pretty melody. She rocked back and forth while he drifted between consciousness. The sun lit the world in its gold and warm embrace, and the beams of light poured into his eyes every time he was close to finally resting them. I think he was in his home, surrounded by trinkets he had grown attached to, but none of it was as fulfilling as his mother's touch.

I didn't understand how he could retreat to a peaceful place after witnessing such horrific deaths, but I grew envious of him. If I were torn apart in my trial by those monsters, where would I go in my final moments? There wasn't a hug or a tender kiss from my kin to draw from, and even though I was accustomed to not having affection or admiration, I was suddenly aware of how awful that was.

I was desperate to have what he had lost, and I was aching from the fact that I had taken away the people he loved. It was selfish of me, but I retreated into Ian's memory to feel the comfort that we both desperately needed. I could hear his mother's soothing voice just as clearly as I heard my father commanding me to slaughter Ian. As I watched her holding her baby boy, I felt her intentions of protecting him. I could feel the love that he felt, and in a few seconds, her lovely song was on my lips.

He began to open his eyes, and I stayed long enough for a swift peek. I knew that I'd never be able to keep him for myself, but I'd never forget his mystifying eyes.

"Wait!"

I couldn't. I jumped back in the water and swam home to beg for forgiveness. I couldn't stay with the humans as long as I wasn't one of them. It was foolish to think differently, even for one second.

I was hoping my father possessed even one ounce of love and compassion that Ian's parents had for him. If he did, I had the smallest bit of hope that I would survive. I swam to where I believed my home was, but I didn't see the crystal walls or my wicked sisters waiting to judge me.

"You won't find Atlantis," my father said from behind. "It's hidden from outsiders."

I was too frightened to face him, but I needed to. "Father—"

As soon as I tried to turn my head, it snapped back from the force of his blow to my face. "You let one of them go."

"I'm sorry! He was only a boy."

"He's a human," he seethed. "He's a filthy, disgusting human. Human explorers killed your mother. Did you know that?" He never spoke of my mother. How was I supposed to know?

"No." I held my cheek and struggled not to sob from the pain. My father was large in stature and very muscular. He didn't need to hit me that hard to get his message across. I could taste blood in my mouth.

"He'll tell others of our existence. More humans will come. They'll kill us, and we'll kill them. They won't be satisfied until blood fills our waters, and I won't be satisfied until their cities are ruins at the bottom of the ocean. There will be no peace." My father was masking his excitement, but I could see the intention in his mind. He wanted the end of humanity, and it didn't matter how many of us had to die in the process.

I had to stop it. "No one will believe him, Father."

"Where is the dagger?"

I clenched my fingers on instinct, and my eyes bucked. I knew I had it when the attack started. I didn't remember dropping it in the water, but I hadn't held it for a while. "I must have dropped it on the rock where I left him. I'm sorry. I'll bring it back here and—"

"You're not welcome back unless that boy is dead." He yanked my hair and pulled me close to his face, so I could see his dark eyes. "I want that dagger to slit his throat and his heart in your hand. Do you understand?"

My family was harsh, but they were all I had. He couldn't expect me to live on my own in the ocean. There was no crueler place in nature. Practically everything ate each other to survive. Safe territory was hard to come by, and it was only safe until something came along to kill you for it. Sharks and giant octopuses were the least of my worries. Other creatures like me were much more dangerous and even stronger. "Father, please—"

"You are no daughter of mine." He threw me away in repugnance. "I am incapable of breeding weakness. You will never be one of us until you destroy that boy."

I was literally shaking, even though I consciously tried to steady myself. It was disgraceful to be fearful of anything, but being alone in an endless world of predators was a death sentence. I wasn't sure if I had anything to live for, but I knew that I wanted to live long enough to find a reason. "There has to be another way, Father. Please!"

"You would forsake your honor and your people over the life of a human boy?" Rage flashed in his eyes, and his trident pulsed with power like the jolt from an eel. The spark frayed my tail, and I whimpered. Every bit of pride he held for me deteriorated like a meal inside a beast's belly. "Has he infected you with his weakness?"

"No, but…" The image of Ian's eyes opening as I sang to him completely overtook my mind. I tried to suppress it. I didn't want my father to experience the intensity of my memory, but it poured out of me. Ian was groggy and terrified. His world had been crushed. The love that I felt in his heart should have been replaced with a need for righteous vengeance. He inhaled from the shock of seeing my face, but the hate never flooded in. Instead, an exhale of relief and awe followed, as if being with me needed no explanation. We were together, as we were meant to be.

I know that I left as soon as I could clearly see his eyes, but I remembered seeing my reflection inside of them. I think I saw a different mermaid than I had ever seen before. Perhaps we were always the same, and I was only beginning to wake up to the truth that she knew her entire life.

I was living in a nightmare, and I wanted to be free.

I had offended my father too greatly to be allowed to live. He thought too little of me to be disappointed. Eradicating me was a matter of propriety. He gripped his trident, and its power rippled toward me. I raised my hands instinctively. The little hairs on my arms began to singe, but before I could burst into dust, I felt my skin beginning to harden. I had closed my eyes, but it felt so odd that I looked to see my skin darkening. I had heard that my father turned an enemy to stone once. I was certain he was doing the same to me, but he seemed startled once he noticed that I was changing.

I might have been mistaken. The light from the trident skewed my vision, and your mind plays tricks when you're certainly about to die. I might not have been sure about what I saw, but my father did see something that made him withdraw his attack.

"Your sisters are weak. You're strong enough to be my heir. I have no respect for you, but I do value your potential." Even admitting that terrible compliment was difficult for him. "You have until the beginning of your seventeenth year."

"To do what?"

"To regain your honor and kill that boy."

My hands returned to their normal color and softness, but I was aching internally. "What if I can't find the same boy? Can it be another?"

"No. It must be him." His commandment rang through me like the crunch of a skull being crushed between his fingers. "It's either him or I kill you both."

And once again, he left me. I had no friends, no family, no resources, and no weapons. I heard the sounds of whales singing in the distance, and I could feel other vibrations in the water. There was danger surrounding me for miles, and I wouldn't have the protection of my family or my father's subordinates.

I didn't have a choice. I returned to where I had left Ian, but he was already gone. I probably could have deceived my father, if I had found the blade, but it was missing as well. I swam around the shore, but he was nowhere to be found. I couldn't blame Ian if he never returned to the water, but if I couldn't find him, I would never be able to return home, the humans would bring war to us, and we would bring hell to them.

"I'll find you," I said to Ian, wherever he was. "I don't care what I have to do, but I swear that I will."

And that's how my story began. I showed mercy to a human boy who should have died with his parents. His life meant nothing compared to the safety of our worlds. I had no choice but to search the ends of the earth until I found him. But finding him wouldn't prove to be the most difficult matter. The man I swore to kill, also became the man that I loved.

Regardless, he still had to die.

Chapter Two

There were days when I could not afford to sleep. Every time I closed my eyes, I felt the monsters in my nightmares shaking my world in a code that prophesied my death.

Magical. Is that what you humans believe the ocean is? Without the magical seal of protection hiding me from creatures, I had to worry about being swallowed by whales. If it weren't for their song being loud enough to shake my bones, I would have been digested in my first week of exile.

My paranoia kept me alive, but unfortunately, not in the best of conditions. I would hide in crevices and dark caverns to keep myself hidden, but it was hard to keep something like that to myself. There were many times when I came to rest and found a vicious animal waiting for me. It was difficult facing even a smaller predator without a good weapon. I had to grab my enemies and slam them against the rocks until they were mushed up and unmoving. I would pull their teeth and bones from their mangled bodies and construct my own set of claws to strap around my hands.

My weapon served me well for a while. The occasional bottom dweller and I got into a couple of scrapes, but I would usually emerge victorious with a few broken spikes to fix. I would replace them with new fish bones, teeth, and so on. I got nicked and bitten a few times. Mermaids heal fast, but there were times when my blood would attract the scent of bigger predators, and I would have to fight for my life once more.

I had an unpleasant altercation with an eighteen-foot shark. It snuck up on me while I was sleeping, and I narrowly dodged before my head was torn off. The shark circled around to come at me again, but I dove under it and stabbed the shark with my claws. It wiggled to get free of me, and its strength proved too ferocious against my worn condition. It gave up its fight, but it also left with my weapon still lodged inside of it. Perhaps I should have gone after it while it was wounded, but I felt like I should be grateful to be alive.

I learned not to sleep much after that. It wasn't safe to bother without a pack. Any creatures that would have been friendly enough to take me in as their own were simply too weak to be of any value. I went an entire week, only sleeping in short doses.

Out of desperation, I swam to the surface. I hadn't noticed that any sharks or octopuses dwelled in that area, so I thought I would be safe. I could certainly fight a dolphin if I needed to. There was a contraption floating in the water with a light circling at the top. It was a huge risk of exposure, but I was too tired not to try something. I rested my eyes, and no one bothered me for a couple of hours. It was the longest and most peaceful sleep I had in days. Eventually, I felt the waves tossing me in an unnatural way.

I opened my eyes, and I saw a boat headed toward me with a light shining directly on my face. A man was shouting at me. I couldn't make his words out, but I think he was concerned for my safety. He must have thought I was a human abandoned to die after a shipwreck.

I almost wanted to let him discover me. I didn't care about exposing my world. My father despised the humans for what they were capable of—my mother suffered their wrath—but I had only personally experienced pain from my family and the ocean. I was beginning to break, and I wouldn't be able to defend myself once I was in pieces.

I even waved to the silhouette of the sailor, so they would see me and know that I meant no harm. But when I thought deeper, I wondered what would happen after they took me. Would they kill me? Would they study me? Would they put me on display? Even those things seemed worth taking a risk for. I could talk my way out of danger. We were supposed to be enchanting to the humans. I could fight my way out if I needed to.

Then, I was overwhelmed with the thought of what would happen to humanity if they hunted for other mermaids. What if they found one that wasn't like me? My father would see any exploration as a declaration of war. He would find Ian. Then, he would find me.

There was no escape, not even on the surface world. For that reason, I dove back into the darkness.

I began sleeping in shallower waters where the weaker fish dwelled, and I got away with that for a long time. I thought I was well hidden amongst red coral reefs, but one night, I was awakened by the swift jerk of my tail being pulled down into darkness. I struggled to reach up, but the more I tugged away from the suction cups that yanked my tail and arms, the stronger the creature became. It was such a soft animal, but its tentacles were surrounded by pure muscle that was nearly impossible to escape, and its body was much larger than mine.

It was pulling me down very quickly. I should have known from its strength that it lived far deeper than where I usually liked to hide. I could feel the tip of my tail beginning to stroke its beak. I raised it closer to my chest to avoid the venom, but it grabbed me tighter and nipped me a few times. My tail was beginning to numb, and I was already exhausted from the conditions of my exile.

Mermaids were the fiercest warriors of the seas, and we were rarely alone and without a weapon. I was not easy prey, but I was worth the fight to most. But I wouldn't allow myself to be so easily destroyed. I was determined to regain my honor and return to Atlantis!

I began to peel each sucker off my skin, one at a time. They left abrasions on my flesh, and the creature's hooks tore me open. I had to fight through the pain, the blood, and the paralyzing toxin that was trying to take over my body. My tail could hardly move, but my arms were surging with adrenaline, and I wanted to live.

I managed to rip the creature off me, and to my surprise, it gave up. I was grateful that I had a moment to rest. But once I noticed where it had dragged me, I questioned if it was acting of its own accord.

I never knew where the horrid Sea Witch dwelled. I only knew that it was forbidden to ever see or speak to her. Her home was said to be built with the bones of creatures it had slain, including other merpeople. My sisters would tell stories about the Sea Witch deep into the night and watch me quiver in fear. They said she would eat her own kind and had tricked many into making deals that cost them their lives.

I had heard less dramatic stories from my father. He said that she was a fierce fighter who was capable of destroying most of our strongest warriors. He told me she was a hideous thing that was apart from any race and had no loyalties. He was never trying to scare me. Fear was weakness to him. I think he might have respected the Sea Witch, but he did hate her. Perhaps that's the true reason why it was forbidden: Father didn't want to be annoyed.

But I was an outcast. If I wanted to venture into the Sea Witch's lair, I should have been able to. I had no inkling why I was even considering it. I didn't want my bones to end up on her wall, but any enemy of my father was worth considering to be my friend.

I touched a few of the remains engraved in the cavern. I shouldn't have gone any further, but I felt the vibrations of an oncoming threat. Something was headed toward me, and I was without a weapon to properly fight it off.

"Drifting in the entryway is rude." I felt her inside my head. There was something very threatening about her essence, but there was also something a little familiar about her, and I didn't believe she was going to hurt me.

I braced myself and began to swim inside. The cavern was lit by strange smokes that were orange, purple, and red, rising from stone cauldrons. I could see her dark eyes glistening from a hole in the cavern wall.

"You're the one I've been warned about as a child?"

"You are a child." Her tentacles emerged from the darkness— all eight of them—and her skinny and frail arms shook as she pushed the rest of her body out. She had nothing but saggy skin on top of bones. Her hair was whited out, long, and tangled. Her fingertips were entirely made from sharp bone. The Sea Witch's teeth were long, thin, and pointed like a fangtooth. The skin on her body was faded and decaying in some spots, to the point where her chest plate was nearly exposed. She certainly wasn't the great warrior I expected her to be.

"Did you send that monster after me?"

"You have an interesting choice of words. That was hardly a monster compared to what you see before you." As she circled around me, I felt a strange energy that was unlike anything I had ever felt before. My father possessed powerful magic—I suppose I did too—but she was special. I could feel the light being sucked out of the cavern, even though it hadn't become any dimmer to my eyes. She might not have been physically strong, but she certainly had power.

"Why did you want me here? Were you trying to regain your honor? Were you seeking revenge? Do you still hate my father?"

She surprised me with how quickly she swam in my face and hissed through her thin fangs. "I will always despise your father, but he has nothing to do with why I have summoned you. I called you for one thing, and one thing only."

I was concerned with my safety—not afraid—but I felt like I needed to know. "And what is that?"

"Your blood." Her long and wrinkly fingers stroked my arm desperately. I noticed a curious symbol on her wrist, a black crescent moon. "I need it for a spell."

I pulled my hand away from her, but not without being marked by her bony fingers. She nearly drew blood. "What sort of spell?"

"One that will restore me."

"Into what?" I asked with a cocked brow.

"A greater me." She hung her head low and turned from me, as she touched pieces of her body that were nearly fading away. "I will be as I once was…" She spoke with such romantics; I wondered if such a creature could truly love another being, or if all her affections were reserved for herself.

I didn't mean to chuckle. Perhaps I was my father's child after all. "You were hoping that wretched monster would be able to kill me and bring my mangled body straight into your den? You meant to spill my blood for soft and glowing skin?"

"Something like that." She sneered at me.

"It was a nice try, but I'm not weak. I'm tired of being underestimated!"

"You certainly do look tired, my dear." She attempted to touch the rings under my eyes, but I backed away. That made her chuckle. "You may be strong, but you are not invincible." She almost seemed concerned for me, but why wouldn't she be? I was a valuable bag of blood magic.

"What if you didn't have to steal my blood?"

Her dead eyes gained a bit of a spark in them. "Are you offering?"

"I have a few conditions." Making a deal with the Sea Witch was dangerous, but how could it have been any more dangerous than the life I was already living? Among cauldrons and the remains of those she destroyed were also weapons scattered about. Some were cast aside, but others were put on display. I couldn't tell if any of them contained magic, but I didn't know there was anything special about the dagger. "I need a powerful weapon."

"That should be simple enough." The Sea Witch gazed upon me intensely. Then she smiled giddily and stroked my hair with her bony fingers. I questioned if she was only after my blood.

"I also want you to promise me safety." Half of me felt weak for asking, but even kings made alliances.

"I will do both." It was strange how the Sea Witch was suddenly drawn to me. I felt her pulling on my magic. It wasn't apparent that I had so much to give until someone else wanted to take it from me.

"I've always been curious about you." I pulled my hair away from her grasp and backed away. "Why were you banished from Atlantis?"

She smiled euphorically. I could still feel her yanking on me and tangling my insides. I shuddered at the thought of what she might be like with my blood flowing inside of her. "I used to be like you."

It took me a moment to grasp what she meant. "A mermaid?" She certainly didn't look anything like me or anything I could possibly become.

"Of sorts." She floated away with her head lowered in shame of the ugliness that had befallen her. "Before you were born, there were several breeds of our kind. Two lived in this area. There was the kind that favored humans more closely—the sort you descend from—and the kind that are usually stronger and more vicious."

"I didn't know this." But I was very studious. I studied my history to avoid my sisters' insatiable appetite for violence. I naively believed my father would give me a pass if I could prove myself in other ways. My father must have had a good reason to block out the truth. "What happened?"

"I was the greatest sorceress in all the land. Your father offered me a bargain if I would betray my race and fight for him."

"Why would you do that?"

"He promised me power and safety…among other things."

I never thought of my father as a liar before, but I felt like a fool for ever believing a word he said. "And then what happened?"

The Sea Witch stretched out her hands toward the cauldrons, and the smoke rising out of them came gushing at us. In the smoke, I could see shadows of warriors, all coming together to fight an army as she described. The ones I recognized as my people had thousands more troops, but they were ripped apart by their enemies. The number of troops disintegrated as quickly as the wind could change. Just when it seemed like the battle was over, the strange shadows continued with the Sea Witch's narration.

"I called upon my dark magic to defend your people. It was enough power to destroy most of your father's enemies, but it had a great toll on me." She swept her hand away, and the smoke dissipated. "Magic always comes with a price, and dark magic has the highest cost. Your father cast me out and stole most of my valuable treasures."

I assumed something as powerful as she possessed some sort of discernment. I could hardly feel sympathy for her. "You were a fool to ever believe my father would honor your agreement."

"We had a bit of a blood oath, he and I. One should never go back on a blood oath. It will cost him his life and his power…one day."

"And why didn't you take it then? Were you not more powerful than him?"

"Not after I gave him his precious trident. It used to belong to my people. Without it, they were easy for your father and me."

"And why have you waited all this time for revenge? Was there no other way you could seek it?"

She laughed at my stupidity. "What has your father taught you about magic?"

"Nothing." I looked at my hands and remembered how exhilarating and frightening it was to have my power flowing through my body and transferring through the blade. "As soon as he discovered that I had any to wield, he banished me."

"Why did he banish you?"

I wasn't sure if telling her the truth was going to gain me trouble from her, but I wanted her to be honest with me. I didn't want her to figure out the truth on her own, and I had a feeling that she would. "I made a mistake. I showed mercy to a human boy, and I saved his life."

"And that made your king exile his greatest source of magic?" She rolled her eyes and scoffed. "That was quite foolish of him."

I was baffled. I knew that my father was excited about my power, but to say that I was his greatest source of magic was unbelievable. "I also left a dagger that possessed magic with a human. It could threaten the existence of us all. He said he wouldn't let me return home until the human was dead, and if I didn't kill him, he'd destroy us both. He thinks I'm too weak. He was ashamed of me."

"Weapons aren't magical themselves. If a weapon gives off any magic, it's because it has traces of magic from its previous owner. That's why the trident is so powerful. My people used it for centuries before your father's greedy hands took it."

"And what happens if it's in the hands of someone without magic?"

"Nothing. If he tries to prove our existence with the dagger, he'll be seen as insane by his own people."

I had been banished for nearly a year. If the dagger posed no threat to our race, then I was punished for a terrible misunderstanding. "Do you think my father knows this?"

She shook her head. "I fought for him, but I didn't give him all of my knowledge. He's a novice compared to how my power used to be."

"And why has it dampened?"

"You ask many questions—"

"And you want something from me. Consider your answers to be part of the payment."

She narrowed her dark eyes in on me. I thought she was going to strike me with her tensing, sharp fingers, but she grinned instead. "Females and males can both possess magic, but it's usually more potent in females. Magic is energy. It can't be destroyed, and it's rarely created. It can be held in a place or an item, but it can also transfer from one host to another. When we have children, our magic is usually dispersed to them."

I knew my expression of shock must have come off as rude, but she didn't look like any sort of mother I could imagine. "You had children and became exceptionally weaker?"

"Not exceptionally, but enough. The magic I passed on mixed in with your father's and created what would have been very powerful offspring."

Again, my eyes widened, and I was stammering for words. "You and my father...?"

"I said we had a blood oath. No oath is greater than a mating ritual." Whatever she had with my father must have been intense and passionate. She hugged her body and smiled as if she could still feel his touch on her skin. "He promised that I would be his queen and rule by his side."

"And he went back on his word once he saw you this way?" It was horrible that my father betrayed her, but I could understand. She was quite repulsive.

"I hadn't deformed yet. What truly made him betray me was when he felt his magic weaken." She was practically hissing as her rage overtook her. "Parenthood is a sacrifice, and he was too selfish for it. He wanted his power back, along with mine."

"And how did he regain his magic?"

She grabbed my face by my chin and began to stroke it softly. I think she was analyzing me. She needed to know if I was ready to hear such a horrible truth. Ultimately, she decided that she was too cruel to care. "By destroying all of our eggs before they hatched."

I gasped and covered my mouth. I knew my father was a monster, but he was a proud and fair king to most. Even though I knew what he had done to me, I couldn't imagine it. I thought his desire for my redemption was a sign. I wanted to believe he was capable of humanity's type of love.

"He absorbed what our magic would have produced and became more powerful than me."

My father cared for my sisters and me, but he cared for his kingdom and his legacy more. I could, unfortunately, believe her words. "And then what happened?"

"I tried to seek my revenge, but I fought a losing battle. I survived, but I was banished. Your father took your inferior mother as his queen."

I almost didn't want to hear any more. My mother looked much like my oldest sister. She had long, golden hair, and she always smiled. She was curious. She liked to swim up to the surface world and listen to the songs of the sailors. I was told she had one of the most wonderful voices in the world. I was looking forward to the time when I was old enough to travel with her to the surface and sing. "I remember that she was affectionate toward my sisters and me."

"She possessed the ability to control magic, but like most mermaids, she had to siphon it from a source, just as your father does with the trident. She was my protégé, so I gifted a golden shell for her to draw from. It was the least I could do for the woman who was supposed to watch after me while I cared for my eggs. I should have noticed that your father was eyeing her. I doubt if he was ever faithful to me."

I wished I could have refuted any part of her story, but I could believe that my father would abandon the Sea Witch for someone younger and prettier. He always told me how much prettier I was than my sisters. I always thought my father was vain, and that's why I believed he cared for me the most and caused my sisters to despise me. "You must hate me for what he's done to you."

"I never hate a good proposition." I had lowered my head in guilt, but she wrapped her bony arms around me and spoke in my ear. "I want your blood."

I dove under her embrace and swam away before she could take a bite out of my neck, but that angered her. "His magic flows through your veins, which means that mine does as well!"

I sensed that she wouldn't stop until she had my blood. My best option was to kill her. If I were armed, I would have stood a better chance, but I could feel her just as she felt me. Inside of her was a pit of darkness with something terrible waiting to pull me down into her depths. Making her my ally would have started my descent, but becoming her enemy now would have been the end of me.

"Will I still have magic?" I hadn't made up my mind on whether or not magic was a good thing. I might have owed her some of my power, but some of it was passed down rightfully through my mother and father. I deserved an opportunity to figure it out.

"Give what you can spare, girl. I know you have plenty."

I looked at my hands. They were in rough condition. I hadn't healed from the attack yet, and a lack of food depleted my strength. I thought the Sea Witch was skin and bones, but after another month or so alone in the waters, I wouldn't have been much better off. "What do you need me to do?"

"I can sink my teeth into you—"

"I'd rather you not." I backed away before she could bite me. I didn't know if the literal pain would have been worse than what my imagination was coming up with, but she made me a bit squeamish.

The Sea Witch stretched out her arm, and a weapon that was mounted on the wall came flying into her hand. It was a sharp disk, but the center had a handle. It was made from gold, but the round, sharp edge was clear and sparkling from the subtle lighting. "Use this."

She placed the disk in my hand. I think I could tell that there was magic inside of it—her magic—along with others. With the diamond blade, it would be a very fierce weapon indeed. "This is quite the gift."

"It's nothing compared to what you're giving to me."

She at least gave me one part of my bargain. I gritted my teeth and slit the palm of my hand. I accidentally cut deeper than I would have liked, and I hissed. "Is that enough?"

My floating blood took on a life of its own and swirled around the Sea Witch's body, along with her colored smoke. I backed away and watched, amazed as her silhouette began to transform. Her tentacles extended out straight until they became a giant tail. Her body bent back, and her sad and sagging bosoms sprang up in her armored bra. She became much taller, and her hair flowed like a magnificent mane.

When the smoke departed, a much younger-looking Sea Witch appeared in front of me. She still looked dangerous, but she was simply threatening instead of a living nightmare. She had a mermaid tail, except the scales were much harder, and she had razor-sharp fins extending from her spine to the tip of her tail. She also had fins on her arms as well. Her skin was a cool blue that glittered in certain lights, and her eyes were so radiantly blue that they glowed. Her knotted white hair transformed into sleek silver. She would never be mistaken for a human or even one of my kind, but she was gorgeous. Her body was slender, yet fit. She even looked better fed than I because her abdomen was pure perfection. I could see why my father would mate with her, even though she was so radically different.

"I believe that was enough blood." She was even kind enough to reach out and touch my bleeding hand. At first, I thought she was going to take more, but when she removed her hand, my arm was radiating warmth, and the cuts and abrasions were gone.

"Should you be using your magic? Won't it make you as you once were?"

"No. That wasn't dark magic, and I only deteriorated so badly because of my age."

"And how old are you?" She now looked much younger than my father.

"Old, and that's all you need to know." But she didn't even look that much older than my eldest sister.

"And you promised me safety. How about a protection spell? Can you give me something to cloak myself with?"

The Sea Witch was so pleased with her younger and agile body that she took it for a test along her cavern, swimming in narrow openings, twirling and circling me. "You'll be safe if you stay with me."

"With you?"

My lack of enthusiasm stopped her in her tracks. "If I need more of your blood, you can donate it. In exchange, I will teach you how to use your magic."

"You want me to be your protégé, just as my mother once was?" I was a little flattered. Perhaps I would feel closer to my mother, but I did feel uncomfortable considering that I knew of their troubled past. But I certainly wouldn't end up competing for a mate against the Sea Witch!

"What other option do you have?" She asked me sweetly, but it also felt like a threat.

I didn't want to be alone, but I mostly wanted to return home. My sisters and father were monsters, but they were my blood. We were once a strong pack. They could forgive me if I made good on my father's terms to bring Ian's heart and the blade home. "Is there a spell to make me have legs, so I can go out to the surface and walk like a human?"

"Of course," she answered cautiously. "I've been to the surface world many times in my younger days."

"Then, I accept your kind offer." As soon as I knew the spell for myself, I would go to the surface world and hunt the human that ruined my life.

"Good." She smiled. "I sense that you have the potential to greatly surpass even me in my prime."

"And is that a good thing?" I sensed that she could be the jealous type. I half suspected that she was only taking me under her tutelage as a means of seeking revenge against my parents. "You would want me to surpass you?"

Her smile increased. She didn't have those long and nasty fangs anymore, but she could still bite me in two. "Oh, it would be wonderful!"

Chapter Three

I thought my time spent with the Sea Witch would be a horrible disaster, but she proved to be a creature of her word. I was suspicious about her resolve, but she made good on her promise to keep me safe quickly by honing my skills. Every morning, I would wake up with her hovering over me with two swords in her hands. It took a while not to be startled, but I eventually grew accustomed to our tradition.

She was very strong, but not physically stronger than my father. When she slung her sword down on me, I had a chance to fight her off. While my father possessed an incredible amount of precision, the Sea Witch had tremendous speed and agility. My father's large stature meant that he was slower, so he made every blow count. He never went easy on my sisters. There were times when I caught them struggling not to sulk over their broken bones. Any blow that the Sea Witch inflicted resulted in her using magic to instantly soothe me.

I didn't get the chance to nick her too often with my blade, but after a few months, I had gotten the hang of her moves and learned to adjust accordingly. When she came in to strike me, I twirled out of the way and slashed my sword across her body.

She hissed and held her bloodied arm, but she smiled with pride. "Well done, my apprentice. I'll make a fine warrior out of you after all." She swam over to some seaweed and began wrapping up her arm to stop the bleeding.

"Why don't you ask me to help you?"

"It's important that I teach you discipline before I teach you magic. I don't need you addicted to your power. I'd hate to see you one day become what I did."

"But if my magic isn't dark, I won't become a monster. Besides, you said that your age played a part in your appearance, and I think I have a long while before I'm anywhere close to—"

"Don't be rude about a woman's age." She took my hand and placed it over the seaweed. "Magic is a lot simpler than you believe. Most of the time, it's about finding the proper motivation. It's a trick of the mind. Once you know what you want to do, you have to possess the will to bring it into existence."

"But I'm a normal mermaid. Don't I need some sort of source to draw on?"

She hesitated before giving me a tiny smirk. "You're special. I know you feel my magic inside of you. You don't possess such limitations like your mother."

I wrapped my fingers around her arm. If magic were so simple, I didn't understand why I needed a teacher or why my mother needed one either. "You're telling me that if I imagine making you better, you'll be better?"

"If it's worth sacrificing a bit of yourself."

"But you heal me all of the time. I give to you; you give to me…" I shrugged. "It seems that we've entered into a cycle."

"I'd like to think of it as our own blood oath." The Sea Witch still had much darkness in her heart. I could even feel it in her magic, but there was still kindness within her. I noticed the further I progressed in my training, the more often a glimmer of light speckled in her harsh eyes. It was satisfying having a mentor acknowledge and appreciate me, even if it came from a witch who killed my kind for frivolous vanities.

"I want to help you."

"Because of our mutually beneficial relationship?"

"No." I smiled at my teacher. We were bonding every day, and I had a trust in her that I never knew in my father. "You've been my friend and mentor. You took me in when my own family abandoned me. I am indebted to you."

"And you will not betray me like your mother and father once did?"

"Absolutely not." I was offended that she'd even ask. "You are my friend." And with barely any thought, magic radiated through my fingers and entered the Sea Witch's body.

She was amazed and ripped the seaweed from her arm. "You are a wonder and a true prodigy."

I felt a slight amount of discomfort, but I was fine. After my display of raw talent, I was confident that I would have a pair of legs on the surface very soon.

The Sea Witch later gathered her weapons to hunt. We had to eat, and she had an insatiable appetite. I wanted to put my new skills to good use, but she insisted on going herself. "Are you sure I can't go?"

"Absolutely not. You're beginning to realize your magic. You can't let it get out of hand. Your first reaction must be to fight and not to use your magic."

"Why are you so afraid of me growing powerful?"

"I'm afraid of you losing yourself."

"That's not a fear you should have." I knew she hated it when I belittled her fears, but it was hard to imagine such darkness taking over my heart. "I'm not like you or my father."

"You certainly are not. That's why you should stay and keep yourself safe." There was often a glimmer of pride in her eyes. Perhaps she wanted me as an apprentice simply because she enjoyed teaching or having a ward. Why else would she offer to teach the young daughter of the woman who stole her lover, especially when that lover slaughtered her children? "I will return with our supper."

"Please—"

"My command is final!" She was indeed kind and compassionate toward me, but she was not always able to keep her ferocity at bay. I tried not to argue with her, and I didn't want to. The only exception was my desire to explore outside of our cavern. But I knew that when her eyes glowed bright blue, and she flashed her fangs at me, it was best to let things be. "Do not test me."

I didn't understand what the Sea Witch thought she was protecting me from. I was confident that nothing would be able to withstand the wrath of both of us. We were too powerful. "Fine. I will stay behind. Again."

The Sea Witch was an interesting companion, but she couldn't always keep my attention. When she departed to hunt, I had to let my imagination go wild.

I liked to look at all the trinkets and weapons the Sea Witch collected through the years. I discovered that I was inventive, and I would dress in new fashions at any available opportunity. There were shells, metals, and nets in our cavern. I created gauntlets, necklaces, and bras for myself. I had no one to flaunt my new looks to besides the Sea Witch when she returned with our dinner. She was always blunt with her opinions, but she often enjoyed my imagination.

She observed my new apparel when we were dining on her latest catch. "It appears that you're running out of materials. You won't be able to accommodate your creativity soon."

"I remember a sunken ship with treasures on it. Perhaps I could use some of the jewels and gold to create more—"

"You are very stubborn, my young apprentice. You are determined to leave my protection, aren't you?" She was trying not to be angry, but she wasn't skilled at hiding her annoyance.

"I only wish to explore." I was getting tired of asking for permission. She was not my mother. She was the furthest thing from it. "I agreed to be your partner, but I never agreed to be your prisoner."

"If you leave without my permission, do not expect to come back."

"Why are you like this?"

"You brought great danger to me and yourself when you decided to live here. If your father finds out that you are under my care, he will bring his wrath upon us. Make no mistake about that."

"And you fear him?"

"I fear nothing, but I know my current limits. Your father possesses some of my magic and the trident. He will believe we are conspiring to destroy him, and he will strike first."

"Is that your plot with me? Are you hoping that I can somehow help you destroy my father?"

"It's a pleasurable thought, but it's not my main priority."

"Then what is? I doubt you need to keep me here. You haven't used my blood since I first arrived. There's something else."

"Remember this: I'm the one who wanted you while your father exiled you. If you want to throw away our relationship for childish explorations, then fine. You're welcome to leave."

I certainly wasn't going to threaten my safety by leaving, but I couldn't stomach being near her. I swam to my shell and pouted for the rest of the night. I thought the Sea Witch would try to brighten my spirits, but she focused her attention on adding the bones of our meal to her wall and powering up our protection spell.

I was furious that she thought it was best to ignore my budding teenage rage. Pretending that I didn't want to escape and explore certainly wasn't going to dim my addiction. If anything, she made it worse.

I was still incredibly bored, but I wasn't going to engage in a conversation with the Sea Witch. There was a jagged stone within arm's length, so I picked it up and began carving into my clam above me. I thought I was making harmless circles, but they ended up misshapen and accidentally transformed into an eye. It was odd to have just one hovering over me while I slept, so I created a pair. That seemed even odder, so I began making a nose and a mouth. I think I meant to make a girl, but the shape of the face was too masculine. It became apparent then that I was drawing Ian's face as best as I could remember. The delicate shapes of his wavy hair were impossible to perfect with a stone, but it was a handsome carving.

I sighed and wondered what Ian was doing. I hoped he wasn't trapped somewhere like I was. That would have made me even more depressed. But I wouldn't be trapped in the Sea Witch's cavern forever. I was determined to return to the surface world, one way or another.

The shark meat could last us for a long while, but the Sea Witch would grow tired of the taste within a week. I thought I could prey on her fondness for me, and I waited for an opportune moment to ask to leave the cave. That moment never quite came, but I asked regardless. I was met with the same tone as always.

The next time she went hunting, I did not bother asking for permission. I checked the cavern for traps and spells, but she foolishly did not leave any preventive measures. Either she believed I wouldn't leave, or she believed I was too much of an amateur to not get caught.

I waited for a few minutes before escaping. It was unbelievable. I expected to slam into an invisible wall or feel like I was suffocating. Her trust in me was astounding.

It had been months since I left. I remembered how terrifying it used to be on my own, but now, I was confident in my abilities to protect myself. I wouldn't be gone long, and I had my weapon attached to my side, thanks to a strap I created out of an old net.

I hardly knew what to do with my freedom. I did want to go to the pirate ship, but I didn't believe I would be able to find it and return before the Sea Witch did. My sisters and I saw it while we were out exploring when I was much smaller.

My desperation for creativity was beaten out by my curiosity about the surface world. I was dying to see how much had changed. It was possible that my father grew tired of my hesitation with Ian's life and launched a battalion of havoc on the humans. I wouldn't have been surprised at all, but a pang of worry spread across my chest.

If he did launch a war for Ian, would it be too late to redeem myself? Would I ever be able to regain my honor and return home? And if that were the case, why did it matter? He killed my half-siblings when they were only eggs to keep his power. I certainly couldn't expect his affection. Did I fear living freely in his ocean? If the Sea Witch was cautious about his power, then I should have been as well.

I returned to the rock that I placed Ian on. I didn't expect him to be there waiting for me, but it was familiar, and I was hopeful that he would return there one day. But it was well worth it, regardless, because I felt the sensation of air coming into my lungs and breathing as a human does. It was almost as exhilarating as beginning my life again, and I allowed myself to pretend—just for a moment—that I possessed the power to heal my home and live in peace.

I rested against the rock and leaned my head back. There was an orb stuck up in the sky, even brighter than the round light of the night, bathing me with warmth. I closed my eyes once I felt its piercing effects stabbing my eyes. Once they were relieved, I opened my eyes to see this light, and a new fascination captured my attention. There was a white creature circling the sky with its long arms. I was a master of the sea. Ian was a master of the land. It was strange to see a master of the sky, and I questioned if the Sea Witch had ever tried to soar through the air before.

The animal landed on my rock and gazed at me as I gazed at him. I tilted my head and smiled, and he followed my lead. I didn't want him to grow concerned for his life and poke my eye out with his yellow beak, but I was so curious about it. Then, it lowered its neck as if it expected me to touch it. Being who I was, I couldn't resist confirming how soft I believed him to be. I smiled when his smooth body grazed my skin.

"I'm glad I don't disappoint."

I drew my hand away in surprise. "I didn't expect to hear your thoughts."

"I didn't expect you to hear mine." It was strange how cognizant he was. Hearing the thoughts of a fish was more like processing their instincts. I could usually only have good conversations with my own kind.

"What's a beautiful human like you doing all the way out here? Were you shipwrecked?" I could feel that he was attracted to me, despite not looking like it.

"I'm not a human." I rolled over and raised my tail. "I'm a mermaid."

"I've certainly heard of them before, but I've never seen one."

"How have you heard of us?" I asked, alarmed. If Ian had convinced others of our existence, I feared that I could never repair the damage.

"Most stories are mythologies born from old sailors, but there are people who genuinely believe. If you travel to Nigeria, many swear mermaids are real."

"That's interesting. I thought most surface dwellers were completely ignorant of our existence." If I expected to one day find and kill Ian, I needed to understand more about the humans. They were more familiar with me than I was with them. "What are you?"

"Today, I'm a seagull."

"What do you mean? Are you something else on other days?"

"I'm only a bird when I want to get around easily." He stretched out his strange, white arms. "Flying is the safest way to travel, especially when you have your own wings."

"I see." I grabbed his wings and observed them closely. It was smooth like skin, but it was layered like scales, and it was much too soft. "What are you made out of?"

"Right now? Feathers. Underneath that? Skin, blood, bones…"

"And what else can you be?"

He flapped his wings to prepare himself. I must have blinked because he instantly appeared on the rock as a bright red crab. "This is familiar to you? I assume you've seen a crab before."

I gasped out loud in shock. I had to grab his claws to be sure I was looking at something real. There was a feather left behind from his transformation; I couldn't have been imagining it. "You possess magic?"

"I do."

"I do as well!" I looked at my hands and began to concentrate. I felt it trying to burst through my skin, but then I thought of the fish I exploded during my father's test. "I wish I could show you, but I'm afraid I could accidentally kill you. It's more of an instinct right now."

"Then I'll take your word for it." I sensed he was a humorous and adventurous creature. I hadn't felt anything so light since I saw into Ian's mind. "What brings you to the surface?"

"I was scavenging. I like to make things in my spare time, so I wanted more treasures."

"Maybe I could help you with that."

"How?"

"Well, you can't go on land, but I can. I will find you interesting things for your collection if you promise to take me below with you."

"You think you can manage that?" He was a crab. He would be slow getting around. Besides, the Sea Witch would eat him for breakfast.

"You tell me." He walked on his tiny legs and dove into the water. I submerged to grab him and found a tannish-colored fish with spots and a blue fin.

"Why turn into a flounder?" I asked.

"It's my favorite fish to eat."

"That seems like a very destructive reason." He probably wouldn't last an hour without my protection.

"I can only become what's been inside of me."

I was certainly intrigued by his magic, but I still didn't trust him to be of any use in that form. "I think I'll be able to help you become a merman."

"How?"

I touched my chest. "I have magic coursing through my veins. I'm sure if I give you some of my blood, you can pose as a formidable merman rather than a very edible flounder."

"Well, that would be ideal." He rose to the surface and emerged once again as a seagull. He rested on the rock and shook himself dry.

"Are seagulls tasty?"

"No. I only had one because I was starving and dying. I'm surprised that I even caught it."

I sensed that I could trust him, but I wasn't sure if my judgment was clouded because I could relate to the pain of hunger and starving for companionship. "I'm curious what you look like as a human."

"Have you ever seen one before?"

"Only once." I realized that I could read his thoughts, but he couldn't know mine unless I meant him too. That was for the best. I didn't need him discovering that I truly wanted to know how similar he was to Ian, and that led my cheeks to redden, and a rapid pace of my heart. I tried not to think of the moment when I looked into his weary eyes, but he often haunted me. Ian's life meant my death, but I strangely smiled at the thought of him living safely and far from my world. I was quite envious of his freedom.

"I'll let it be a surprise," the bird gently insisted.

I very well couldn't let him become an imposter merman if he knew nothing about my people. It was too dangerous. "Bring me enough trinkets, and I will give you some of my blood when I feel satisfied."

"I'd hate to pass up on a perfectly good opportunity to be around a beautiful girl!" I felt his immediate embarrassment. It must have been awful that he couldn't hide his thoughts from me. I would know every intimate detail that his mind projected. It was an unfair advantage, but I didn't need to be a magical mermaid to know what a young male was thinking around a mostly naked girl.

"We have a deal."

I was ecstatic. I found a human who could teach me about the surface world, and he could disguise himself as one of my kind. He wouldn't have to fear that my father would kill him on sight.

There was, however, a legitimate chance that the Sea Witch would have his head. "I'll be back within a week. Meet me here in the same spot."

"I can do that. My name is Napayshni, but you can call me Napa."

I always knew when someone was referring to me because they placed their thoughts into my head. There was no mistaking myself for anyone else. I had no use for a name before, but if I wanted a pair of legs to find Ian, I would need one. "What is the bright light in the sky when the rest of it is dark?"

"The moon?"

"Yes!" I thought excitedly. "You can call me Moon."

"That's terrible! Do you not have a name?" I sensed that he was amazed and amused by me.

"I don't know what's appropriate for a name."

"How about Magena? It means the same thing to my people. Or how about Luna? She's the Roman goddess of the moon."

"Luna?" I spoke it with my lips to hear what it might sound like. It had a nice ring to it after a few pronunciations. "I like it."

My stomach began to rumble, and I was reminded of the Sea Witch. She must have been finishing up her hunt by then. "I have to leave. Someone is expecting me."

"A young merman?" he asked with unmistakable sadness.

I grinned. "It's not any of your concern, but no. My guardian is expecting me, and she'll be wicked if I don't return before she does."

Napa lowered his head. He had such wonderful freedom, and yet, I caged him. "I will return a week from now. I'll be waiting for you patiently."

"Until then, Napa." I dove into the water and swam to the Sea Witch's lair as fast and furiously as I could. Luckily for me, she had not returned yet. It shouldn't have taken so long to return from a hunt unless she was searching for a particular prey.

A considerable amount of time passed with me being alone, and I became extremely concerned. What if I were spotted near the Sea Witch's lair, and my father sought horrible vengeance upon her? I would probably never find her body. He would have turned her into ash like Ian's mother.

She was right. I was the death of her!

"Calm your mind," she spoke to me from outside the cavern. "Worry will cause wrinkles."

I smiled and swam to meet her at the entrance, but when I laid eyes upon her catch of the day, I was horrified. I had eaten many before, but it was too much of a coincidence that she would return with a net full of red crabs.

"You look like you've seen a spirit, my child. What has you so frightened?"

I wouldn't be able to tell the difference between Napa and any other crab by looks, but I didn't hear him begging for his life. Still, I felt very threatened by her tone of mind and her smug smile. "Why did you decide on crab tonight?"

"I thought you could use the shells for something wonderful."

I pressed a smile to my face and did my best not to think. We didn't usually shield our thoughts from each other, so I didn't. I simply focused on the shells and the unique armor and jewelry I could build from them. "I'm glad you thought of me. I'm quite famished."

"Well, you know how much I care for you." She dropped her net and gently stroked my cheek. "You're under my protection, and nothing can get in the way of that."

Yes, she was much kinder to me than my father was. He was a monster, but that didn't mean I hadn't traded up for an even greater monster. She needed me for something. It might have been a matter of power or to use me against my father, but there was more to our relationship than I understood, and she'd kill anyone to make sure that I fulfilled my task.

"Thank you. I appreciate that."

Chapter Four

Each time we dined on crab, I had a chill in my bones about my new friend, Napa. I tried not to think of him at all, but I took the Sea Witch's threat seriously. But if the Sea Witch killed him, she risked losing my cooperation. She might have been maniacal, but she wasn't insane.

We ran out of crab in a week. I wanted everything to appear normal, so I offered to hunt with her again. She cocked her brow in suspicion, but her usual response came next. "You are not to leave the cavern. It's too dangerous."

"For who?" I asked. "I do not fear my father, and neither should you."

"You're no match for your father until you learn how to fully control your magic."

"My father doesn't want to kill me. He wants me to prove myself as a fierce warrior." I was putting on too good a performance, but I was genuinely angry. "Is that why you're so slow to progress our training? You don't want him to welcome me back. Do you?"

"Do I think that you should fall back in line with the murderer of my children, so he can abuse and use you like he once did to me? No. I want more for you than that."

"And why is that?"

She hesitated. "Because you're valuable to him, which means you can be valuable to me. If you're valuable to me, then you're a threat to your father."

"Do you honestly believe that you can use me as a tool for revenge? I don't want him dead. I'm not a killer."

"And I don't want you to be. Ever." She was convincing, but I also knew the Sea Witch was a master at deception. She never outright lied to me—not about important things—but she hid the truth in places too obvious for one to look. It was a useful skill that I was afraid to learn.

"Fine. You go. I will stay and be weak, even though you want me to be strong."

She continued to glare at me. I was certain she had figured me out, especially when she leaned in closer. "I'm glad we have an understanding."

I couldn't have a moment of relief until she took her sword and net, and then left. Again, I waited a couple of minutes before I decided to make my way to the surface. I jumped out of the water and flipped my hair back as the sun poured down on my body. The water was my home, but the fresh air was the only freedom I had come to know for quite a while.

When I turned to the rock that the seagull was standing on, it was in awe of something. Not a single thought was passing through his simple mind. There was only a radical feeling of admiration, bursting through into something uncontainable. "It's good to see you again, Napa."

"Luna!" He flapped his wings in excitement. "I've been looking forward to seeing you all week."

"That's flattering. I've been excited to see you as well." I swam closer and rested my arms and head against the stone. There was a red velvet cloth tied together on its ends by a piece of rope. "What have you brought me?"

"I brought you a couple of things that human women like. Maybe you'll like it too." His beak grabbed the knot on the rope, and he pulled until everything spilled on the rock.

There were lots of things I had never seen before. Some of the items were shiny; some seemed dull. There was something silver with spikes sticking up on one half of it, but it wasn't sharp. It was firm, but it moved as my fingertips guided. "What is this?"

"It's a brush."

I was drawn to my reflection and picked up another item by its black handle. "And this?"

"A mirror. Women use those to look at their reflections. They do their hair special to make themselves look pretty."

There were crystals and reflective surfaces down in the depths, so I had seen my reflection before, but it was clearer to me now. My sisters were very beautiful, and as I moved my face in different positions, I could see how similar I was to them. I didn't believe I had any masculine features, but from some angles, I saw my father. But it was strange, truly seeing myself in the light of day. The version I was accustomed to was incomplete, and I couldn't quite put my finger on why I was suddenly so rattled. I felt as though someone had peeled off my skin and revealed someone else.

As impressed as I was with my beauty, I was also unnerved. "Well, what should I do?"

"Pick up the brush and press it against your hair."

I grabbed the brush and did as instructed. It ran through my hair in some parts, but yanked it in others. It was sort of painful. "Like this?"

"No. Start from the top of the head and go all the way down. Don't be so rough. You don't want to yank it out. Your hair is too pretty for you to go bald."

"Is my hair unusual?"

"Blue hair? It used to be. Nowadays? Not so much. But it certainly isn't natural."

I started from my scalp and brushed down to the ends. I did it slowly and gently, so I wouldn't rip much of my hair out. When it got caught, I stroked the tangle continuously until my hair was smooth and fluid. "And what now?"

"Take that black thing. It's a hair tie." He tapped his foot on it. "It's made to stretch. Put your hair through it."

I picked up the black ring. My hair was considerably long and thick. I didn't believe I could put all of my hair through it, but the ring did bend to my will once I pulled it open wide with my fingers.

I looked in the mirror to observe any major change, and I wasn't significantly different. The shape of my face was now more obvious without so much hair hanging from everywhere, so the odd feeling of familiarity only became worse. "Do you like it?"

"You look beautiful either way." It was strange feeling the emotions of a smitten bird. I wished he were like me, or even Ian.

"It's certainly different." I picked up the other gifts he brought. I slid one of them through my hair, and it left a pretty gem exposed. I could use what he brought me and make more. "I'm inspired to do many things now."

"You could do a lot more on dry land. It's too bad you can't go back and forth like I can." He had been a crab, a flounder, and a seagull. He was impressive, but I was beginning to question if he was making a fool out of me.

"When will you show me what you really look like?"

"When it's the right time."

I picked up another item. It was smooth, black, and as long as my index finger. I pulled on it, and the top half easily came off. Inside, there was a red stick.

"That's lipstick."

I continued observing the black shell. As I twisted the bottom, the red part popped up. It had a strange smell to it, but it seemed edible.

"Don't eat it!"

He warned me a little too late. I took a chunk out of it, and as soon as my tongue made contact, I spat it right out. I had to lick the smears off my teeth. "That's disgusting."

"You're supposed to rub it against your lips."

I frowned. If I didn't want it on my tongue, I certainly didn't want it on my lips! But I decided to be obedient and circled it on them. "Like this?"

He raised his beak and chirped in amusement. I could sense he thought it was hilarious.

I rubbed my hand against my lips to wipe it away, but I still felt it on my mouth and hand. "I look like a fool."

"You just need to master it. Anyone can master makeup. It comes naturally for some, but women like you rarely need an enhancement."

If Napa knew how to properly apply such things, then I wanted to as well. I tried to see into his mind as clearly as I did Ian's, but it was muddied and dark. He wasn't open to me, and I didn't want to force and take what I wanted from him. That would have been dangerous. "I think it would be easier to see your memories if you weren't a bird. It would help me understand more."

"I'm not ready to reveal myself to you yet." I didn't understand. He was not embarrassed, so he must have been a glorious sight to behold. Why didn't he take the plunge if he truly wanted to impress me?

"Fine." I began packing up my things in the cloth. His hesitancy made me rethink everything between us. "I'm going to withhold my blood for a little while. I want to know that I can trust you. I assume you don't trust me. That's why you won't let me see your face."

"I like you. I just don't know you."

"Fair enough." If I were truly trustworthy, I probably would have told him about how the Sea Witch subtly threatened his life. He deserved to know I was putting his life in danger, but honesty might have alienated me. "We can meet in a week again."

"Alright. I'll see you then." He flapped his wings and flew away. He was headed for the closest plot of land. Surely, Ian must have headed there after I saved him. Convincing the Sea Witch to give me a pair of legs wouldn't be enough. I needed information, and I needed Napa's cooperation for that.

When I returned home, I felt the cold presence of the Sea Witch before I even crossed the threshold, and I questioned whether I should enter her lair. My father would offer me a quick and brutal death. I imagined the Sea Witch would use her magic to make my suffering last.

I didn't want to be afraid of her, and I doubted she would truly make a move against me anyway. She still needed me for her twisted plans, so I braced myself and entered.

I carefully swam to our dining area. Her back was to me, so I couldn't see her face. My eyes focused on a sharp blade in her hand as she cut hooks and beaks off squids. "Are you hungry?"

"Of course." It seemed strange to me that she could eat what she used to so closely resemble, but that was our way in the sea. That's why I had to be on my guard as I took my place across from her.

The Sea Witch was very quiet. She focused on her task of cutting. She returned with an assortment of creatures this time, and I welcomed the variety. I reached for another blade sitting on the stone, but she slapped my hand with her knife and accidentally nicked me. "What's your problem?"

The blood from my hand rose and swirled around into a perfect circle. As clear as I saw my face in the mirror Napa gave me, I could see myself speaking with him on the rock. The supply of crabs from last week was not a coincidence.

I waited for her scolding. After that, I figured an attack would do. Was she only cutting up her latest victims to intimidate me? Perhaps. I couldn't be too sure.

"If you use your magic aggressively, you may accidentally turn it dark. I don't want that for you." Her eyes slowly came up to mine, and I realized they held genuine concern. It was a very rare commodity in my realm. I had only seen it expressed through Ian and his parents.

"Why does it matter to you whether my magic is light or dark if it can somehow help you defeat my father?"

She turned her head and shook it in disbelief. "You don't know me at all."

"That's your fault. You're keeping things from me—"

"I told you about your father's past with me." She threw her knife into the stone slab and banged against it in rage. "How intimate do you need the details to be? Do you want to know how he made me feel when he touched me? Do you want to know how foolish I was when I looked into his eyes? Do you want to know if I loved him?"

I had to look away. It was difficult seeing the pain in her eyes while feeling it so strongly. It was soaked into her bones. "I've never heard anyone talk about love before…"

"That's because of your father's rule. He took the trident and created an entirely different world. He chose power over love. I might have been cold, but he became cruel."

I certainly trusted her over my father, but her words wounded me for some reason. I couldn't stand to believe that she was the victim. "You killed your people for him. You murdered hundreds—"

"Thousands," she corrected without remorse. "They were vicious warriors, but they didn't possess the vision that he did for world domination. Land and sea are his goals, and he'll resort to genocide to achieve them. His thirst for blood can't be quenched, and it's my obligation to put an end to him."

"For revenge?"

She opened her mouth and shrieked until my ears began to bleed. I covered them and backed away, but her magic had a significant reach to it. I don't think she meant to hurt me, but her fury was incredible enough to tear open a portal of truth, and neither of us was quite ready to cross over. "He broke our blood oath! You don't get to wipe the slate clean when it comes to magic. There's always a price, and I need to collect."

I wasn't sure if the room was shaking or if my vision was that severely impaired. "What does all of this have to do with me?"

"I can't afford for him to have you. He could kill you and try to steal your magic."

"If he wanted to do that, he would have." He might have banished me immediately after, but the pride he had in his eyes after I displayed my magic was real. I could almost feel his unusually comforting touch. "He told me that I was his true heir. He wants me to become like him. He wants me to take over his vision if he can't succeed."

"And will you? You have his blood flowing through your veins."

"But I also have my mother, and I remember that she was kind—"

"My apprentice was a whore! She's hardly an example." The temperature surrounding us lowered drastically, and it became darker, even though the bright lights from the cauldrons never extinguished. Her bright blue eyes thrived in that darkness. I couldn't possibly lose sight of her beaming hatred for my father.

Perhaps mentioning my mother wasn't the right course of action. I tried to warm my body by holding my arms, but I became more concerned once I felt the frost on my flesh and my skin hardening. "Please, stop this! I'm nothing like either of them."

The Sea Witch closed her eyes and raised her head to the roof of our cavern. She pressed tightly clenched hands against her chest as if she were praying for her dark reign to end. She was afraid that I would give into the temptation of dark magic, but she was the one out of control.

Maybe it was compassion driving her to protect me. She might not have wanted me to fall prey to my potential.

My body began to warm once again, and the brightness was restored to its original setting. The Sea Witch opened her eyes, and I saw shame in them, instead of vengeance. She wasn't the invincible villainess that I heard about. She was just a woman trying to find her way back into the world with bright blue eyes—the same eyes that I had seen staring in my mirror.

Chapter Five

We spent our dinner in silence while I tried to loosen the threads that bound my identity to the Sea Witch. I had grown accustomed to her company, but I had no desire to replace the woman I believed to be my mother with the focus of my adolescent nightmares. I had a few memories of my beautiful mother, but I did recall chasing after her glittering orange tail as she glided through our kingdom. I was the smallest among my sisters, but I was faster than most of them. Before I could catch my mother, I was flung backward and smacked by a stream of flapping tails. By the time I tumbled through them all, my face was bruised, and my lip was busted. I refused to whimper and create more trouble for myself, but my mother realized that I was cast aside and came to my aid. She held my tiny shoulders to steady me. It wasn't an embrace, but it was the closest I had ever been to one.

"Girls, leave the little mermaid alone. You know that she's special." My mother tapped under my chin to raise my head. At the time, I took her words and gestures as profound affection. My sisters hissed at my mother's favor, but they did not raise a hand against her. She was respected among us all, and they would not come to harm me again while in her presence. But after seeing genuine love through the eyes of Ian, I recognized a coolness in her emerald eyes and a melancholy tone in her mind. There wasn't even a sliver of a smile on her thin lips as she gazed down at my tiny body.

Were my memories suddenly tainted by the Sea Witch's disdain for her, or did I genuinely know better now that I had witnessed how parents should have beheld their children? I was special, but I didn't know if I was anything out of the ordinary to her. She took care of my father's every need, and he needed a worthy heir. Was she loving me for us or grooming me for him?

The Sea Witch avoided total eye contact with me, so I couldn't compare our facial features too closely. I tried to find comfort in our differences. I was still growing into my body, but my shoulders were broader. Our hair color was an obvious difference, and her hairline was a smooth arch across her forehead, while mine was made up of two that met in the middle. Of course, those were traits I inherited from my father, but they comforted me at the time.

But the longer we sat together, the more similar our mannerisms became. At first, it was blatantly obvious when we reached for the same tentacle and drew our hands away. Instead of reaching an agreement as to which one of us should have it, we both moved on to the next tentacle on the right side of me. I pulled my hand away in frustration and decided to stop eating, but she continued. I studied the way she slouched forward and realized that my body was leaning into our table. I immediately straightened out, but I didn't feel any better. The uncertainty was driving me mad.

"I was wondering about my mother…" I was so timid; I was amazed that I managed to think my request loud enough for the Sea Witch to hear.

"The incessant whore?" She might have been annoyed, but she still managed to smile wickedly.

"Do you have to be so cruel when it comes to her memories?" I didn't expect any better from the Sea Witch, but if she happened to be anything more—anything at all—she should have been able to see how important it was for me to hold onto one semblance of a happy childhood.

But, in true form, she sneered her nose in disgust at her young pupil. "She took from me what did not belong to her. She'll always be a whore."

I understood her hatred well enough, but it did feel deeper than what she let on. "Are you really that angry about not having my father?"

"Don't insult me," she snapped quickly.

"Then what else did she take that did not belong to her?" The Sea Witch's head was raised toward me, and I witnessed the pain that had struck them. She was not any more prepared for my questions than I was for the answers, but I knew—at the very least—that it was right to genuinely ask.

The Sea Witch paused. She was such a horrible and unsympathetic person. The Sea Witch winced as she struggled through the mental torture of searching for a compliment. "For the time that she watched over me, she was thoroughly attentive to my needs, and…" She sighed long and heavily. "…I assume that she was attentive to you."

I jerked my head back in surprise at her astonishing feat. "She was."

She attempted to scowl, but the Sea Witch allowed a spec of a smile to graze against her lips. I think it was a sign of relief. But why would she care about how my mother treated me, especially since our time together was so brief?

I excused myself without explanation. I didn't possess the courage to confront the Sea Witch about my true origins. Besides, she claimed to have disclosed the important details involving her and my father. Why would she be honest if I came out and asked her directly?

I thought I had all the proof I needed anyway. The mirror Napa gave me cracked from the Sea Witch's screeching, but I could still see that the shape and color of our eyes were the same. Our hair shared a similar thickness and texture as well. Both of our faces were heart-shaped, and our lips were pouty and full. I always had a shorter torso compared to the length of my tail, and I noticed now that the Sea Witch did as well. My sisters teased me about it on occasion, and I never understood why I was so different.

I couldn't sleep. I tried, but my mind never quite got to rest. I wondered if the Sea Witch heard my distressful thoughts. I was trying to keep her out of my head, but I was mentally screaming for her to answer my questions.

I must have dozed off eventually because when I opened my eyes, the Sea Witch was hovering over me with a sword. I was unnerved by the fact that she wouldn't attack, which was an odd thing to be disturbed by. "Are we fighting today?"

She narrowed her eyes at me. "I need to know why you were talking with a seagull."

I tried to imagine what she would look like without blue skin and silver hair. I thought she would have been an older version of myself. Our noses were a bit different. Mine was a bit rounder in favor of my father's. "You threatened his life."

"And?" she asked, rather bored with my concern.

"He's a human that can shapeshift."

Her brows rose in surprise. "I've heard of such magic, but humans couldn't possibly possess it. Have you seen his human form?"

"No, but—"

"Then you don't know what he is. What does he want from you?"

"He brings me gifts in exchange for the promise that I will one day help him become a merman. For this, he requires my blood." I waited for her to scold me, and I braced myself for a vicious slap against my face. That's what my father would have done. "Are you angry?"

Her body tensed up, and her fingers gripped into tight fists. I thought she would release her rage, but her hands instead loosened and cupped my face. "You are playing a very dangerous game. Your father kills humans whenever he can get away with it. Exposure to the surface world will provoke him into war, and his army will easily follow. Why would you risk such a thing?"

"Because I..." I felt like such a foolish child. "I wanted a friend."

I expected her to be ashamed of my actions, but she instead turned her disappointment inward. "I will allow you some freedom. You may come and go as you please without fear of me, but you must be cautious. Your father cannot discover that you are under my care."

She must have known what I expected. I couldn't get her out of my mind. Why wouldn't she come clean and confess or deny? It was the least she could do. "Agreed."

"Good." She smirked. "We should continue training."

I smiled in our brief solidarity, but I realized I had much to fear and nearly missed her sword taking my head off. I dove out of the way and picked up my favorite weapon—the first gift she had ever given to me—to defend myself.

She was ferocious, but I knew that she was never truly out to hurt me. Her goal wasn't to break me like my father, so he could piece me into his liking. She wanted to beat the impurities out of me, so I could be a more perfect form of myself. She was far from wonderful, but she was proving to be a much better caretaker than my father. But if she truly were my mother, I found it hard to believe she would leave me in the care of the two merpeople who betrayed her.

To no surprise, she did not speak of my concerns. When we were exasperated after our battle, we stared each other down awkwardly until she decided to take her sword and abruptly leave to hunt.

I probably should have accompanied the Sea Witch and forced her to tell me the truth, but I also didn't want to know. I stayed in the cavern sulking. I couldn't wait for a week to pass, so I could swim to the surface and join my friend at our usual meeting spot. I arrived early, but he was already waiting for me with another bag. "How are you doing, Napa?"

"I'm fine, Luna. I brought you some more treasures for women." I could tell he was excited. He pulled the rope with his beak, and jewelry poured out. There were very lovely gems in each piece. I wondered if the surface world was littered with such jewels that a seagull was able to take so many.

I took one necklace and held it against my chest. It was an emerald that complemented my hair, eyes, and skin. "These are beautiful, but I already make pieces like these for myself. I want to be educated about your world. If I ever had to visit your land, I don't want to seem like an outsider."

"Are you planning on growing a pair of legs any time soon?"

"There is a way." I had no desire to take advantage of his feelings, but I also had no other options. "I need you to help me find someone."

"Who?" He asked with just enough hesitation to let me know that he was jealous.

"There was a human boy that I saved a long time ago. My family killed his parents for traveling in our waters. For reasons I cannot explain, I saved him. Now, he risks exposing me, and my father will not allow that."

His bird neck jerked his head back in surprise. "You want me to help you find a boy, so you can kill him?"

I panicked internally once I sensed how alarmed he was with my request. "I know this is asking a lot, but my father will kill me if I don't. I don't have a choice."

"Your father would really do that?" Napa was radically more upset, but his guilt subsided. "Who would believe a kid rambling on about mermaids?"

"He has a dagger that he took from me. If he convinces a few people, then we've already lost." I dipped further into the water and pressed my chest against the rock. I needed to be closer to his eyes. "Please, Napa! I swear I'll give you my blood if you do this."

"If I take your blood to transform, I'll be using blood magic. I've been taught that it's complicated magic. It could be dangerous."

"Well, I'm not going to let you eat me!"

"I'm not fond of that way either. Shapeshifting is sacred to some of my people, while others think I'm a demon. Maybe I am. I know I seem impressive to you, but I don't exactly have a good handle on this."

"How so?"

"Well, when I first turned into an animal, it was a complete accident. I turned into a chicken."

"And what's that?"

He flapped his wings, and his body grew larger and shorter. His white feathers turned to black, fading into a vibrant red and orange. His head had changed. It was as if he wore a strange coral headpiece. I stroked his new feathers, which were larger and silkier. He was less pretty, but I was fascinated.

"I was trapped in this form for days. My family thought I was dead. I was almost eaten myself!"

"Do you taste delicious?" I laughed aloud.

"It would depend on who plucked and cooked me. My mother would have done me no justice."

I could certainly sympathize with being something's intended meal, but I could laugh at the irony. "And how did you escape?"

"I pecked her hand and ran away when she was distracted. I fell asleep once I was safe. When I woke up, I was human again."

"Have you forgotten how to be a human? Is that why you haven't shown me your true face?"

"To be honest, I did something my people deemed as unforgivable." Strangely enough, I didn't sense his remorse. "Ever since then, I haven't been able to change back, and I can't acquire new forms unless I do it as a human. I've been trying to break the curse, but I've never met anyone like you who could understand me."

I thought he was just a curious creature, but now, I could see that he was just as alone as I was. I did not mean to smile at his misfortune, but I was pleased to have such a kindred spirit. "How can I help you regain your body?"

He flapped his wings and jumped into the water. I thought he would drown, but his body grew slimmer. His feathers became gray, fading into brown, and his head was a vibrant green like my tail. He still had a beak, but it was much longer. "You should follow me for a swim. You can protect me from sharks."

It was dangerous for him, but he glided on the water so gracefully that I was inclined to watch. I swam on my back and stayed close to him. It was unfortunate he couldn't be what he was born as, but he had dominion over the land and sea. "Do you have a formidable form?"

"I have a few. I was also very capable as a human."

"And how will you become a merman? Even if we break the curse, you don't want to do blood magic."

"I think there's another way to acquire your DNA. I'll test my theory when the time is right."

"DNA?"

"It's the tiniest bits that form you. When parents have children, they share their DNA and create a uniquely new individual, but you can always see a trace of where you come from."

Humans certainly were fascinating. If it were possible to know definitively that the Sea Witch was my mother, I certainly wanted to possess such magic. "How?"

"If we were on land, a scientist could probably show you. The simplest way is to look for similar features." I had stopped swimming, but he circled around me and made a strange and loud sound from his mouth that was very brash and alarming. "Are you questioning your father's paternity?"

"My mother's, actually..."

"Wow. That's tough." He made the sound again. I could recognize it was simply his response to my scandalous position. "I'll find Ian for you. What you want to do afterward is entirely up to you."

"Thank you, Napa." I raised him out of the water, and he batted his wings in sudden fright. I was a bit startled by his reaction, but I laughed. "Now, tell me everything about your world."

Napa quickly became my beloved companion. We began to meet twice a week. I told him what I knew about Ian, and once I had gone over the horrific details of my banishment, my mind clung to the strangest details. I wanted to know more about the strange hip-hop he performed with his feet. Napa thought this was odd and blurted his strange sound at me again, but he told me that it was a form of dancing. I remembered how happy Ian was and how amused his parents were when they watched him. They didn't think he was very good, but he captivated me.

I was envious of humans and their feet. Isn't that ridiculous? A human like Napa longed to see my world, and I desperately wanted to see his home. His family was a part of a tribe. He said they were very proud people and appreciated nature. He didn't grow up with many valuable goods, but they were skillful hunters. Everything he had, they fought for. He was much like me, except he didn't live in such dangerously extreme conditions.

The Sea Witch never seemed remotely interested in meeting Napa, but she always wanted to know about our comings and goings. I told her things about him, but I never bothered to arrange their meeting. Honestly, I was always a little afraid that he'd end up as one of our meals. But she didn't have a true reason to hate him. I continued to stay hidden from my father and his subjects, and I still spent plenty of my time training with the Sea Witch. My life became a constant routine between the two of them, and I was content.

I soon discovered that Napa wasn't as satisfied with our arrangement, and his desire to travel with me had only increased. I tried to warn him continuously about his delicate flounder form, but he was stubborn. One day, when I went to meet Napa at our usual spot, he was late. In a year of knowing Napa, he had never been late for a single meeting. I think he was always afraid that he would miss me for some reason. It felt like he was courting me, in a way. Mermen were very fierce competitors when it came to winning the affection of a beautiful mermaid. I didn't need Napa to viciously rip a competitor to shreds to have me, but I certainly wasn't going to mate with a flounder or a bird. Even if he somehow found a way to become a merman, I didn't know if it was right to let him continue courting me. I had to wait and see if Napa was capable of making me feel something new toward him, other than perpetual friendship.

I felt vibrations coming from the water below. It was something relatively small, so I wasn't afraid. However, I learned to be cautious and dove back down to defend myself, if necessary. "Napa?" Yes. It was an unmistakable flounder. "What are you doing in the water? Where are you coming from?"

"I knew you would never take me exploring in this form, so I went without you to prove that I could handle myself."

I fumed up my face in anger. "Not dying doesn't prove that you can handle yourself. It only proves you've got luck, and even that runs out eventually."

"Relax. I want to show you what I found."

I crossed my arms. I didn't appreciate him taking such a major risk. What if he had gotten lost and I never found him? He was at odds with his family, but I knew that he did want to see his mother again. "Napa, I don't feel comfortable with—"

"You're strong enough to protect me," he thought uncomfortably. "I mean, I don't want you fighting my battles for me, but I trust you. That's why I'm not afraid. Besides, I can move this tail pretty fast."

My fear was valid, but I didn't want to coddle him like the Sea Witch constantly did to me. Besides, my curiosity had been piqued. "Lead the way."

Napa made a decent enough flounder, but his speed was nowhere near my ability. He seemed to know where he was going. We headed the opposite way from my home. If something happened, the Sea Witch wouldn't know where to find me. "Napa, how long have you been down here?"

"I've been doing some exploring for the past couple of days…"

"Napa!" I swam in front of him and crossed my arms. I couldn't believe that he would risk himself. What if he had been eaten by a bigger fish? What was going to save him? His chicken powers? "You don't understand how vicious my world can be."

"I've gone fishing before. I get that it sucks being a fish, but I've been careful. Besides, I wanted to surprise you."

"Surprise me with what?"

He swam around me and continued. I wanted to force him to turn around, but I was also genuinely curious about what he thought he could find in my domain that would surprise me. I saw coral reefs bursting with vivid colors found in a child's imagination, inhabited by schools of friendlier and non-threatening fish. I could understand if Napa was excited about the bright and alluring palette, but it wasn't anything new to me.

Still, I had a very uneasy feeling and kept flexing my fingers, in case I needed to draw my weapon and defend us. "Are we close?"

Napa stopped once he saw the strangest sort of rock in the world, lodged between two other rocks. I was curious and touched it. Oddly enough, it was soft, and I could squeeze it easily with my fingers. "I've never seen anything like this before."

"It's wreckage from a crash. It's a chair from an airplane."

"What's an airplane?"

Napa was excited and pressed further into deeper and darker waters. Close by the chair was a strange object that had to be from the surface world. It was a lighter color—perhaps white—and hard like a stone. It was large and long like a giant eel, but it had hard wings. One was broken, and the tail had been snapped off. The Sea Witch wouldn't have wanted me to explore inside a surface world object, but my curiosity was beckoning me. "Is it dangerous?"

"It's not alive," Napa said, "but it did do incredible things like fly humans from one side of the world to another. It would have been even faster than your best swimming stride."

"That's incredible..." I didn't feel any vibrations in the water that would signify close threats. I figured we'd be safe, and I swam up through the broken plane to see inside. I wasn't quite expecting to be looking inside a graveyard of human corpses strapped into their seats.

I paused. I had seen dead bodies before. The Sea Witch's cavern was still decorated by the bones of my people, but there was still flesh on those bones. The smell of the dead hadn't spread. They weren't even decaying. I swam over to a child sitting next to her mother. She had some sort of contraption on her face like a shell, but it was bendable and connected to something clear and fragile to the touch like a jellyfish. Most of the other humans had it on their faces. I wondered if it was some sort of measure that was meant to save their lives. "Napa, what's the meaning of this?"

I knew then that Napa didn't go exploring inside before bringing me there. His mind went into a dull gray blaze of misery. I couldn't hear his thoughts for a long while. It was incoherent emotions. I had to pierce through a wall of solid pain to make sense of his fish mind. "This area above the water is known as the Bermuda Triangle. They say there are always weird things like planes and ships disappearing here. I don't know if that's true, but there was a recent wreck. The humans are talking about it nonstop."

"Well, I can certainly explain sailors going missing. My father likes to send our people to kill many humans as a warning. That's how I ran into Ian. But if this were in the sky..." I swam to the top of the strange flight carrier. It was made out of some sort of strong metal, like some of our weapons. It must have been incredibly heavy. "How is it possible for something like this to be up in the sky flying?"

"Science. Technology. Innovation. Men wanted to fly, so they made it happen."

"It's fascinating…" Finding a pair of legs wasn't only about finding Ian, I must admit. I was so curious about humans and their world. Napa made it seem like such a marvelous place. I was sure that if I mastered magic, I might have been without limitations, but the creativity and ingenuity of humans proved that "impossible" was a meaningless word. "How did this plane fall?"

"It's still being investigated. No one knows where the plane fell or where it went off course…except for me."

"Wait…" I could feel rattling in the water pulsing from an oncoming threat and shaking through my body. There was a group of mildly large creatures heading our way, and it would have been difficult to fight them by myself. I could possibly outswim them, but Napa was a concern. "Does your formidable form have teeth?"

"Yes, but it can't live underwater. Why?"

I didn't have time to explain. I held Napa close to my chest as I swam out of the airplane. "What's going on?"

Oh, as if he cared! He was concerned for his safety, but he reminded me that he wasn't a fish as he flopped against my breasts. "Can you control your thoughts? I'm trying to save your life."

"Well, you've gotta be more careful where you stick me." He slipped from my grasp and put a little bit of distance between the two of us. "What are you doing?"

"I'm trying to protect you!"

Napa's mind went blank as a hot flash of fear overcame him. It was disappointing that he wasn't strong enough to have the mental capacity to warn me of the danger, but I could feel it behind me, and I swam up and flipped over the predator that desired to tear me apart. When he failed, he swam around so he could try once more.

"Shark!" Napa would have screamed if he could have, but it certainly felt like it in my head.

I didn't have time to be afraid or to stop. There was a part of me that wanted to battle it out with the shark to prove that I was capable of surviving, but my warrior would have gotten my nurturing side killed. Still, I turned around for a brief moment to consider my options, but there was a sudden change in vibrations that commanded my attention. Just as I turned my head, my eyes caught the shine of black eyes and bright teeth. Another shark hid in a cave, and it sprang right at me masterfully. If not for my quick reflexes and nimble body, I would have been one inch too far to the right and had my arm removed.

I spun around, and my back hit the rocks that the shark emerged from. There was a prick and a sting as I rolled off it, but I had to continue swimming. The sharks had to turn around, but after that, they were an unstoppable force.

"You're slowing down!"

My vision also began to blur. The sting in my back spread, and the pain rapidly intensified. I held Napa closer to my body, but I had no control otherwise. Instead of swimming for my life, my body was suddenly drifting helplessly in the dark emptiness.

"Luna?" Napa slipped from my numb fingers and swam behind me. He took a clump of my hair in his mouth and began pulling, but it was useless. He'd have a better chance if he abandoned me, and he'd still fail. "Come on, Luna. We have to go."

Humans are such ridiculous creatures to fantasize about the wonders of an underwater world. They're absurd enough to believe they can tread upon our domain and not feel the wrath of a mother shark protecting her young, or a jellyfish stinging some fool that wanted to have fun with its oily body. They don't even realize that there are even more dangerous creatures with the strongest poisons in our world, the sort of poison that I had just stumbled upon by complete accident.

"Luna!"

I saw the two sharks coming for me. I would never flee fast enough now. I tried to reach for my weapon, but my knuckles felt like they were breaking when I tried to stretch my fingers. The pain was blinding as if every nerve in my body were being mercilessly ripped apart. I grunted and tried to force myself to fight, but the poison only spread faster.

I did not want to die there, that day, or in such a horrible manner. Sharks were not the kings of our domain, and I could not let myself be another trophy for their reputation. I possessed magic, and I could feel it bubbling up inside of me. It was a force and had its own rhythm—like a heartbeat—and a mind. It was indignant and refused to be destroyed by such insignificant creatures.

"Ahhhhh!" Something within me exploded, and the effects of the poison faded as my hands raised toward the two sharks coming my way. There was a flash of colors that were so bright, I went blind for a moment. I felt my magic surge out from my body and connect with the sharks. It pierced their flesh and broke loose every fragment until they were blown apart into specks of dust, and they dissolved even further into nothing.

I opened my eyes to see what I unleashed. The water was still radiating from my power, but my vision was no longer impaired. As a matter of fact, it was much sharper than before. The little demon that pricked me was a fish camouflaged perfectly with stone, because of its bizarre shades of brown and red, paired with its coarse texture. I hated those pesky things. One of my sisters pricked me with a poisonous quill as a prank. She was jealous of the attention our father doted on me. I bet she was enjoying every moment of my exile.

At least I was recovering quickly. The pain from the toxin was a little more than an ache now.

"Uh, Luna…?"

"Yes?" When I turned around to see Napa, he was still very frightened about something, but I didn't sense anything dangerous near him. I looked back to where the sharks used to be, and they were certainly wiped from existence. I didn't understand why he was so afraid. "I warned you that I could blow you up with my magic. Did you not believe me?"

"Luna, you're different. Your hair, your eyes…your skin!"

"What?" I looked at my hands. My skin was milky white with a hint of pink, but it was different now. It was an icy blue. My nails were never very long before. I always broke them while I was tinkering, but I suddenly had claws at the ends of my fingers. My beautiful blue hair had changed into an illustrious silver. It was shining in the light of my power.

"Is this something that happens to you?" I could feel his fear. I had yet to figure out if he was afraid of me or if he was concerned for my well-being.

"I…?" My tail was different as well. I wasn't an enchanting fairytale for lonely sailors to dream about. I was a monster. A demon. I was a…

"Sea Witch…?" She warned me about using my magic too quickly. I was only defending myself. Had it already turned dark? I couldn't bear to be what the Sea Witch was or what she once was before having my blood.

"Luna, where are you going?"

I was in such a panic that I abandoned Napa. I had to find a way to reverse my fate. Only the Sea Witch could give me a cure for my appearance, so I swam home as fast as I could. In my new form, I noticed that my speed had at least doubled. If I weren't so terrified, it would have been invigorating!

I sensed the Sea Witch was not near when I arrived home. I went inside my clam and hysterically moaned. What had I done to myself? How could I make it go away? There had to be an answer. I couldn't accept otherwise! There was a strength within me that I had never truly known. I never thought I would be tempted, but I was curious to know the depths of my dark powers and how far I could go without being crushed.

Chapter Six

"Luna?" I was surprised when I felt the Sea Witch reaching out to me. It was a name that only Napa used. I thought if she ever did, it would be to mock me. "Luna, why are you upset?"

I was hidden inside my clam. I had closed it shut to hide from the world, but it seemed insulting to be so ashamed of my new form in front of her. "Why are you calling me that?"

"It's the name that shapeshifter calls you." She peeked inside the cracks, and I saw her light blue eyes. "You like having a name. I thought hearing it would make you feel more at ease."

I was practically shaking at the thought of someone seeing me, but I had to ask myself if it would have been so horrible to trust her. After all, the Sea Witch was acting as my guardian. "I need you to help me."

"Help you what?"

I braced myself and pushed the clam open. I don't know what her first reaction was, because I shut my eyes tight in fear. "Turn me back."

Nothing happened for a while. I opened my eyes, one at a time, and she just stared at me blankly with no thoughts passing through her mind. She began to reach for me, then drew away. I didn't mean to break her. Disappointing her was a burden I wasn't quite ready to bear, and I collapsed back into the clam, holding my wretched arms and moaning.

The Sea Witch snapped out of her trance and pulled me up for a better look. I was still too ashamed to look her in the eye. "How did this happen?"

"I was in danger. There were two sharks about to bite me, and I had been poisoned by a stonefish. I didn't have any choice, and then, my powers emerged. I killed the sharks with my magic, and I was like this after the battle."

"And why do you think this happened?" she asked carefully.

I thought it was obvious, and I snapped at her. "Taking two lives has caused my magic to go dark."

She smiled, but then she chuckled at my moral dilemma. "That's hardly enough to make you go dark."

"Then why am I like this? Why am I like you?"

"You were weak. You took on a stronger form to ensure your survival. That's all. You should return to your normal state soon...I think. Probably when this heals." She noticed something on my back and touched where it was sore. I didn't realize I still had quills from that stonefish inside of me until she yanked them out. I hissed and glared at her, but not even my menacing appearance could frighten her. "This poison is very potent. It would have killed anyone else in your position."

I took the quill from her hand and looked at it myself. I wasn't familiar with poisons, but I trusted the Sea Witch was well-educated in such an area. Besides, I did feel the crippling pain of the poison prior to taking on my new form. "Can all mermaids become like this?"

The Sea Witch's eyes widened with surprise at my question, but she lowered her brows and scowled at my cowardice. "Luna, ask your question."

I knew then that it was true. Even if she denied it, I knew. It made too much sense. I could feel her too deeply within me. I didn't know if I'd ever escape her. "I shouldn't have to."

She didn't speak with words, but a rare smile came to her face as she gently held me with her hands. It wasn't that she didn't smile, but it was usually due to the thrill of killing prey or intrigue. This was different. It was tender. It was...loving. "Yes. I am your blood mother."

I couldn't doubt her. I saw her face in me when I looked in the mirror. I wondered how similar we looked now that I had taken the form of a sea witch. I wished I could find some sort of comfort in the truth, but I was truly terrified. "Why didn't you just tell me?"

"I thought nothing of you when I had you dragged down to me. I didn't know you were mine until I used your blood. Even then, I didn't understand. I thought you died with all the others…"

I slipped away from her grasp in shock at her words. "Are you telling me that my father tried to kill me and steal my magic?"

"Yes, and I thought he succeeded." She had no delicacy or appreciation for how horrible a revelation that was for me. I wasn't surprised she was so blunt. "You must have been strong enough to fend him off. You must have been dormant for all these years. That's why you're so young—"

"Please, explain everything." I swam backward before she could touch me again. Everything was changing too rapidly. "Hold nothing back."

The Sea Witch nodded and swam to her cauldron. She had to mix a few bottles of various eyeballs, odd roots, corals, seafoam, etc. Within a few moments, her colored smoke rose and spilled out of the cauldron and surrounded us. I was alarmed and moved in closer to the Sea Witch. She closed her eyes, and the smoke circled us faster until I couldn't see past it. When the Sea Witch opened her eyes, the speed of the smoke decreased and appeared as something almost solid, like a screen of ice that displayed her memories.

Within the illusion, I saw a kingdom of dark stone and crystals occupied by many who looked like her. Some of them had different colored hair and eyes, and their skin tones varied in shades, but they were mostly like her. They didn't appear to be dark or vicious like the Sea Witch. I saw a young girl inside the walls of a small palace who looked so similar to me; I knew it must have been my mother in her youth. She was laughing and happy as she studied magic over a cauldron with her teacher.

"One thousand years ago, our world was a different place. Merpeople came in different forms, and there were several different empires. Your father was only a prince back then, and I was a young priestess who would eventually lead, due to my power. Like humans, we warred with each other over minor differences. Eventually, it led to segregation and hatred. But I didn't hate your father. I loved him at first glance."

I saw her looking for spies in her magic smoke and gazing upon a young scout who had my father's unmistakable eyes. It was odd to see him without his beard, and I had no idea his hair was originally blue like mine. For whatever reason, she became smitten when she saw into his eyes. She was breathless, and I saw a brightness within her eyes that I didn't know she was capable of.

She had to sneak away from her people to escape the protection barrier. It was the only way for my father to see her, and once she revealed herself, he was also in awe. Her memories jumped through time, and I saw them experience the world together. They spent time just talking amongst each other on the surface under a full moon, and they swam far away from both of their kingdoms just to be free from other eyes. I saw her show a demonstration of magic by freezing the water around her into an ice ball. He smirked, and she failed to recognize that his intrigue was wicked and ambitious.

"We met in secret, and he'd whisper such wonderful lies to me. We vowed to be together, but our kingdoms were at war." Through their brief flashes of time, I saw how hard she fell for my father. He didn't seem disinterested. Her physical differences didn't deter his attraction. When he held her, it seemed as if she were a possession, and she was caught too deep within her fantasy to recognize that he succumbed to a darker nature, and his only goal was to corrupt her.

I saw them returning from their day of flirtations to a battlefield of death. There were only a few dozen blue bodies among the dead. My father looked on at the scene in incredible anger, while the Sea Witch was overcome with guilt and fear for the inevitable. "I knew my people. We were going to wipe out Atlantis until there was nothing left. Your father lost seven older brothers to the war. He also would have been killed. It was only a matter of time."

"So, you betrayed your people to save him?"

"He told me that if I got the trident for him, he could save our people and force a truce. He said I could find asylum in his realm. I was skeptical, but he suggested making a blood oath. It was dark magic, but I agreed. The power we would provoke would seal our agreement."

"And what was your agreement?"

"If I gave him the trident, I would give him an heir that would inherit all that was his."

"And you said nothing in your agreement about being faithful to you?"

The Sea Witch tensed up her hand as if she wanted to slap me, but she resisted the urge by tightening her fist. "I didn't think I would have to. Besides, I did add that I would destroy him and his entire kingdom if he went back on his word. I thought that was more than enough incentive to keep our bargain."

Her memories flashed again to their moment of intimacy, and I averted my eyes. The Sea Witch snickered in amusement and forced her memories forward. I was grateful that she spared me from watching them writhe up against one another in pleasure. Instead, I bore witness to the deed afterward and the mysterious new mark on her wrist. "We mated and performed a blood oath. I could feel his seeds inside of me, and it gave me the motivation to succeed in stealing the trident."

I wondered if my father also bore the same crescent mark. Every time I saw him, he wore gauntlets around his wrists, so there was no way for me to know if he was still bound to her after all these years.

"I thought I would do it peacefully and quietly, but I was discovered. I had to fight my way out, and I killed the high priest. His death began plummeting me down a dark path." I saw blood floating around her, the priest's searing body, and her magic glowing so vibrantly in her hands that I thought it would broil her. Adding onto her evolving magic was the power of her priest, leaving his body like a stream of wispy blue lights and piercing her skin. The optimistic and loving girl that she once was hadn't faded all the way. She had too much remorse to let go completely, but she had become much closer to the woman I knew her as.

"The only light I could feel was inside of me, and I had to protect the future of my children. I had to protect my family. I fought my way out through anyone I had to, in order to return to my beloved."

It was difficult to watch her stumble through her home and fight off family and friends reluctantly. With each kill, her heart became a little bit blacker and colder. It became easier, and that's what frightened and thrilled the Sea Witch. "And then what happened?"

"My magic had been corrupted so much that I thirsted for battle...for blood. Your father didn't have to do much convincing for me to finish the fight." She spared me the grizzly details, but I did see my father by her side as she held the trident up. There was a hot, bright light, and the sheet of ice dissipated into a puff of smoke. It faded away until nothing but the taste of death remained in my mouth.

"And what happened next?"

"I moved into the palace with your father, but I stayed in a secluded corridor. It was in secret because he hadn't told the king about our arrangement. No one even knew that your father had the trident, besides a young mermaid that your father trusted." By the scowl on her face, I knew she had to be referring to the woman who raised me. "I took her on as my apprentice—for added protection—while your father was deciding on what he should do. He knew his father wouldn't accept me. We spoke of overthrowing him. In the meantime, I laid my eggs, and I waited for you to hatch…"

"Were you deformed yet?" I couldn't imagine my father bothering to lead her on if she were in such a horrible physical condition.

"No, but the darkness was still strong in me, even though my powers had waned. Your father noticed the decrease as well. He had a difficult time operating the trident. That's when I told him about the price of parenthood.

"I thought he took it well, but as I slept…" I knew that she didn't want to show me. She closed her eyes tightly as if she were experiencing the trauma all over again. She was unable to contain her sorrow, and I saw flashes in my head of her waking up out of her sleep to a room pulsing with light. The silhouette of my father stood over a nest with the trident aimed at my family and me. "I heard cracking, and I felt an intense blast of heat. I woke up just in time to see my eggs exploding, and the magic that we created being absorbed into his body."

I shut my eyes and hit my head, forcing out the image of the Sea Witch shrieking in horror. Her heart was shredded to pieces at the sight of my forming siblings exploding into dust and streams of light.

"I didn't understand. How could I understand or comprehend it? What he had done was so…it was monstrous! I attacked him, but with his increase in power and the trident, I was no match. He nearly killed me, but I escaped."

Her rage was palpable. Flashes of bloodied faces kept coming to my mind, and it gratified her more and more each time. "I ran amok in the palace, killing anyone I could find. It wasn't long before I ran into his father. He tried to put me down, but I ripped out his spine through his chest. I thought that would hurt your father. I did it right in front of him, but I had done him a favor."

Amongst the flashes of her memories, I saw my father's smug smile. I wondered if there was ever a time in his heart that he cared for her, but as her magic grew darker, his ambition blotted out everything.

"He blasted me again, and I narrowly escaped. I tried to return once I had recuperated, but someone used one of my spells to put a barrier around Atlantis."

"My mother?"

By the sneer on her face, you'd think she thought I was the woman who barely raised me. "My former apprentice. Your father had been wooing her. Apparently, he never felt comfortable loving someone as powerful as me. It was too great a risk. She was weak enough for his heart."

Even after seeing so much and experiencing her pain, I still found it difficult to believe. "If that's true—if any of this is—then why did my father keep me alive?"

"By all accounts, you should be dead. Something protected you. Perhaps it was your own power. He probably couldn't hurt you. But he probably also realized that keeping you alive served a greater purpose."

"Why? So, he could keep his blood oath to you?" I guessed. "Why would that matter to someone like him?"

"Everything. A blood oath cannot be broken without consequences. I promised that I would destroy him and his kingdom. I failed. That is why I became the beast that I once was. I should have let myself die in agony and shame, but I refused to die without revenge. That's why I lured young and stupid little mermaids into my den of iniquities. I give them a piece of paradise as long as I get what I need in the end."

Her lack of remorse didn't surprise me, but it was certainly disturbing. "Their lives for your youth?"

"Don't look at me like that. I told you that my betrayal took place over one thousand years ago. Your 'mother' and father must have been stealing lives to keep themselves relatively young. He probably waited so long to bear children in fear of having his magic dissipate again. I'd wager that it was an accident. Lucky for him, his daughters were destined to be weak."

"Why was I born one thousand years later?"

"I don't know, but your magic protected you. It made you strong. It's ingrained in your blood and your bones. It's potent." She grabbed my chin and eased me closer to her. "You have the potential to be the greatest sorceress that's ever existed in this world—on land and sea—if you want it."

No wonder why she fell so hard for my father. She might have slipped into darkness over love, but she also had a thirst for power. Why couldn't she see where her greed led her? "I don't want any of this."

By her widening eyes, I could tell she was genuinely surprised. It wasn't that I lacked interest, but I certainly didn't want to reap the sort of consequences that she did. "How did something so pure come from your father and me?"

"Maybe it's because you bore me with love." I was aware of how ridiculous I seemed, and it was obvious by the scowl on her face that she thought I was insane. But I saw a light in her, even if she didn't want to see it herself. "He might have promised you lies, but your heart was true. And you wouldn't have been filled with such rage and grief if you didn't love me in return."

"Perhaps," she answered slowly.

I didn't feel like I had any good options. They were both mass murders. "You desire to kill my father."

"I do."

The revelation of her revenge suddenly dawned on me. "And my sisters and my kingdom! You expect me to help you?"

"You don't have to kill anyone—"

"But if you don't do it soon, you will eventually need my blood to hold off the power of the oath. Won't you?" Her silence was more than enough confirmation. I gritted my teeth to conceal my rage. My sisters were vicious, but they weren't unreasonable. My father was the problem—not my entire kingdom. "Why should I aid their murderer?"

"Because if you don't help me continue to be a monster, your father will eventually force you to become one." She smiled once she noticed my brows slightly elevated. "You can't survive on your own. You need one of us, and out of the two of us, I'm the only one motivated to keep you pure."

"I don't know if I want to kill him."

"He killed my children. He threatened your life! If you don't want to kill that human boy, I have to destroy him."

If I returned to my father, my magic would be at risk of corruption. I didn't want him to force me to kill Ian. I trusted that the Sea Witch didn't want me to go dark, but I wasn't without my suspicions. What if I stopped her revenge fantasy? Would her hatred of him overtake her urge to protect me? "How do I know that you even care about me? Maybe you only want to steal my magic."

She took a deep breath. "I have no intention of stealing it. But if you one day decide to give it to me, I wouldn't refuse."

I trembled from my desperation of wanting to trust her. "Is that what you were hoping for when you took me in?"

"It doesn't matter what my intentions were. It matters what they are now." She tried to touch me, but I moved away from her again.

"Is your revenge more important to you than me? Your daughter?"

"I would like to restore what I lost—what your father took from me. But I can guarantee you—because I know him better than I know my own black soul—he will separate us from one another. Is the family that betrayed you worth my life?" There was only one answer for her that wouldn't be offensive.

"You're wrong. I'll find a different way. We can do it together."

I was taken aback by the soft and tender smile that came to her lips. "I wish I could say that I believed in your hope…" She swam to my face quickly and shoved her thoughts in my mind as loud as she could. "But I'm not nearly that idiotic."

I was overcome with anger—which I'm sure was born out of frustrations about my dark future—and I retreated to my clam. In my world, I wanted to turn back to my original form, live peaceably with the Sea Witch and Napa, and return to my kingdom with my birth mother by my side. I wanted my sisters to be kind, my father to be loving, and my mother to be forgiving. I knew that outside of my world lived the truth, and I'd have to embrace it eventually. I would make a decision about my allegiances, and I'd confront my father about my attempted murder.

But until I was ready to face that world, I would sulk in my own.

Chapter Seven

The Sea Witch left me alone for a good while. I fell asleep, and when I woke up, my hair had returned to blue, and my tail was in its normal shape. I touched my face and was relieved to be my normal self. My fingernails weren't going to accidentally peel the skin from my bones.

I looked up and wished a good morning to my outdated carving of Ian. It was ridiculous that I was relieved to be pale-skinned for him. Humans wouldn't understand something like a sea witch. I never expected to see him again, but sometimes, I'd play a game and pretend that wasn't the case. I wanted to remain beautiful in his eyes, and believing that I was, gave me comfort. Silly, huh?

The Sea Witch was nowhere to be found, so I assumed she must have been hunting. It might have been considerate of me to wait for her return, but I cared more about poor Napa. What if he had gone on a search party and ended up as something's lunch? I had to go to the surface to check on him.

I was a little surprised when he was resting pitifully on a rock as a seagull. I should have known that he'd be waiting for me to return. It's not like he had any family or friends to go home to while he was still an animal.

"Napa?"

He raised his head and began flapping his wings in excitement. "You're alright!"

"In some ways…" I patted his soft head. He was the least complicated person in my life, and I appreciated our friendship. I never wanted that to change. "The Sea Witch is my mother."

"And…" I could sense he was trying to ease around my feelings. "…is that a good or a bad thing?"

"I thought it would be horrible—it sort of is—but it's fine. It's a bit of a relief to have a mother again, and I know she cares about me in her own way."

"And why did you turn…" He tried not to think about it once he saw my face, but he couldn't stop. "…into that thing?"

I chose not to be offended, especially since my emotional reaction probably should have offended the Sea Witch. "It's another form. If my life is in danger, and I need that power, I'll become that way again. It's a defense system."

"Well, I'm glad you're okay. I was afraid I'd never get to see the real you again."

"Well, I hope I'll get to see the real you soon enough."

If he had a face like mine, I imagined that he would be grinning from ear to ear. It was no secret that Napa was smitten with me, and his feelings were only becoming stronger. I grinned hard, but it was difficult to reciprocate such feelings with a bird. Besides, love was foreign to me. I had only seen it briefly through the eyes of the twisted Sea Witch and…well, Ian. I recalled the affection he felt for his parents and how his entire world exploded in front of his eyes.

"When do you think I'll be able to see your human face? Why can't I know your plan to turn back into a human?"

He ducked his head down in embarrassment but raised it again. "Have you ever heard of 'true love's kiss'?"

"No." His wave of adoration caused me to blush, though.

"It's from fairytales. Most think it's a stupid myth, but I think some people can experience it. It's said that true love's kiss can break any curse. There are a couple of examples—"

"You think if I kiss you, you'll change back into a human?" It seemed like a very simple task. I would have done such a simple favor for him ages ago.

"Not exactly…" Poor Napa. He rubbed his feet against the rock as he sulked in disappointment. "Let's just say that I'm gonna surprise you one day, very soon."

Napa was the kindest person anyone had ever been to me. If he were a man, and I could somehow gain a pair of legs, I imagined that I could have a comfortable life with him. I doubted that he could gain a tail and live in my dangerous world. I wouldn't feel right asking him to, but I already knew that he would agree. Still, I wasn't sure if blind devotion equated to love. It either meant that he was a great friend or a great fool.

"If I were in love with you, how would I know?"

Napa flapped his wings nervously and nearly flew away. He was such a silly bird. I didn't mean to laugh, but I expected him to be a little bit bolder if he were going to bring it up. "It's just a strong feeling that you get. It feels like irrational logic. You know the intensity of your affection can't quite be explained, but it can't be refuted."

"Well, my mother experienced an irrational affection for my father. It didn't turn out so well for her."

"Did he love her back?"

"I don't know. It doesn't seem like it." Loving each other at first glance seemed strange, but that's what my mother claimed. Her feelings intensified, but I never saw a man who loved her. However, she was pulling memories from her own mind. It's possible that her truth was corrupted by her pain.

"Well, I don't know what love is like for merpeople, but humans fall out of love. Sometimes, people end up together too quickly, and they jump into relationships without knowing each other. Then, you have couples that have been together for so long that they fall into a pattern, and they don't know how to admit they're not happy."

"There are different forms of love, though." I could certainly see that in Ian's life. He perceived his parents' love for one another to be real, but they certainly loved him differently. They were his providers and protectors. In time, it was possible to learn to feel the same way for the Sea Witch. I would have to heal from her betrayals first.

But even though I didn't know who else cared for Ian, I still knew that his life was fulfilled before I came along with my family to ruin it. "You don't have to be intimately involved with someone to truly love them."

"…that's true, but…" Napa didn't really think of anything else. His mind was blank, but his emotions weren't. It was like coming up on the surface, expecting to see a clear night sky, and being encompassed in thick fog instead.

I didn't mean to upset Napa, but I simply couldn't offer him more than companionship while he was trapped. There was a part of me that questioned if he was lying about being a human, and I had enough lies to last me a lifetime. "Since we are on the topic of your world and the way humans do things, why don't you tell me about your lands?"

"Well, I used to live out in the forest, miles away from any town. My dad taught me how to hunt, and I was crazy good at my age. I used to run all the time, and I'd climb trees all day."

"What's a 'tree'?"

"It's a very tall plant. They have leaves on them that are sort of like flat reefs—usually green. I'm sure you've seen a wooden boat before. That pirate ship you talked about would have been made out of wood, and wood comes from trees. They can be wide or thin, young or old. Those are trees out there."

He pointed his wing out toward the shore. I knew about the sand, but I didn't see any reef ships. "Where?"

"Up high. Do you see the crowd of green in the distance?

"Yes." It didn't look so wondrous from afar, but I assumed it would have appeared very big if I were up close. "That looks nothing like you've described."

"Well, you're welcome to paint a better picture when I turn back into a human. You can go inside my mind and see my memories. You can truly experience the world...unless you just come with me."

I grinned hard. "That would be lovely, but I don't know if I should risk going to the surface unless it's to get rid of Ian. My father might take it out on the rest of the humans."

"So...you still need to get rid of Ian before you can be free?"

"I think so." I leaned against the rock and frowned. Everything inside of me broke when I thought about the light in Ian's bright blue eyes being extinguished forever.

"Well, we're gonna figure this out. We're going to save you from your dad, and I'm going to learn how to become a human again." I appreciated Napa's optimism. Napa had learned to handle his curse gracefully—assuming his story was true—and I admired him for that. He certainly kept my life interesting.

"Thank you, Napa." I wished I could completely trust him. He hadn't given me a reason not to, but my parents taught me that trusting others would only end in agony.

I didn't want to be like them, though. I wanted to trust my friend and learn to love someone in the future. Perhaps that would one day be Napa or someone else. But if I were going to learn to trust anyone, I thought it would be best to start with myself.

When I returned home to the Sea Witch, she was sharpening a sword with a stone. She didn't speak about where she had gone, and I did not ask. We both accepted the new truth of our lives, but we certainly didn't address it. She was my mentor, and I was still her protégé. "When will you teach me about magic?"

She set her stone and sword down before turning to look at me. "You're not too afraid of what will happen?"

"The only darkness that I've experienced has come from my parents. I'm not afraid of what's inside of me. I control my own fate. If I can master my magic, I can determine its outcome."

I could tell the Sea Witch still believed I was being naïve, but she smirked with a bit of pride. "Fine. We will continue our combat training, but I will include some teachings of magic."

I was thrilled. I don't know why it suddenly mattered so much to me. Perhaps it had something to do with the fact that there was a growing amount of trust between the two of us. "When do we start?"

"Tomorrow." She went back to sharpening her sword. I didn't want to wait, but I also didn't want to press my luck with her. She agreed to teach me, despite the fact that aiding my parents led to her betrayal and banishment. Gratitude was the proper emotion, not impatience.

The next day began like most of our other days. The Sea Witch woke me up with a savage attack. I learned to sleep lightly while in exile, but I perfected the skill, thanks to her. I thought I had already received her best, but she was demonstrating a much faster and more agile warrior than I had ever encountered before. It wasn't long before our battle turned into me trying to get away from a decapitation. "Is this level of ferocity necessary?"

"It's always necessary. Don't ask foolish questions." I tried to twirl out of the way of her strike, but her sword took a slash to my back. I hissed in pain, but after the next swipe took a chunk out of my shoulder, it became clear that I certainly would not receive mercy. "Fight like your life depends on it!"

"But it doesn't!" She was clearly trying to provoke me into my stronger form—the form that resembled her—but I was determined not to become that. My father might have been the mastermind behind her genocide, but I still saw her monstrous hands commit those atrocities. I had to fight in my own way. "You can't force me to become like you."

I tried fighting back with my sword and deflecting her attacks with my rounded blade. That became the most effective technique. Just when I thought I had the upper hand and was determined to bring my sword down on her head, she outstretched her hand, and a force blew me back against the cavern wall.

My back made a violent impact, and I bounced off and drifted for a few seconds in paralysis. The feeling came back to my skin first. There were slight sensations of pain triggering my senses. Then, it all flooded in like an eel, jolting me with power. "That would be useful to learn."

The Sea Witch threw her weapon on the ground and clenched her fingers into fists with much pride. "Magic isn't a force that comes from nothing. There's a trace in it everywhere. It's the energy within us. I used my energy to produce such a blast. It's advanced, but you could learn to do the same."

I had a feeling that the dose she gave me was minuscule compared to what she could truly do, so I composed myself and ignored my aching body. "And how do I do such a thing?"

"You should take care of your wounds first."

I looked at my bloody shoulder. We did take care of our wounds quickly. We didn't want any uninvited guests coming into our territory by the scent of our blood. "I've never healed myself before. I thought healing was about sacrifice."

"When I heal you, I'm only giving you enough of my magic to accelerate your body's natural ability to heal. The worse the wound, the more power you need. It's trickier to draw from your own magic. It requires a greater will. The stronger you are mentally, the easier it will be."

I closed my eyes and focused, but there had to be a catch. I had never seen her heal herself. If it were all a matter of will, she should have been a master. "I'm trying."

"You know your body better than anyone," she scolded. "Using magic is a way of manipulating our world. You should only manipulate what you already understand. There is instinctive magic, but it's erratic and dangerous."

"Well, you would know," I mocked.

"Yes," she admitted hesitantly. It was still a sore subject. "Creatures like us can use reactionary or impulse magic. Most can't.

We're powerful, but we're dangerous. And if you are solely relying on your own energy for magic, you can risk using too much and destroying yourself."

"And where else would I impulsively draw from?"

"Dark magic. Even I don't know where it comes from, but there is a direct source. It touches everything, and it has infinite wisdom and power. I don't know if there's any spell outside of its capability. Sometimes, when you think you're using magic on instinct, it's actually guiding you."

"And it can corrupt anyone?"

"Yes, but it varies. It's had a hold on me ever since I did that blood oath with your father. I opened a passageway. I can reach out to the source, but it can reach back to me. I don't want that for you."

I certainly didn't want that either. "So, I need to draw on my own magic to heal my wounds, but I shouldn't use too much?"

"Correct. You know how strong you are, how strong you should be, and where you expect to go. These wounds cannot stop you. Rise above your pain. Rise above your weakness."

I knew she was trying to be insightful, but it all seemed a little too simple to me. Still, I closed my eyes and concentrated. I let myself be still and rocked with the water as it gently tussled me from side to side. I listened to the sound of my heart beating in my chest until I could feel my blood pumping and rushing through my veins. I began to feel my power waiting inside my stomach as if I had swallowed something alive. It bubbled up, and the pain from my cuts was centralized until they faded away. I couldn't see the mark on my back, but I could feel it closing and my pain subsiding.

"That is quite useful." I touched my back to be sure and looked at the Sea Witch, amazed. "How come I've never seen you heal yourself?"

"While in my prime—as I am now—I heal quite fast on my own. When I lived alone, I usually let my body do its natural work. If you choose to rely on your weaker body, you may have to tap into your magic to save your life. But you must remember, you are not an unlimited source."

My fatigue was greater than when I used my magic to heal her. It humbled me—in a good way—to know that I wasn't immortal or all-powerful. "Will my magic be stronger in my other form?"

"Didn't it feel stronger?"

"Maybe…" I didn't want to fully admit the truth to her. Jumping into my powerful form meant that I was capable of so much more, and I had to make sure that I wouldn't be tempted by the power I had access to as my normal self.

"Napa—the shapeshifting human—needs to acquire a piece of an animal to transform. He usually consumes them. Is that his way of understanding those forms before manipulating his body into them?"

"I don't know much about your little friend, but I would assume that is the case. Transmutations can be a bit complicated, though." She was still uncomfortable with Napa, but I had moved beyond the fear of him ending up as dinner.

"You said that you know how to gain legs. Does that mean you've met a human before and figured out how their body works?"

"It does…" she answered slowly. "Why are you still interested in getting legs and going to the surface world? I know you don't want to kill that human. You don't want to darken your magic."

"What are you suggesting?" I asked, startled.

The Sea Witch crossed her arms and got right in my face, smirking deviously. "When you saved the human, did you kiss him?"

My entire face heated, and my heart raced. "I breathed air into his mouth, so he wouldn't suffocate. Why?"

I had misinterpreted the Sea Witch's intentions because her smile softened into amusement. "Do yourself a favor and never tell your father."

Considering that my father exiled me for saving Ian, I certainly never planned on discussing the intimate details of how. "I had no plans to!"

"Good." I had a feeling that she knew more than what she was letting on, but I was too embarrassed to press her. "Your magic has mostly been about defense. When you feel threatened, that's when it manifests. You need to activate those emotions without letting them control you."

"Like the night you nearly froze me to death…?" I regretted my smart comment as soon as I thought of it.

But the Sea Witch was more amused than angered. "I did. Rage is a powerful motivator, and so is grief. You'll be your greatest enemy, but if you master yourself, no one will be able to defeat you." She held onto my shoulders and shifted behind me. "Imagine being alone and afraid while something is waiting in the dark to rip you to shreds. Your father expects you to either become a killer or be killed.

He'd feel no grief if you were to die. He would feel little pride if you succeeded. You're only a tool for him to use."

I closed my eyes and tried to feel my rage behind her words. I had every right to feel angry or neglected for the hell he had put me through. I thought of the intense pain of my stomach carving itself out of existence from starvation. I thought of how shattered my mind felt from the lack of sleep. I thought of the neglect and how weak I felt for wanting him to welcome me home, when the truth was that he always abused my sisters and me. The world would be a much better place if he were dead!

But I still couldn't get anything to form. "I feel something, but it's not enough."

She sneered. Her rage for my father was palpable. "I don't understand how you lack the proper hatred of your father to succeed."

I tried to focus on my hands as I thought of my father's trident pinning me down, and the look of disgust on his face. He thought of me as a failure. He tried to murder me. He murdered my siblings. But even with all the atrocities he committed against me, I found myself feeling incredibly sad for him. Perhaps my instincts were telling me to pity my father instead of opening myself up to rage and darkness. "Maybe there's another way."

"There is…" she suggested hesitantly. "Defending yourself out of fear is a sure way to hurt yourself and others that you may wish to protect. Rage creates incredible magic, but it burns through you quickly. Instead of operating in fear or rage, love can also be a powerful magic. That way, your magic can be used for protection. It's unlikely you will cause a mistake and darken it this way."

I thought operating off love would be easier, but when I closed my eyes, I realized that I didn't know where to begin. I barely remembered my mother, and she was currently tainted as a fake and an accomplice to the murder of my siblings. My father's sparse affection felt like a scheme, and I knew the details of why his praise and attention were so shallow. My sisters were petty and jealous. I didn't even know what love was until I saw Ian's smiling face and heard his laugh—any laughter—for the very first time.

"I can't think of a powerful enough memory to draw from."

The Sea Witch's shoulders dropped, and she stroked my cheek sympathetically. "I know, and I'm deeply sorry for that."

I didn't realize that I wasn't being honest with her. There was a spark of something in the pit of my gut, flickering. I was simply too afraid to seek out what it truly meant. It was an impossible feeling to search through. It honestly frightened me.

"I'll show you some meditation techniques. I'll teach you some of my spells, but I can't make you tap into your potential. That's something you have to do yourself."

I nodded. I knew the Sea Witch cared for me, but she didn't embrace me like I knew Ian's mother once did to him. Finding strength from my real mother would have been the easiest way to tap into my potential, but I wasn't going to lie to myself. She trained me, fed me, and kept me safe. I think that's all she knew to give, and it was all I required of her for a long time.

Chapter Eight

Nearly two years went by until our routine was broken. When I opened my eyes, the Sea Witch wasn't hovering over me with a weapon. She was lying beside me and just…watching. It was unnerving, and I kept wondering if she was about to ram her sword in my chest. I tensed up my body as her fingers came at my face, but her sharp fingers were surprisingly gentle. She softly stroked my skin and made me feel at ease.

"What's going on?"

"I was curious…" She grinned maniacally and touched the faded carving of Ian's young face. "…how long has this been here?"

I was so embarrassed that I turned my back toward her and covered my face. I never expected her to find the carving. I honestly didn't think it was anything to fuss about until that moment. My face was warm, so my cheeks were probably red. I had to force myself to calm down and face the Sea Witch. It was the only way to belittle the significance of Ian. "Why are you in here?"

"It dawned on me while I was grabbing my favorite weapon to best you—"

"You wouldn't have bested me today—"

"I always do." She grinned sadly. I had become extremely formidable, and there were one or two occasions that I could have considered a victory, but the Sea Witch always made up a technicality, and she insisted that I cheated. Other than that, she usually won. "You're nearly of age, and we're coming to the point where we need to make a decision."

My smile fell as I realized what she was referring to. We didn't talk much about my inevitable demise. It led to heated arguments that I wanted to avoid. It was a little too late to avoid it all now. "Do you think the two of us can defeat my father?"

"The only sort of defeat he'll honor is his death, Luna."

I sat up and clutched onto her hands desperately. "What if we run away together? You know how to give us legs. We can go to the surface and live as humans!" She knew that it was a deep desire of mine. I turned her lair into a museum of surface world artifacts. I told her all the stories Napa shared with me about his world, despite her appearing uninterested. I had been preparing myself to escape, just in case I had to.

"Your father also knows such spells. He'd find us."

"He hasn't found us yet." She gave herself too little credit. Her barrier spell kept her safe for one thousand years, and it was her spell that kept me from finding my way home to Atlantis. There was no reason why we couldn't try it again. "We have a chance up there. We don't have to kill each other."

"Luna, I've tried that already."

My desperate smile faded, and the intensity in my shoulders was swallowed up by numbness. She mentioned that she met a human before, but she never gave me specifics. I imagined she had gained her ability to grow legs from observing sailors as they passed by, and nothing more. "You lived on the surface world?"

"For some time." Her eyes darted to the crescent symbol on her wrist. "I wanted to see if it was even possible to leave who I was behind, but I couldn't. I'll never be free as long as I have the blood oath."

I became instantly furious with her; my body was shaking. I was outrageously saddened by the fact that she tried to live as a human and failed. That stripped away every fairytale I dreamed about when I closed my eyes and wished for a world where I could be safe. Honestly? I felt as though she betrayed me.

"Maybe things will be different," I begged for both of us. "You'll have me."

She slightly shook her head, while her eyes stayed focused on my hands gripping hers. I wasn't used to such a somber expression on her face. She usually replaced her sadness with indignant fury. "I need to show you something, but I don't know how you'll react."

"You've kept another secret from me?" I'm not sure why I was surprised or hurt. I don't know if she loved her secrets, but she certainly needed them.

"Yes. I thought training you would create a proper bond between us, and I thought you would sway in the direction I wanted, but…"

I let her go as the situation became clearer, and I became even more outraged. "You're disappointed that you couldn't turn me into a hateful witch like you?"

"I thought I knew you, but we're not that much alike." She chuckled with relief. "That's a good thing."

I could sense from the Sea Witch that whatever she had to show me was going to rip me up inside. I was disappointed she didn't have more faith in my strength, but I was hesitant to push through her mind and see the secret weighing on her. "What will this change?"

"Everything." The burden she held was too great, and a fragment of it pierced my mind. For some reason, the shard was an image of young Ian. She provoked a memory I had of him unconscious on the rocks. I watched his small chest and noticed it barely moving as he struggled to breathe, and his body trembled from the cold. He was so naïve and fragile. I questioned how I could ever believe something so weak could be so beautiful.

I knew that I was too young to remember thinking this, but I wanted to kiss him. I had pressed my lips against his already. I knew what they felt like, so it was more than curiosity. But he was very handsome as the sunlight rested on his skin and glittered off the beads of water caught in his slick hair. I wanted our kiss to be different. I needed it to be.

I gasped and pulled myself out of my tainted memory before my younger self could lock lips with Ian. I had instinctively swum away from the Sea Witch and out of my clam. She cocked her brow in confusion. If she hadn't planted the vision of kissing Ian inside my head, I didn't understand what that could mean. "I need to see it."

She raised her eyes to the top of the cavern wall. I didn't appreciate the Sea Witch's constant struggle with who she thought I wanted and who I needed her to be. The truth was, I needed her to be somewhere in between. Unfortunately, she only dealt with absolutes. "Let's go."

The two of us didn't travel together very often. I wish I could have said it was nice swimming beside my mother, but she was unnervingly quiet. She was also moving at a rapid speed, so I pumped my tail furiously to keep up with her. I didn't bother asking her to slow down. She'd probably scold me for preferring to stay pale and weak instead of blue and powerful.

I began to feel an eerie recollection of my environment. I was so focused on keeping up that I didn't take notice of anything until I saw a chair from the airplane lodged between large rocks. "We're headed toward the sunken airplane?"

"Yes."

I lost my motivation to keep up with the Sea Witch. I thought I was unfazed by death—since I had monsters for parents—but the horror of Napa's emotions was hollowing out my insides. To think of how frightened those humans must have been—knocked out of the sky and falling without any sense of control or chance of a miracle—was maddening. All my life, I had been fighting to survive. My spine was tingling at the thought of having no options and not even a chance to fight.

The Sea Witch stopped swimming, but I didn't see the plane. I knew we had traveled far enough. "Shouldn't it be here?"

"I cloaked it." She raised her arm and pressed her open palm against an invisible force. Her magic pulsed against something large, and it quaked with her power. I was amazed at her level of mastery, but I didn't appreciate it fully until the plane was visible again. "I didn't want any humans tracking it here. It would have led to more bloodshed."

Napa told me once that he expected humans would be able to find the plane. He said they had ways of tracking it with technology. Her magic must have shielded more than just physical appearance. "And what do you care?"

"I care because I know that you would." I knew she could feel, but empathy wasn't a strength of our kind, and her tone didn't convince me that she was an exception. "Touch it. Tell me what you feel."

I touched the outside of the plane. I merely glanced at the inside. I didn't have the stomach to look at the humans. The stillness of the dead children often bothered me. In Ian's memories, he was an energetic boy who could never be quiet or still. I imagined all human children to be so full of life. To see them frozen in death was such an egregious injustice to the fantasy surface world I created in my mind. "It feels smooth and cold…"

"What else?"

I closed my eyes and tried to let my other senses guide me. I did feel a tingling in my hand. It was mild at first, but it jolted throughout my arm. It didn't hurt. It almost felt natural, like it was a part of me. But then, it lingered and drenched me in a rush of cold that left me quivering on the inside. I could feel the breath of death inside my chest. "This magic is like mine and yours…"

I opened my eyes and turned to her, amazed. Once again, she had to reveal a horrible truth that I didn't want to accept about my father. "It wasn't an accident, Luna. Your father has been leaving messages for you. He causes some sort of massacre on the same day, every year. I suspect it's happened since the day you were exiled."

There were no yearly celebrations in my culture to honor the day you hatch. Napa told me once that humans call such things "birthdays." What a terrible gift my father had given me on my thirteenth birthday, nearly four years ago. "Then, he's about to do something horrible in a few days."

"And he won't stop until that boy is dead."

Again, I saw a flash of Ian in my mind, but my memory was altered. I could feel my father's commands throbbing in my brain, but it all dulled once I pressed my lips against Ian's. He was stunned and inexperienced. I remembered him blinking hard and his eyes opening even wider than before. Our hearts were rushing—and that wasn't so odd, considering that I was saving him from being murdered—but they stopped. For the few seconds we had together in our first kiss, we were drifting in a strange assurance that we were going to survive. Somehow, we would find a way to live together. And when I felt my heart revive, it synced itself to his.

"Kill him!"

I shrieked and held my head as I tried to get my father's wrath out of my mind. I could remember the weight of my panic and desperation dragging me down like an anchor. I didn't want to feel that way ever again. I had become too strong! My magic wouldn't tolerate it. I could feel my power bubbling up in my stomach and scratching against the inner layers of my skin.

"Why didn't you tell me?" My magic was surging throughout my body. My skin was hardening, my gums were sore, and my vision was sharpening in on the witch that focused my fury. "How could I not know he was doing this?"

"I wanted to protect you from it." She was unfazed by my changing body and my magic. The temperature of the water around us was rising rapidly. I was going to hurt her, and she didn't even care. "Your heart is different than ours. You feel compassion. I didn't want him to provoke you into killing that boy."

"If it'll save the lives of other humans—if it'll save my life—then what does it matter if he dies?"

"I think you know the answer to that."

"I don't!" I held my head and tried to concentrate. Maybe the Sea Witch didn't care if I broiled her skin and cooked her alive, but I certainly did. I also wanted to stop my transformation. I wasn't ready to know what I'd do with more magic at my fingertips. I had never lost control before, and it was frightening. "I don't know why that boy is doing this to me!"

"But you feel it. You just don't understand it…yet." The Sea Witch's eyes glowed bright, and her purpling skin chilled back into the coolest shade of blue. I was doing my best to keep my magic from leaking out, but the Sea Witch began to ease hers out on purpose. It took time for me to feel the temperature drop, but I recognized her power spreading, and my skin began to numb.

I breathed in deeply. She was trying to help me, and I let a wave of her magic sweep through my body and cool me down. The Sea Witch was not my enemy; it wasn't her fault those people were dead, she didn't want Ian to die, and I was the only one who had the power to save him. "What are we supposed to do?"

"I have to kill your father, but I cannot do it alone." Her shame quaked inside of me. She didn't want me involved, but the Sea Witch knew she was too weak.

We didn't communicate for a bit. She didn't need to ask, nor would she. I knew what she wanted anyway. It was clear from the first day I met her. I honestly felt as if I owed her for years of protection and training, but when I wanted to agree, I trembled. "I don't know if I want to give up my magic."

I was dirty, covered in ambition like tar I couldn't remove. I looked at my hands and nearly screamed at the thought of not feeling power flowing through my blood. With every heartbeat, it rushed through me. My pulse was linked with the universe itself. My potential was infinite. "I like having power," I whimpered. "I'm ashamed to admit that."

"Don't be." Her arms swept around me so quickly that I thought she was going to rip me open and take my magic by force. It's sad, isn't it? I didn't know she was embracing me as a display of affection. "It's your power, and you inherited it from me."

My arms slowly raised, and my fingers landed against her back. I had to believe she was capable of more than I thought. She knew love once before. It wasn't supposed to be impossible that a mother could love her daughter. Love was something that humans dreamed about in fairytales, but dreaming of something impossible was the only way to escape a nightmare.

"I know him," she told me. "He won't kill you. If you are not his heir, the same blood oath that infects me will inflict him. But he can do far worse than kill you."

"But you can't defeat him without me, and you'll need more than just a few drops of blood." I tried to pull away, but she grabbed my arms. I looked into her ruthless eyes and finally grasped what she was doing. If she couldn't convince me to give up my magic—and seeing that I was her daughter, she must have known that was unlikely—then she needed me to stand beside her in battle. But I never had a desire to kill my father, though she did what she could to widen the trench between us. The revelation about my father's massacres was supposed to be the final rift. "What if killing my father makes my magic go dark?"

"I'll be the one to kill him." She struggled not to seep out any excitement. "He's my responsibility. I should have protected you from him a thousand years ago. I won't let him destroy you or your heart."

I cocked my brow. "Are you sure we can defeat him?"

"He's nearly invincible with the trident, and he's increased his power since the last time we battled." She stretched her hand toward the inside of the plane, but I looked away. I still couldn't stomach it. "These humans died tragically. There should be a massive amount of energy left behind, but there's nothing here. Your father is feeding off death to make himself more powerful."

I certainly had no idea how I was supposed to know whether the dead left power behind in the living realms, but I did know the origin of the bones embedded in our home. "Is that really so different than what you used to do when you killed my people for your youth?" I sneered at her hypocrisy.

She snatched my arm and burrowed herself deep into my eyes. "I'm not making excuses for myself. I'm also not apologizing for what I've had to do to survive. Your father made me into what I am, and I am his reflection…except when it comes to you." She grabbed me by my chin and raised my head. She claimed that we weren't alike, but I could feel her admiring her own young image. "I want to do right by you."

I narrowed my eyes at her. Her magic and intentions felt impure. The smell of death was on her skin. I could nearly see the odor, like the colored fumes that rose out of her cauldron. "When my father dies, and the barrier around Atlantis falls, what happens to my sisters and the rest of my people?"

She didn't even possess the decency to pause. "I have to fulfill my blood oath, Luna. You know my answer."

I laughed shortly and out of hysteria. Deciding to help her kill my sadist of a father wasn't a hard decision, but it was a difficult one. Deciding whether I should help my unstable and cruel mother destroy the barrier that was protecting my people was much simpler.

But I didn't have much of a choice in the matter, and I hated it. "I need time to think."

She jerked her head back in disbelief. "You don't have much time left, and the only other option is to kill the boy and return home as a murderer, to the monster who killed your siblings."

"There's more to this world than the war between the two of you, and I don't believe my people should be eradicated because they're led by an evil king."

She scoffed and rolled her eyes as if I had said something outlandish. "Even fools have to pay for their ignorance."

"Even if I were planning to go around you and fulfill my father's wishes, I have no idea where Ian is. I'd never find him in time."

"There are greater forces at work here. They can't control you, but they position you exactly where you need to be for the desired outcome. You'll find him soon. I'm certain of it."

A shiver came upon me, but after my body involuntarily convulsed, I knew it wasn't from the cold. "I have to meet Napa."

I didn't allow the Sea Witch to distract me. She hated that I would risk going by myself out in the open to see Napa, but my life wasn't worth living without taking a couple of chances, and there was a strong possibility that I would be dead soon anyway. Besides, I needed someone else to communicate with besides my estranged mother.

When I returned to the surface, Napa was spewing with pride in himself and anxiousness. I thought he would have a new treasure to put in my collection, but he didn't have a pouch with him. "What has you so excited, Napa?" I needed some good news to take my mind off my horribly violent fate.

"I think I've found the boy you're looking for!"

"Ian?" My heart began beating so fast that I thought it would escape out of my mouth. I swallowed just to keep it safely inside of me, but I still felt ill. "Are you sure?"

"Well, his parents were killed while he was out at sea. He's around the right age. He has black hair and blue eyes, though humans can change those features."

"Like you?" I asked, amazed.

"No, not quite like me. But his name is Ian. He's been traveling with a group of Nigerians."

"They believe in mermaids." I remembered him telling me that some time ago.

"Yes, and they're near."

I wondered how Ian's life had been after so many years without his parents. I didn't think a human orphan would have it quite as hard as I did, but I was—sometimes—fortunate to have the Sea Witch take me in. Perhaps those Nigerians looked after him. "What else do you know?"

"I'm a bird! I listened, but it's not like I engaged in much of a conversation. Once I was sure, I got excited and wanted to tell you."

I didn't know what to think. Did the Sea Witch know he was sailing in our waters? It was impossible! She had never even met him. It could have been a coincidence, or she could have been prophesying a horrific end to my short story.

"Are you still willing to kill him?" Napa asked as if his heart would break if I gave him the wrong reply. "I don't want you to die, and if it would save other lives—"

"Then, I should stop the unnecessary bloodshed. Absolutely." Every kill I made was for food, out of self-defense, or on pure instinct. Would killing Ian truly be that different? I was a survivor, and I couldn't allow him to be the end of me. Fate should have respected the choices I had to make to protect myself and my family. "Show me where you spotted him."

Napa took off into the air, and I followed him in the water. I was always fascinated when he flew, but he couldn't fly faster than I could swim. My slow stride was only making me more nervous. I often thought of Ian and the sound of his laughter. He was so boisterously happy before I came into his life and ruined it. I wondered how much his voice had changed. He couldn't possibly be the same.

I had changed. I was malnourished and weak while I was alone in my exile, but I grew stronger, longer, and more beautiful as I became older. I wondered if he would be as enchanted with me as I was with him long ago.

I was beginning to sense something close and moving relatively slowly. I breached the surface, and I saw a boat from far off. Ian came from a small yacht when he was young. Napa said that only wealthier humans could afford to have them. This was a fishing boat, rusted and gliding slowly across the water. I often wondered if humans lacked resources so much that they had to take from us, or if they were gluttonous creatures that never learned to stop invading.

"Are you sure he's on that boat?"

Napa dove into the water and immediately transformed into a flounder. "I'm pretty sure, but you'll have to see if you recognize him."

I still felt so strange about seeing Ian again, especially with Napa by my side. What if there were trouble? He was so helpless before. I didn't want to risk him getting hurt, but Napa wouldn't leave my side. He was too stubborn. "I think I should go see the Sea Witch. She should probably know what I'm about to do."

"You want to tell her?" he asked, amazed. "I assumed you'd want to keep this a secret from her. I get the impression she's a little—"

"Strict—?"

"I was going to say scary and insane, but you'd know better than me."

I grinned. He wasn't wrong about her. She was certainly someone I wouldn't want to update about Ian, but Napa didn't need to know that. "I'll make a decision about what I'm going to do afterward. I'll meet you back tomorrow in our usual spot."

"But what if they get away? You don't want to miss this opportunity."

"It's better to be safe than sorry, Napa. Go on."

Napa was disappointed. I sensed that he also thought I was being dishonest, so I played my part and began swimming toward home. Once he thought I was gone, he turned into a bird and flew away.

I waited a little while before heading back to the boat. I approached it from underwater and emerged to the surface when I was very close. I heard several different voices coming from the side of the vessel, but I stayed hidden and listened.

"Where do you think you're going?" a man asked angrily. His speech was different than the few humans I had heard on the water, and his pitch was quite low.

"I'm going for a swim." This voice was more familiar and higher than the other man's. I couldn't be sure if the voice was Ian's matured, but my heart was beating so rapidly that I felt my chest vibrating. It had to be him! My imagination wasn't that absurd.

"Knowing what's out there in the waters? Are you insane?" another man yelled.

"If I were afraid of water, I wouldn't be out here. Besides, I've been freediving for years. I know what I'm doing."

I heard a splash and felt the ripples of his dive. He was being honest about his diving ability. He was moving faster than I thought a human would be able to. As he dove, his thoughts became clearer to me. He was focused and driven; once his mind was set on a task, he tore into it with a set of vicious teeth. He was searching, and he had been since the moment I left his side. His desire to find my kind was consuming, and even if it devoured him whole, he would press on.

Was he chasing me with that ferocity? If so, what would he do if he found me or another one of my kind? I needed to know if he meant me harm or if it was only curiosity that held his world together.

I knew both of my parents would have strongly objected to it, but I dove back into the water to get a good look at Ian. His body was lean and muscular like many of our warriors, except he had those long and beautifully strong legs. If I could get a hold of him, I knew I'd be able to grow a pair and walk among the humans.

I was curious how far he could dive. He must have been down three hundred feet with no sign of stopping. Was he really such a fool? He could easily find something willing to kill him, and he only seemed to be armed with a light strapped around his forehead and a belt with several compartments.

Then, I noticed there was something about Ian that I could feel calling out to me like something had its own life, rhythm, or magic. "That fool brought the dagger with him!" If I could sense it, I assumed my father could as well. It wouldn't be long before he sent someone to investigate, and I couldn't let him find me observing Ian while he tried to prove my existence!

I swam as fast as I could to Ian. He felt my presence, but Ian only turned his head just as my arms wrapped around his waist. He tried to push against my hands to force himself free, but I only squeezed tighter. His light was knocked out during our struggle. After a while, he became still, and I grew concerned that he was going to drown. I could have solved my problems right then and there, but pulling him down until he suffocated should have been his original fate, and I suddenly thought of my father's orders in my head. It made me physically ill—forsaking Ian to appease that psychopath.

I had to get him out of the water, but returning him to his boat wasn't an option. I couldn't afford to expose myself to his crew.

Napa and I had done many explorations, and I knew a few spots of land abandoned by humans. I came on the beach, dragging Ian's limp body. I was concerned that he was dead, but when I pressed my hand against his chest, he felt very much alive. His pounding heart left a pulsing sensation in my hand. I began to feel a strange warmth that baffled me. I recognized it from that spark that lived deep inside of me, and now it was growing and forming into something greater.

"Ian!" I was determined to revive him if he were between the edge of life and death, just so I could understand what sort of power he held over me. But when I dove down to press my lips against his, his arms grabbed hold of mine, and he rolled the two of us over and further from the water. I was stunned. He was alive, well, and on his feet, clicking some sort of device that he quickly retrieved from his belt.

"What are you doing?" I tried to block my body from his attack, but nothing seemed to be hurting me.

"I guess you creatures don't have cameras, but I'm getting the proof I need to show the world I'm not crazy."

I had seen a form of camera before. Napa brought one to me, and he told me they captured moments in time, so humans could hold onto memories. I tried crawling toward him, but he took out the dagger and held it up to me with his other hand. I was insulted that he thought he could successfully fight me off, but I didn't know what sort of magic he possessed.

I concentrated on the camera in his hand. I didn't want to hurt him, but my very survival was at stake. And when I thought about the frustration from failing those dead children on the plane, it wasn't difficult to turn it into power.

Ian hollered as the camera flashed bright with wavy colors and puffed up with smoke. He dropped it and shook his hand to dull the pain. "What was that?"

I wasn't exactly sure. The camera was still brightly lit with warm colors that wiggled with reckless abandonment. The camera began to crumble and ooze. I had never seen anything like it. "What is this?"

Ian was angry and probably wounded, but he quickly scooped some sand on top of the warm colors and the camera until it was gone. He moaned about his device being destroyed, but he put it back inside one of his compartments on his belt. "You can make fire, and you don't know what it is?"

I remained puzzled.

"I guess that makes sense—the not seeing fire part—but you're, apparently, more powerful than I thought." He still held my father's dagger tightly in his hand, but I didn't believe he would use it. I had seen the eyes of warriors determined to kill. He didn't possess such eyes.

I, however, could often make such difficult decisions when my life was threatened. His confidence in his safety was almost insulting. "I save you from possibly drowning, and this is how you repay my kindness?"

"Ever since you saved me, I haven't been able to drown. I was only pretending to be unconscious, so I could trap you on land while I got some answers."

I thought the Sea Witch asked about kissing Ian's lips because she was curious if I held affection for him. I had no idea that I had somehow bestowed a special power on him. "It must have happened when I breathed into you when we were children."

I wondered how deeply he had changed since he was a boy. He was taller and stronger, and his features were more masculine. Seeing a sculpted and bare torso wasn't very odd, but it had been such a long time since I was among any males. His physique was foreign, and it stirred feelings I didn't know how to describe.

But was he more of a challenge than he was presently presenting? He was reasonably strong, but did he possess more magic? It was possible. I did feel a sensation between the two of us, and he acquired an unnatural ability.

"It's quite the gift you've given me, but I'd much rather have my parents back."

Parents didn't seem like such a gift, considering my father. "I'm not the one who killed them."

"But you know who did." There was unrest in his heart. His vividly blue eyes shook with fury as if he constantly looked at the images of his parents' horrible deaths, every day since it happened.

I often thought of their blood and ashes coating the water. The poor soul couldn't even mourn over their bodies. He never saw them again after I carried him away. "I can't offer you revenge for what my father and sisters did. They are powerful, and I've been banished ever since. If you return to the water, especially with that magical dagger, they will find you and finish what they started all of those years ago."

He looked at the dagger and twirled it in his hand. Clearly, he had kept it close. He must have naively thought it could keep him safe or kill one of my kind, but I could tell he lacked the conviction required to kill me. "They banished you?"

"Yes, because I'm not like them."

His face softened just a little. He gripped the dagger once more, but ultimately, he decided to put it in a holster attached to his belt. Then, we both breathed a sigh of relief before he knelt on the sand in front of me. "You risked a lot to save me. Why?"

I hoped I wasn't being too bold by touching his body, but I was always an overly curious person. His face was sharp and very detailed. His nose was perfectly straight until the appropriate bulge rounded it out; it wasn't too wide either. After tracing my fingers across his jaw and cheeks, I was confident I would always remember how his skin rested on his bones, and the way his lips pressed together into an almost mischievous smirk, while I pressed his bushy brows in with my thumbs. It was surreal to be with a man, but it felt incredible as well. I couldn't stop myself from staring into his eyes and allowing myself to get lost in the sound of him breathing in the same air as I did.

"I saw that you were kind. I saw that you loved. I didn't know what that was like. I was curious what it would feel like to be…"

"To be loved?" He grabbed my hands to pull them away, but only so he could feel my face as well. I shuddered at the touch of his thumb grazing my cheek. The sensation I felt became a shockwave inside my body. I could accept it if it were mere attraction, but there was something more to it than that. I didn't know if the world was becoming madder or if it was finally making sense, but when he talked about love—when I looked through the prism of his mind to feel and know what it was meant to be—I knew, wholeheartedly, that I was finally discovering it for myself.

"Have you been looking for revenge this entire time?"

"Maybe." That saddened me, but Ian chuckled as if he really didn't know. "Mostly, I just wanted some proof. No one believed me. They thought I suffered such a trauma that I made the part about mermaids up. I had to have therapy and finally stop talking about it, or I would lose control of my family's fortune, and I couldn't even protect it in the end anyway. It's not easy living in a crazy world knowing you're the only one who is sane."

It was difficult to understand all he had gone through, but it was clearer when I went into his mind and recalled his feelings of grief, loneliness, and betrayal. Those things weren't so foreign to me. He deserved vengeance, but if I couldn't help the Sea Witch, I certainly shouldn't have helped him. "You mustn't bring humans to us. My father has been waiting for an excuse to destroy the surface world. I've seen him wipe out kingdoms before. He can and will do it again."

Ian snickered and fell back on his butt. "I doubt he could stand up to us. We have too many weapons. We'd burn the entire world before we'd allow ourselves to fail."

"And he has magic!" I couldn't afford for him to be so blinded by his arrogance when he understood nothing about real power. "Don't throw your life away on a vendetta. That's not why I saved you."

"Thank you for that, by the way…"

"For what?" I was afraid to breach too far inside his mind. I felt pain and fear so intensely from his childhood. I could see a young Ian being met by men in white, carrying him off. He looked back at a man screaming with tears in his eyes, and the man slipped out the tiniest smile. That was only a small portion of the betrayals he suffered because of my family. "For bringing such darkness into your life?"

"No," he smiled, "for saving me." His lips made contact with mine, and I was at a loss. It had been such a long time since I pressed my lips against his, and I knew that it was innocent. I was in such a panic to save his life. Now, I was suddenly aware of how much he had changed. His lips were succulent and full. I slightly gasped in shock of his advancement, but I didn't pull away. I thought I would. I even pressed my fingers into his shoulders, but I found myself gripping onto them instead.

I didn't want to lose myself to a stranger that I could never be with—one who I should have killed—but that was the logical part of me, and it was retreating deeper into the recesses of my mind. My instincts were telling me that there was nothing to fear or be concerned with, because the touch of his fingers pressing into my back, and his tender kisses on my lips, were telling me that we were compatible enough to see our attraction through to the end. Then, there was also the emotional part of me that connected with him so deeply. We had both suffered at the hands of my father. I felt guilt and obligation, but he was also my first connection to real love.

Whatever the reason, I couldn't bring myself to escape the desire he had for me. I don't know if I could have pulled away from the intensity of our affections. It was Ian who finally pulled away from my lips, laughing a bit hysterically. "A mermaid. I can't believe I'm making out with a mermaid…"

"Well, I can't believe I'm kissing a human. This isn't a normal thing for me either." I knew mermaids were nothing more than a fable to humans, but I wanted him to know that he was also a rarity. "Did you ever doubt that I was real?"

"No. Even when the doctors tried to convince me that I was insane, I could still remember your face. I could still hear your voice. I remembered when you breathed your breath into me. I knew you were the only reason I survived. There's nothing anyone could have done to take that memory away."

He spoke pretty words that were making me collapse under the weight of his romantic whims, but before I completely allowed myself to be crushed, I gathered my strength for reality. "So, were you searching for my family or—?"

"I was searching for you."

That spark inside of my gut began expanding. My affections were rapidly increasing, but I also knew it was power. It was a source of magic that was the key to my safety and the Sea Witch's.

Ian chuckled. "I don't know what I expect to do now that you're in front of me—we're from two different worlds—but I'm glad that I've seen you again. I just feel a little bit lost now."

I knew what my father wanted me to do, but I had no intention of killing Ian if he proved to no longer be a threat. "I need that dagger back."

"Why? It's the only thing I have from your world to prove something happened that night."

"That's precisely why I need it back." As a treasure collector, I sympathized with his desire to have more rare and beautiful things. I honestly felt a little horrible for asking. "You got to see me again. Do you honestly need anyone else to believe in mermaids if it would endanger your world?"

As he held the blade, it became apparent that it was more than just a knife to him. His mind went to a time right after his parents' murder. He presented it before a room of older men and women who seemed to be listening very carefully at first, but the more he talked, the more they whispered amongst each other. They dressed alike in dark blue uniforms and had golden shells on their chests. They should have been protectors in Ian's mind, but they weren't. They coddled him and spoke false promises, but they never offered him belief.

"No." He turned the dagger and pointed the handle toward me. Before I could grab it, he pulled away. "But I have some questions I need you to answer."

I wondered what the Sea Witch would think of us. She would probably slit his throat to protect us both—if she thought she had to—but she also seemed to know that there was much more to that boy than I originally fathomed.

"I'll make you a deal." I was being a fool, but my heart was telling me foolish things. "If you can make the pirates leave, and if you promise to never again speak of mermaids and the secrets I tell you, I will answer whatever questions you want to know."

Chapter Nine

"Fine. I agree."

I eyed him suspiciously. He agreed a little too quickly for someone who searched for me their entire life. "You'll never speak of mermaids again?"

He raised his arms and laughed. "No one has believed me. Unless I want to drag you to a lab and have the media declare that you exist, I might as well let this fantasy go."

His smile was incredibly warm, and he was inviting me into his persona of being a respectable and kind human. I didn't see that he was lying in his mind, but he literally had a history of obsession with my people. "I don't know if I can trust you."

He scooted a little closer to me and stared right into my eyes, shaking his head until he cracked a smile. "I think you know that you can."

I closed my eyes and concentrated on his thoughts, but I was bombarded with a tidal wave of emotions toward me. I was so overwhelmed that I had to immediately jump out. But just because I removed myself from the immensity of the ocean, didn't mean I was free from its presence. It was on my skin, my hair, my lungs, and it burned my eyes. Ian was, undoubtedly, infatuated with me. "Ask your first question."

"Am I under a spell?"

My face began to warm up, and I smiled so hard that it hurt. "What sort of spell would you be under?"

"In legends, sirens are beautiful creatures that lure sailors to their deaths. Their voices are enchanted. Men will do whatever they say."

My sisters had experience in that area, but they weren't hypnotic. They drew men in to kill them, and that was the end of it. "Have you done everything I've said?"

"Point taken." After all, he still had my dagger in his possession. "Are you capable of manipulating me in that way?"

I felt embarrassed and turned away, but I forced myself to resume power by smirking in his face. "Mermaids are wonderful at seduction, and men are curious and sexual creatures. We don't need magic to trap and kill you. Mermaid songs are lovely, but I haven't sung since that day I saved you."

"Why?"

"I don't know." It wasn't because I had never gone back up to the surface. Napa would have loved to hear me sing. "I'm sure there's probably a siren song or two, but I've never learned such magic, and not all mermaids possess magic."

"Why do you?"

I hesitated. I had only confided in Napa, and he hardly cared. Ian might have judged me harshly for it, so I mumbled my great shame out quietly. "My mother is a sea witch."

I braced myself for his disgust, but he chuckled again and shrugged his shoulders. "What does that mean?"

I felt as though I were going to explode right out of my skin, but the rest of my head followed forward in awe. Surely humans must have dealt with magic in one form or another. "Mermaids usually have to siphon magic from a source, so they are capable. A sea witch is born with magic, and my mother is very powerful."

"So, what else can you do besides blow things up?"

I wanted to show Ian something without endangering him. I pressed my hands deeper into the sand and felt the texture. Each grain was like a tiny crystal, but together, it could move like water. But if compressed tightly, it could make an impressive force. I concentrated my energy and moved it through the sand. I could manipulate the grains with my will and proper concentration.

"What are you doing?" Ian rose to his feet in alarm as the ground beneath him began to shake. The beads of sand swirled together, underneath and behind me, until they formed a modest throne to sit in. I figured it would be more comfortable for me to sit and be at eye level with Ian as he stood in awe of me. "How did you do that?"

"I've learned a couple of spells from the Sea Witch. It's mostly about manipulating the energy around you. If you can feel something's energy, connect with it, and understand it, you can alter it."

His brows rose, and I couldn't tell by his expression whether he was impressed or intimidated.

"I've learned to fight with magic as a defense. I'm not great at it, but I'm a strong enough warrior on my own to get by."

"Are you now?" he asked with an amused smile.

"I am." If he were mocking me, I'd have to show him a demonstration of my power. "I've also learned a little about transmutation, but I've never practiced."

"Wait…are you saying that you could maybe turn into a human?"

"Perhaps." I looked down at my tail sparkling in the sunlight. Napa was determined to become what I was, but he knew what it was like to have legs. Maybe being a human wasn't a satisfying lifestyle at all. I only needed legs to kill Ian, and I—apparently—had no intention of doing that. "I don't see a point in it though."

Ian folded his arms and laughed off my answer in disbelief. "You wouldn't like to see my world?"

I shrugged my shoulders. I was curious, but it wouldn't matter in a few days. Even if I ran away and my father never found me, that still meant abandoning the Sea Witch.

"I could show you impressive structures built by men that reach out and touch the sky. We could go flying and soar above the clouds." I appreciated his hand gestures as he explained, and how wide his eyes became as they filled with glorious memories. "I could treat you to the most incredible food you could ever taste, and—"

"Would you teach me how to dance?"

He was so stunned; his face was frozen for a moment. After a few seconds, he backed away uncomfortably, but he kept a smile on his face. "Yes. I would most definitely teach you how to dance."

I grinned. He could show me skyscrapers, but I'm sure he would have been just as amazed by the mountains and caverns in my world. Flying might have been thrilling, but he couldn't compare to Napa's expertise on the matter. Dancing was the experience I was most curious about.

Still, Ian seemed uneasy about it. "Are you sure you don't have me under some sort of spell?"

"No spell." I raised my head and leaned back on my throne. "I'm just very charming."

Ian's demeanor changed into a more somber expression, and he cautiously took a seat on the armrest of my throne. I scooted over to distance myself. "Your father banished you for saving me...what are your people really like?"

My heart shuddered inside my chest. I don't know why I became so nervous. There was nothing I could explain that would be worse than what he experienced. "There are other tribes or types of merpeople. I've never met them before, so I can't answer for them. My home is full of warriors, and we're merciless. My father believes it's best to kill potential friends in case they're potential enemies. He believes humans are a threat that pillages and pollutes our waters, and he wants to see them eradicated. He hated that I spared you. He saw my compassion as weakness."

I expected Ian's eyes to fill with disgust or at least outrage, but they softened and his brows furrowed into concern. "What happened to you after you saved me?"

"I was alone for almost a year. I barely survived. I'd probably be dead by now if my mother wouldn't have found me..." That was the first time I had admitted to anyone how much I needed the Sea Witch. My warrior pride would have never allowed me to be so soft before.

"And is your mother different from the rest of you?"

"No!" I laughed sadly. "She's just as fearsome as my father—probably more so—but she cares for me. She would do anything to keep me safe and make me strong. If that meant hurting me, she would..." I looked out to the waters in fear of the Sea Witch coming ashore to slit his throat. "You should be afraid of her, but I care for her as well."

"Why did your people attack my parents?"

"Because they love to kill." I saw the horror and sadness form in his eyes. It was too much of a blunt force rammed against his fragile heart. With everything I had endured, I thought I was stronger, but his pain was shredding me up inside. "I don't have an answer that can comfort you, Ian. My father has done worse to humans in retaliation for what I did for you, and he'll do much worse. You have to leave our waters while you still can, or you and your crew will be killed."

I tried to touch his arm, but he pulled away from me and began walking toward the water. "And how do you know me?" He turned back around before his feet could hit the wet sand, and I saw that his fury was made from pain. "My name, my mother's song…any of it."

"I can see in your mind. That's how we communicate."

I never thought entering one's mind was intrusive before, but by his wide-eyed expression of betrayal, he was obviously violated. "Your advantages seem very unfair."

"That's why you can't let others know of our existence. You don't want to begin a war."

Ian combed his fingers through his silky, dark hair as he paced around the beach. His eyes shined, and his voice quivered. "I don't know what else I should ask. I feel like I've prepared a million questions my entire life, but the most important one was understanding why my parents died. Now that I know there wasn't a real reason—that it was pure savageness…"

I thought the tears in his eyes were from weakness or fear, but I knew I had misjudged him by only gently tapping on his mind. He was inquisitive like I was, but the answers he received were maddening. "So many times, I've wished that I just died with them…"

There were times when I hated myself for sparing Ian. I felt like a fool for torturing myself over an ungrateful human, but…my heart was aching at the thought of changing that decision. If I had seen him torn to pieces or blown to dust, it would have haunted me.

"My father wanted me to find you and finish you off. I thought it was just about being cruel and hating the fact that his daughter was weak, but it was about corrupting my magic. He wants it to become dark. I'm not sure what will happen if it does, but he thinks he can control it."

"And?"

"If I hadn't saved your life and lived my life of exile, I may be like him now!" I didn't realize the revelation until I heard the words that left my lips. If I wouldn't have fallen flat on my face, I would have leaped from my throne. "He would have control of my dark magic, and your world may already be gone. I'm not trying to justify anything, but maybe there's a bigger fate working everything together for the good of the world."

"You're quite the optimist for an evil mermaid," he spoke bitterly.

"I'm trying to comfort you." How could he not see the value of his life? Our paths led us right back to each other. It must have been Fate. No sane person would go freediving after the circumstances of his parents' murder, and he was very adamant about not being insane.

"We were meant to know each other, and…" He turned to me, wide-eyed and alarmed, and I didn't know what else to say. How can you describe a feeling rapidly growing inside of you that envelops your entire life in a matter of seconds? How do you explain a passion that overtakes you with no rationality behind it? There was no justification for my aggressive internal struggle, but I was beginning to lose a war with myself.

"If you don't want them to find you, you should leave. I have a tracking device on my belt, so they'll find me here and pick me up. Hopefully, anyway."

If he had the courage to look me in the eye, I might have taken him seriously. "And that's it? After searching your entire life for me, you're willing to let me go?"

He placed his hands on his hips, raised his head to the sky, and laughed to himself in disbelief. "The thought of seeing you again was consuming me. I thought it was about finding answers, but now I know it's something more."

"More?"

He looked at me again, and I quickly identified him as a wounded man. His emotional complexity wasn't the most attractive quality. As a mermaid, I was taught to look for a strong mate who would be a fierce warrior and worthy of taking my father's place, but I couldn't dismiss the hurts caused by myself and my family. Besides, I began to feel his ache inside of me.

I wanted to understand. I needed to! So, without his permission, I dove into his mind.

Ian was sitting up in something comfortable that I equated to the clam I slept in. He had a cloth over him that covered his body from the center of his waist down. His chest was bare, and his garments were tossed on the floor. There was morning light peering in from the window, and he was taking advantage of the light by chiseling ink onto a small tablet with what Napa called a "pen."

"Hey, I brought you some coffee…" A beautiful young woman came in from a secret opening in the wall and sealed it back up once she entered. She held two white containers in her hand. She gave one to Ian and sat beside him.

"Thanks." He set the tablet down on a platform before taking her coffee.

She smiled hard, but she was unsettled. "I know men well enough to know that when they hide something, it's best to find out why. Don't screw with me." She placed her hand on top of his leg. "Please, let me see."

He sighed and handed her the white tablet. The details of his carving were simple, but it was clearly meant to be a picture of my face as a child. The young woman scoffed and shook her head. "This again?"

"It's just a doodle. You know I'm into that stuff."

He tried to retrieve it, but she ripped off part of the tablet and crushed it with ease. "Yeah, but this isn't one of your little anime fetishes, Ian. I talked to your uncle."

Ian's smile slowly began to morph into a scowl. He narrowed his eyes and nearly seethed out his words. "You did, huh?"

She threw her hands up. "He approached me when he found out about our plans. I told him to go screw himself, but he made a good case when he showed me dozens of sketches of this girl. You're obsessed with this story about a mermaid saving your life."

Ian set his coffee down on the platform and leaned back against a wooden board. He was still visibly furious, but he spoke calmly as if his words were rehearsed. "I know that I imagined the whole thing. I was in a boating accident and washed ashore. The mermaid story was just a way to shield my mind from the trauma."

"If your mind was shielding you from trauma, you wouldn't tell stories about your mother being blown to pieces by some man-fish on steroids." She walked around so she could get right in his face. "You still believe in this fairytale, and it's driving me nuts! It's unhealthy."

"Why?" he exploded in frustration. "Just because I see her in my dreams?" Ian's face landed in his hands, and he breathed in and out slowly to calm himself, but he released his hands to growl out his remaining rage instead. "This is the face of the girl who saved my life. What if it were an angel that revived me? She kept me alive!"

The strange woman was not moved by his plight. She seemed angry and exhausted, and her eyes began to shine like moonlight bouncing off the unsettled sea. "I've wondered why you and I weren't going anywhere—"

"I just turned nineteen, and I'm already engaged—"

"But you won't set a date, even though marrying me is in your best self-interest. I've finally figured it out—accepted it—that you've created a perfect woman in your head. No one can compete with a figment of your imagination."

"What are you saying?" He asked his question as if he weren't looking for an answer.

She sat beside him and placed her hand on top of his. She wore a ring around her finger with a sizeable diamond, and I noticed that he wore a plain silver band. She didn't strike me as a normally affectionate person, and he seemed a bit surprised by her gesture. He also seemed a little disgusted, but her concern did appear genuine to him. "I'm saying I think you should consider actually taking the medication your doctors prescribe, and you should go back to your shrink. You love something that can never love you back. I kind of get what that's like."

I felt Ian's hot rage instantly flare up, and as he pulled away, I was pushed out of his memory. "I don't understand..." I could tell he romantically cared for her, and I felt a pang of jealousy. I felt like a fool—knowing full well that I had captured his affections—but she was a pretty woman. She had dark hair and wore garments that were dark as well. Even her fingernails were black. She wasn't someone I expected Ian to be entangled with, but the more I got to know him, the more mysterious he became. I thought Ian would bring me light, but I questioned if he had a darkness that he was also fleeing.

"There are people in my life that I should have embraced, but I could never fully commit to them. Now, I know it's because I've put you on such a high platform." He laughed, but I believe it was an expression of relief. "I thought I was searching for answers, but that's not the truth. I needed them, but I really just wanted to be with you. No relationship could ever compete with the fantasy I had in my head. I always argued and fought with people and myself. I was trying to convince everyone that I wasn't messed up, but being this infatuated with you...it's not right."

I thought of my father and the Sea Witch. I imagined they would both believe I was completely insane for the nauseating feeling in my stomach, which still made me feel joyful. I was conflicted and confused, but it was clear that I was caught up in a net that he never meant to cast. "What if I told you that I feel the exact same thing that you're feeling?"

His brows raised a little bit, and he gave me a tiny grin, but he still seemed very sad. "I would say that you're still a mermaid. I'm not crazy enough to try and make this work, and you obviously don't want to leave your mom."

I took a hard swallow of the facts. If I did somehow figure out how to give myself legs and live a human life with Ian, the price of the blood oath would continue to rot at the Sea Witch. "I'm afraid of what would happen to her if I did."

He turned and shook his head as if I had betrayed him for agreeing.

"She needs me," I pleaded. "It wouldn't be fair to abandon her after everything she's done for me."

"I thought so." I sensed such sadness in his voice, and it only made me feel worse.

"Maybe she would come with me to the surface world." I was optimistic while I was blurting that out, but by the time I could catch my next breath, I knew how much of a fool I was being.

If killing Ian wasn't an option, I had to destroy my father. I didn't know what that would mean for my future.

"Maybe..." He opened one of the pouches on his belt and pulled out a strange-looking rock, but it was blinking red. He sighed and put it back inside. "Should I help you back in the water?"

I was genuinely surprised he was satisfied with our short time together. I knew that I wasn't. "If you don't mind." No one had ever carried me before. I couldn't even remember my father holding me. A part of me was uneasy—as if I were insulted that he was wrapping his arms around my back and under my tail—but those feelings melted away once he lifted me with a jerk, and I fell into his eyes.

"Are you okay?" I chuckled. "I'm a lot heavier than I look."

"You're probably the only girl that could say that with a smile."

"Well, if I've got to be an evil mermaid, I might as well be an honest one, too." I managed to get a chuckle out of Ian, but there was something pathetically sad about it. As he carried me back toward the shore, I felt a stirring inside of me that tickled and radiated through my insides. I wasn't sure if it was simply emotions or something more, but I swore that I felt stronger while in his presence. I wanted to figure out what sort of strange magic he possessed over me, but our story felt like it was coming to its close as soon as he put me in the water.

"Are you sure you want me to go?"

"No." He finally placed the dagger in my hand. "But I want you to be safe."

"And you must leave immediately," I begged. "Don't search for my father. He'll kill you and any human near here. He always has a massacre on—"

"On the anniversary of my parents' death." He spoke with an undertone of vitriol, and his jaw tightened. He wasn't very surprised, though. "That's how we found your position. Some refugees were killed last year. There was a plane that disappeared, a ship before that…"

"I'm sorry that I didn't know. The Sea Witch said he was trying to send me a message."

He flashed his beautifully pure teeth with a smile, but his shining eyes gave away his rage. "Well, I thought there was something important about the date. I didn't realize he was intentionally trying to hurt you for saving me."

I had a horrible feeling that he wasn't going to listen to me. He had no way of fulfilling any revenge fantasies, but he wasn't satisfied. "May I have some of your hair?"

"For?"

"To remember you," I lied. If I ever needed to find him, I could locate him with his DNA. Blood would work better, but I had nothing to trap it with.

Ian turned, so I could pick a lock from the back of his head. He had such beautiful hair, but it wasn't long. I was careful not to cut too big a chunk. I had a loose strand of rope peeling away from my bra that I ripped off to bind the strands of hair together. Hopefully, I would never feel the need to find him, and I could just use the lock as one of my many keepsakes. "Good luck, Ian."

"You too…?"

"Luna." I had forgotten to introduce myself. I finally met a human to say my name with his succulent lips, and I nearly forgot to use it. "That's what my friend calls me."

"Luna." He spoke my name as if it were a song, and I almost begged for him to sing it once more. "Goodbye."

I thought of kissing him again. I truly wanted to feel the touch of his skin against mine. I wanted to wrap my tail around his body, as his hands pressed into my back to pull me in closer. I wanted him to gently whisper my name as if it were a normal rite for such a creature like me. I wanted to burn the look of his eyes into my soul and brand us together as one.

But I didn't. I eased away from him and watched his face become possibly more miserable than mine. When he was a blur in the distance, it was still difficult to turn away and dive back into my mess of a world. He finally turned around to sit on the beach and wait for his crew, so I hurried away.

I finally had the dagger in my hand. I could make my own fate now, but I didn't know what I wanted. If I returned it to my father, would he be able to tell my magic wasn't corrupted? If I told him that I didn't wish to return, would he force me? Would he hunt down the Sea Witch to make sure I didn't have an option?

Even if I didn't have my father's wrath to consider, how could I go on with the Sea Witch as if everything were normal? Would I stay with her until I died? Would she take someone else's youth? Would she force me to stay young, so we could both be bitter monsters until the end of time? No. I doubted that.

But the only other option was to kill my father. The only way to stop the Sea Witch from killing my people was to break the blood oath. I didn't even know if it was possible, and I was running out of time.

My mind was so unsettled that I hadn't been paying attention to my surroundings. There were vibrations in the water from something skillful in stealth. I searched around, but there was nothing visible for miles. There were some rocks and coral that something small could have been hiding under, but I felt something larger—at least my size—close by.

I closed my eyes and focused. I didn't necessarily need to feel the water tugging and pushing on my body. There was a force vibrating and giving off magic, just as my dagger could.

I heard a scream and felt a rush of bubbles that sprang up on my back. I turned around just in time to have my back slashed by something that felt like a sword. I twirled around, but I still didn't see who was attacking me. The siren scream was familiar enough for me to remember.

"What are you doing here?"

I saw movement through bubbles and waves, but my opponent was still invisible to my eye. I moved out of the way once I felt a jolt of vibrations, but I wasn't quick enough. Another cut appeared on my shoulder, and I swam backward to get away.

"Now, this is curious," her voice echoed in my head. "Why is my little sister so close to forbidden territory?" It was my eldest sister. She was seven years older than me and determined to be my father's successor. She hated me long before my exile.

"What does it matter where I go? Our father exiled me. I can't go home. I might as well go where I please."

"Is it a coincidence that you're so close to the Sea Witch?" she asked. "She's one of Father's greatest foes. Someone must have taken care of you all this time. You're too soft to survive on your own."

"Oh, I'm a lot stronger than you think!" To cloak herself, she must have been drawing from some sort of powerful force. If I could concentrate on the magic itself, I could separate her from it.

The vibrations came at me again, and I was able to dodge out of the way. Her blade only nicked my stomach. My sister was beginning to aggravate me, but I had full confidence that I would overcome her. I could feel more clearly where she was.

I tried to think of what the Sea Witch would advise me to do. I was relying too much on my eyes or even my natural senses. Whether I wanted to admit it or not, I wasn't just a mermaid. I was a Sea Witch. Magic was natural to me—not her. I closed my eyes and focused on the only thing that mattered. "Come at me."

"You always were a weak fool," she said. "You won't be missed."

I could feel the source of magic so strongly, it was as if I had never closed my eyes at all. It looked like a gem that pulsed through her entire body, and suddenly, her form was made clear to me. The next time she came for me, I didn't have to dodge. I latched onto her pendant and tore it from around her neck.

She gasped and retreated backward as she became visible. "How did you do this?"

"I don't need to steal magic like you. I have my own." The power in the stone wasn't nearly as powerful as some of the trinkets the Sea Witch had in her lair, but it was almost too much fun not to use her own trick against her. The stone shone in my eyes and warmed my fingers. Each speck of light bounced off a different edge of the stone, and I instinctively understood what the stone was designed to do. I could feel the light around me, and I knew that I could bend it to my will.

"How are you doing this? It took me months to master that."

I smiled. The Sea Witch might have been right about my uncanny abilities. Perhaps I shouldn't have taken so much pleasure in being superior, but my sister deserved my smugness. She always treated me like a child, but I should have been her elder. "You shouldn't have underestimated me."

I thought back to when I was fighting the Sea Witch and how she summoned her magic as a defense. My life wasn't in danger, so I had no fear to push my powers out. Even still, I knew that I could somehow do what was impossible for me before. I could feel my power itching to come to the surface. My fingers began rubbing together instinctively, and it bubbled from the inside out until I could see it gathering with my own eyes.

I had never seen my sister filled with such fear before. It was a bit amusing. "You have been learning magic from the Sea Witch!"

"This is my own power. It has nothing to do with her." I slung my arm forward, and a wave of unexpected power followed my sister's direction. She was swept up in a wave of radical energy. Her life was in my hands. If I willed it, I could have pulled her insides out of her body. The Sea Witch would have killed her without a moment's hesitation. It was the best way to keep her safe. It was the best way to keep me safe!

However, it was also a risk to make my magic go dark. It was also something I genuinely didn't want to do, despite what she and my father did to Ian and his parents long ago. I didn't want to be anything like them.

I lowered my arm, and the assault on her life ended. My sister was stunned and unable to move for a little while, but I could still feel her heart beating. She had blood pouring from her nose and ears, but her fingers began twitching a few seconds later. She would survive. "Leave here and never return. I can't guarantee your life next time, especially if the Sea Witch is near."

She gritted her teeth and screamed through them. Her entire body convulsed from pain, but she was able to shake her tail enough to flee from me. I did feel a small sense of satisfaction in her defeat, but I also had a dreadful feeling poking me in the back of my head, telling me that I had made a horrible mistake.

Chapter Ten

When I returned to the lair, the Sea Witch was much too distracted gutting her catch of shark to care much about my adventures. She had no idea that I had found Ian and kissed him. I wanted to keep it that way. For all she knew, I spent my day with Napa, and I most certainly didn't fight my sister to the almost death. I made sure to heal my wounds before she saw me.

I hid the pendant, dagger, and lock of hair in a satchel and hoped the Sea Witch wouldn't be able to sense the magic. I also hoped she wouldn't sense any special magic in me. It was odd that I wasn't fatigued from my battle. Instead, I felt energized. My magic was leaking out of my body. I tried to keep my movements limited and to remain completely calm.

Unfortunately, somewhere between the chewing of our dinner, the Sea Witch cocked her brow at me in suspicion. "Did Napa bring you a new gift?"

"Why do you ask?"

"I sense new magic."

I panicked on the inside, but I would not allow that panic to surface in my thoughts. Of course, she would have been able to sense the pendant. I reached into my satchel and handed it to her without any fuss, and I hoped she didn't ask any questions about the other item of interest. "Napa didn't know any better."

"Interesting." It only took a moment for the Sea Witch to analyze what it could do. I don't know why I was so surprised when she disappeared. "This would be more useful on the surface world." She tossed it back to me and became visible once more. "Quite interesting."

"Very." I grinned hard and continued feasting, but I sensed she knew I was hiding many details from her. It's not that I didn't trust her. I just wanted to make sure she would take the news well, so I didn't have to worry about her killing everyone outside of our immediate sphere.

It wasn't easy. I wanted to tell her about Ian's infatuation with me. It was flattering after my father threw me away. I wanted to tell my mother how his smile enchanted me, and now, I was under his spell. I tried to get him out of my head, so the Sea Witch wouldn't find out, but while I brushed my hair and stared into the broken mirror Napa gave me, I began to imagine that I was staring at myself from his point of view, and I knew I was truly as beautiful as he made me feel. The thought of never seeing him again was crushing my heart and suffocating my insides. There had to be a way to see him again beyond tricks, smokes, and mirrors.

"Luna, what's wrong?"

I saw Ian's face too clearly in my mind. She must have known I was thinking about him, but that wasn't so strange. I could still hide the truth, for a little while. "Why would something be wrong?"

She floated in front of me with a furrowed and curious brow. "Because you never sing."

I hadn't even noticed. I was singing the same song I sang to Ian when I first said goodbye. If he had his hooks in me that deeply, was there truly any escaping him? "You'll think I'm being a fool."

The Sea Witch surprised me and held me by my shoulders from behind. "Out of the two of us, I'm the one who made a blood oath with your father. You could be foolish for a thousand lifetimes and not end up as foolish as I once was."

Perhaps I was being unfair to her. If she were trying to be a real mother, she deserved a chance. As my elder, she might have sound advice to put my mind at ease. "Napa told me that humans believe in true love. I know it sounds childish, but I think I'm experiencing it. I've found true love."

I was so embarrassed that I kept my eyes focused on the teeth of the comb in my hands. I was responsible for ruining Ian's childhood, and I delayed his life afterward. I didn't deserve to feel such a consuming joy, especially if Ian were the root cause.

"I've heard of true love." The Sea Witch nicked my chin to force my eyes into her own. "The humans teach it like a fairytale, but true love is not a myth; it's mystic. It's a force in the universe that draws two people together, resulting in incredible power, for either good or chaos."

"Chaos?" I laughed. Frankly, it was difficult to believe there was an actual explanation of how I felt. Napa referred to love as "irrational logic". I wasn't sure if having a legitimate reason was worse or better. "How can what I feel ever lead to destruction?"

"I'm not saying that it will, but true love is a dangerous magic." The Sea Witch got uncomfortably close to my face. I tried to back away, but she swam around to observe me fully. Nothing about me had changed physically, but I'm sure she wasn't seeing with her natural eye. "I can sense it on you. Your magic is stronger."

I thought of how quickly I defeated my sister, but then, I pushed that out of my mind. "How is that possible? Is it just because I have feelings for Ian?"

"No. That would be ridiculous, but it is possible that you're drawn to each other for a reason." She, once again, became agonizingly uncomfortable. I didn't back away or cower from her glaring and curious eyes. I tried to be firm while I blanketed my mind with thoughts of training battles, meditation, and the past few lonely years of my life. I would not think of Ian, and I certainly wouldn't think of the kisses we shared!

Except, I completely did.

I don't know if my sudden memory of Ian's kiss was vivid enough to burrow into her brain, but she certainly seemed more suspicious after I indulged in it. "You must have seen him again!"

I covered my face. I would have hidden in my clam, but she was already inside of it with me. She grew impatient and pulled my hands away from my flustered face. "I did. Napa found Ian, and I went to see him. He gave me the dagger I had been searching for, and we spoke."

"That's not the only thing you did."

I straightened out my body and tried to look a little taller and more mature than I had been acting a moment ago. "We did share a kiss, yes."

Instead of lecturing me, she twirled around the cavern, shrieking in delight. I hadn't seen her genuinely happy or excited about anything, so I was a little terrified. "Did he have magic?"

"He didn't seem to have knowledge of having magic."

"Perhaps he's an amplifier," she suggested with much intrigue.

"What do you mean?"

"They are extremely rare, but an amplifier can increase your magic, even without being able to use it." She swam to me, clasped both my hands, and smiled. "If you were to mate, you could create new magic for your offspring and leave your own power intact. If that's true, you should definitely mate him."

"Uh…" My mouth opened in shock. The desire to feel and be more of an adult was ripped away from me. "I'm not ready for this conversation."

"Why? Do you love him?"

"It's preposterous that I love him!"

"But you do!" She chuckled. "I see it in your eyes. I feel it through your magic. He's made you more powerful. If Fate is pulling you to love this man, don't push back. There's no sense in fighting what will be."

Was it truly possible that Ian made me feel stronger? Was he the reason why I could use my magic to fight my sister so effortlessly? Even if it were true, what did it matter? I only wanted to control my magic so it wouldn't accidentally go dark. I had no desire to be the greatest sorceress in the world.

It was silly to think that I could take human form and live with Ian. I hardly knew him. But, for some reason, the thought of leaving to discover the world with him began to fill my chest and gut with a ticklish light that turned into a glorious rumbling. I clutched my chest as I felt it vibrating. My entire body was radiating heat. I tried to convince myself that I was merely embarrassed, but my hands were tingling.

"The thought of escaping with that human is causing your magic to burst from you," the Sea Witch said. "You can't deny what you want or may very well need."

I looked at my hands. My skin was glowing, but I also felt it hardening. I feared that I was beginning to transform into my other form—my sea witch—so I did my best to calm down. Instead of dwelling in the shared kiss or basking in the glory of my future, I reminded myself of my reality. "What would happen to you if I left?"

She shrugged nonchalantly, but her eyes weren't nearly as cold as the rest of her. The Sea Witch could pretend all she wanted, but I could see a change in her. Something about finally being mother and daughter was bringing her back to a time when she had nothing but hopes for our family. That's why it was so difficult to imagine leaving her.

"If you don't want to end up looking like you once did, you need my power to fend off the dark magic of your blood oath. The only other option is to fulfill your promise to kill my father and destroy his kingdom. I can't let you do that."

"You couldn't stop me if you wanted to—"

"Mother!" I flipped my tail in defiance.

She took me seriously but smiled, nonetheless. "What do you suggest?"

"Maybe there's another way. If Ian can truly amplify my magic, what if we found a spell to undo the blood oath?"

She rolled her eyes. "There are dark forces that expect me to keep my promise of annihilating your father. If I don't, that darkness will destroy me." Whether she was right or not, she was still making excuses. Every time she spoke of my father, her hatred was palpable.

"My magic isn't dark, and you said I was potentially the strongest sorceress in all the world. If we add Ian into the mix, I'm certain that we'll be able to overcome the oath."

She pursed her lips together as she pondered the absurd possibility. Had she never thought of a way to break it? Was her only goal in life to seriously destroy my father, my sisters, and all their subjects? "It's not impossible…"

"Then we should find Ian now!" I squealed. I didn't mean to want him so badly, but his eyes were endearing and captivating. Every fiber of his being screamed that he wanted me, and I had never been wanted for reasons that weren't selfish. He made me feel like a brand-new being—like I was truly worthwhile—and that might have been the most glorious benefit to our bond. "He could still be around."

"Or he could be on land or sailing halfway across the world. Optimism is annoying enough. Don't be foolish."

I grinned at my mother and dove for my corner of the cavern, where the most treasured pieces of my collection were. I had placed the satchel inside a chest after dinner. I removed my silly keepsake and placed the satchel back inside. "I have a lock of his hair. Can you find him with this?"

"Clever girl. I should be able to see him." The Sea Witch gathered ingredients and poured them into her cauldron until it began smoking vivid colors, as it did when she showed me her life story. A new and more curious ingredient was the broken mirror Napa had given to me. I reached my hands out to stop her, but she grinned and smashed it hard enough against the stone, making all the pieces of glass fall inside. "Now, add his hair."

I instinctively clutched onto the strands. It was such a fragile memento, only being held together by a small piece of string. In case it was all I'd ever have left of Ian, I didn't want to let go. But if there was even a chance that I could have him forever, I needed to take the risk.

I dropped it into her vat of magic, and the fog began to rise, encircling the shards of glass until it expanded into a grander, shimmering mirror. It was broken up like a handful of tiny crystals, but it was only reflecting our image. "I don't share a connection with him, Luna. You have to complete the spell."

She gently raised my hand and poked one of my fingertips with her bony claws. I was too curious to react, and a drop of blood fell into the mixture and rippled throughout the shards until it was a solid and smooth surface.

The reflection of us also rippled, and once the glass settled, I saw him. Ian's beautifully sculpted face was being pulverized by dark men. Two of them stood behind Ian and forced him to his knees, while a third man continuously punched him and yelled. We couldn't hear what they were discussing, but Ian definitely spat up a small puddle of blood and rose a little higher. This enraged the man, and he began to beat him once more.

"What's happening? Why are they hurting him?"

"What sort of men was he traveling with?"

"They're pirates from a land called Nigeria. Napa told me that they believe in mermaids. Ian wanted to convince the world of our existence. He has a very lonely life, and the humans think he is insane. He probably boarded any ship with a crew that would believe him."

"He absolutely is insane if he's been running around with pirates." The Sea Witch's vague references to an exciting and interesting past never ceased to amaze me. "What sort of man is Ian?"

"One in danger, apparently!" The truth was that I didn't know. I had seen into his mind, but there was so much I didn't understand. I was so happy to know he had been searching for me that I disregarded the fact that he was also hunting my kind. He had a difficult time with a human woman, but he was with her. His memory suggested they might have been intimate. I hadn't thought everything through with Ian, but I very well couldn't piece the mystery together if he were dead. "Can you save him? Please!"

She wasn't unaffected by my pouty lips and mopey eyes, but she eventually scoffed. "I wouldn't dream of putting you in harm's way. Humans are resourceful, and they may be ready for you. If they expose you, you'll force your father's hand. I'm not risking your life for a pirate."

"But Ian—"

"They roughed him up. That doesn't mean they're going to kill him." To further belittle my emotions, she swiped her hand across the mystic mirror, and it faded into wisps of smoke.

"I can't take that chance…" The smoke continued to fade, but his bloodied and bruised face was still clear and present in my mind. In my heart, I knew he was taking a beating for me. I ruined his life from start to finish. If I had stayed with Ian a moment longer after saving his life, he might not have obsessed over me. If I hadn't come to his boat, he would have never confirmed my existence. He was protecting my secret. I could feel it in my bones.

I spared him once from death. I should have let him be, but the love he had in his life compelled me to search for something more. If I allowed him to die now, I'd feel like an ungrateful fool! "I won't allow you to stop me."

"Luna!"

I swam for the entryway as fast as possible, but I hadn't bested the Sea Witch yet. After a head start, she caught up with me quickly enough to nearly bite my tail with her fangs. Even if I invoked magic, I'd never be able to outswim her. The best I could hope for was to stall her.

I summoned magic in my hand, dove under my body for a quick flip, and forced out as much as I could muster. The Sea Witch bounced back against a wall of white and golden-lit magic. She was physically fine but angry enough to hiss and shriek at me. "I'm sorry, but I have to save him."

She beat her fist against it in fury, and the entire wall shook. That small bit of gratification replaced her rage with a smug smirk. "I can break through this barrier. It's childish and sloppy."

I raised my head a bit defensively. "I don't doubt it, but I can slow you down."

I was aware that my magic was stronger, but the level of boldness I just exhibited was beyond what I thought I was capable of. I did have a horrible pang of guilt, clawing up my insides, about forcing the Sea Witch to stay behind. I also felt a good deal of fear about what she might do once my barrier was broken. I was also heading into danger with no weapons. I only had magic that I hadn't yet mastered. I hoped that was good enough.

I returned to the shore where I had taken Ian, but it was a long shot that proved frivolous. He was nowhere in sight, and neither was the boat. I should have tried to see if it was possible to salvage the strands of Ian's hair for a locator spell. I practiced once with the Sea Witch, but I had one of her weapons to draw from. I had nothing of Ian's.

But if I couldn't find him, perhaps he could find me. I opened my mouth and began to sing a melody that was slow and haunting, in an oddly beautiful way. It was only the second song I had ever sung, but every note came out naturally. I didn't believe my voice would give me dominion over all men who heard it, but if I lured sailors like my sisters often did, I would be pleased.

I focused on Ian's face and imagined holding him in my arms. I closed my eyes and envisioned myself whispering my song into his ear. If my magic was somehow connected to him, then I had to believe that he could somehow find me. In my heart, I could feel the strength of our magic radiating through my song and making it more powerful.

I dove into the water and headed back toward where I had found Ian on the boat earlier. I felt more vibrations the closer I got. I knew that I was actually feeling the boat, and I wasn't alone on my journey. My sense of smell wasn't as keen as some creatures', but I could smell blood, and I could certainly tell if it possessed magic.

"Ian?" His body was clothed in something slick, black, and skintight. His face wasn't covered, though, and his body was surrounded by blood floating in the water. I could see it seeping out of his right arm from a cut. He appeared to be unconscious. Thankfully, he was unable to drown, but he was more than capable of freezing. He was encased in some type of cage.

I grabbed onto the rails and began to pull and shake them. When I lived between my world and the surface, I had seen fish get caught in human contraptions. I had never seen a human in one before. "Ian!"

If I didn't get him out soon, I'd be fighting off sharks rather than pirates, and I was in no mood to contend with them. I could feel them getting closer in the water. "Ian!"

He opened his eyes slowly as if he were under some sort of haze. "Luna?" But he shook it off and desperately grabbed onto the bars once he realized I wasn't an illusion. "You shouldn't have come!"

I was distracted—only for a moment—and something behind me hugged onto my back and enveloped me. It was another human trap that I was more familiar with—a net. I was accustomed to ropes or material that would have been slicker and tighter, but this was different. It was hard and scratched up against my skin. As I struggled to break through, my scales snagged on the material. I hissed as they pulled and fought harder. Before long, I was shrieking in anger and panic as I was raised to the surface.

"Look what we've got here!" one of the men said from the deck of the ship. I recognized his voice from earlier.

My mind was hot white with terror. I knew that my father would never forgive me for being caught by humans. I felt that burden suffocating me. I couldn't properly think to control my magic, but I knew an outburst was out of the question with Ian so close to me. I felt my body harden as the will to live overtook the rest of my senses. I didn't want to be blue. I didn't know if Ian would understand that part of me yet, but I might not have had a choice!

"Put her out of her misery. We don't need a pissed mermaid on board."

I felt several stings around my body and looked back up to the deck. Another man had a weapon pointed at me. I was furious that they dared to attack me and use Ian as bait. The other man also attacked me with flashes similar to what Ian did when he used his cameras. I had no choice but to go on deck and destroy any evidence they had of my existence. But as they reeled me in, I became exhausted. I couldn't even reach out my mind to Ian and see if he was alright, before collapsing in their clutches.

Chapter Eleven

My hearing returned first. I heard the subtle clanking of chains from above, and there was a rapid and louder clank across from me. I heard my breath and took in the fact that I was alive. The profuse huffing and puffing coming across from me sounded like Ian. He was even grunting and mumbling to himself.

"Ian?" I opened my eyes, and my vision was blurred. I realized my arms were strung up, and I looked above my head to see what had me bound. I was chained up against metal railings, and so was Ian. I blinked again, and the world came back into focus. "What's going on?"

He shushed me and began to focus his thoughts for me to hear. "I told my associates I got caught up in a tide and ended up on that beach. They didn't believe me. They said I had been enchanted by the mermaid. They're very superstitious, and one of the crew members claimed he was attacked by one when he was young."

"That's probably a lie. He wouldn't have survived the encounter."

"I survived mine."

I sighed. He might have had a valid point, but I still didn't believe it. "Where are they now?"

"Celebrating. They have their proof. They haven't had a signal, so no pictures have been uploaded to the internet, but they feel very satisfied."

"I don't know what that means."

"It means that if we can get out of here, you've still got a chance to prevent a war between our species."

We were in a crowded room with many things. It reminded me of my section of the cavern where all of my treasures were. Our chains were tied around big, thick metal that wrapped around the walls. I pulled on it to see how strong it was. I thought I might have had a better chance of ripping my chains apart. "How long have I been asleep?"

"Not long at all. It's probably been half an hour. They thought you'd be out half a day, at the least."

"They underestimated me. I get that a lot." I grabbed onto my chains and prepared to pull on them.

"Wait!" he shouted in his head. "If you break it, they'll come in with guns, and I don't know if your magic is strong enough to stop them."

The idea that pirates would pose a legitimate threat insulted me. I straightened my pouting face once I reminded myself that I was captured. I was caught off guard, and they used my feelings for Ian as a weakness. Those fools couldn't possibly know that he would also be my strength. "I'll have to fight them eventually, Ian."

He shook his head and cursed himself under his breath. The poor boy looked like a mess. He was shivering—his lips were even blue—and his cut wasn't properly tended to. The pirates must have cut him in hopes of luring me out. He needed a healer, whether it was from magic or human means. "Why did you come back for me? You risked everything."

I immediately began to blush. It seemed like such a strange thing to ask. After all, he was the one being tortured for keeping my secret. He could easily answer his own question. "I feel drawn to you."

At first, I felt like a child for holding onto such whimsical fantasies. I turned my head and wished that I had my sister's amulet, so I could turn myself invisible. I waited for Ian to say something—think anything—but the only sounds I gathered from him were his intense and focused breaths. I could feel him, though, the longer I listened. There was an intensity to him—a purity—that began to quake inside of me. Suddenly, as I turned to face him, I didn't feel like a child anymore. He was clearly, and without any remorse, gazing upon me with enough desire to fill the seas themselves. It wasn't even a matter of lust. He simply wanted me, and I was reminded, once again, that I was worth wishing for.

"I…I wish I could hold you right now." It alarmed me once I felt a warm stream of water slip from my eyes. I was baffled as to what was happening, but I was embarrassed and rubbed my face against my arms.

"I won't let them hurt you, Luna. I will protect you." His steely gaze gave me much comfort, but I was ashamed for giving him the perception that I was afraid. I certainly wouldn't rely on his protection, but I welcomed his sentiment.

I offered Ian a small smile in return, but it quickly fell once the ship roughly jolted. The items in the room began to spill over, including a wooden crate that landed on my tail. I clenched my teeth to suppress the quick shock of pain.

"Are you okay?" Ian asked aloud.

I heard the sound of a man talking and a thumping that increased in volume as he got closer. Then, the wall opened, and he came barging in with a laugh. He glanced at me, but he didn't notice me. I believe he was prepping himself to mock or question Ian, but his eyes widened after a few seconds had gone by, and he snapped his head back at me. "So, the harpy is awake?"

He was a very dark man with dim, yellow eyes and a sunken face. He was bald and very slim. His teeth were stained, and he had an unusually long pinky nail. When he got close to me, I got a whiff of his pungent musk. He came very close to me and grinned wickedly. "She is a very pretty mermaid. It's a shame she's such a devil."

I turned my head in revulsion, and he began to chuckle. I thought of flinging the heavy crate, but I noticed a black metal object on his hip that looked like a weapon. I decided to restrain myself until I understood him more.

Ian was offended on my behalf and attempted to lunge, but he was obviously restrained. "Eya, what are you doing?"

He turned to address Ian. "We were sailing clearly until we were caught up in a fog. Then, we crashed into a thick sheet of ice, as if we were trapped in the Arctic. It must be this witch's doing!"

"She literally just woke up. Leave her alone."

"Something unnatural is happening here."

He wasn't wrong. I could feel great magic surrounding us, and it was familiar. As each second ticked by, I was encompassed by palpable anger that tasted bitter. The hairs on my arm immediately rose, and a small quake shot through my back. I was breathing in literal rage, and I was dwelling in the spirit of vengeance.

Loud noises were coming from above as if someone were spraying thunder. It was accompanied by screaming and some kind of ferocious blaring from an animal. There was some sort of battle going on, and by the look of panic on Eya's face, he knew he was losing. "What is happening?"

He grabbed his weapon of choice and pointed it right at my head. I didn't know what it was. I defiantly glared at him, but Ian was panicked. "We don't know what's going on! It sounds like a dog or…a wolf."

"A wolf?" I asked. I felt a jolt in my stomach. Intuitively, I could confirm there was certainly something supernatural happening, and it was certainly on my behalf. "Is that an animal?"

The men glanced my way in confusion, but they ignored my odd question.

"Unchain me," Ian demanded. "I have a right to defend myself."

Eya practically headbutted Ian and seethed in his face. "You deserve to die with your witch." I didn't understand what the black device on his hip was, but I knew he intended to cause harm to Ian once he reached for it, and I couldn't tolerate that.

"I've had enough of this!" I used my tail to fling the crate that had fallen on me straight toward his face. Eya tried to block it with his arms, but he was disoriented and knocked on his back. The gun was still in his hand, and I tried to destroy it in a similar manner to Ian's camera, but I wasn't sure how I had done it. It was very instinctual before, and now, I was overthinking something I didn't even understand.

Whatever was happening on deck was beginning to spread below. I could hear pounding in sync with the tapping of claws as a creature ran across the floors. There were grunts and growls, but the screaming from the pirates had stopped altogether.

"You've pissed off a sea witch," Ian warned. "You should never piss off a sea witch."

Eya sat up groggily, but also enraged, and pointed his gun toward me. "Let's see if your sea witch can survive this."

I slightly shook my head. "I'm not the sea witch you should be worried about." I almost felt sorry for the fools. They had no idea what sort of power they were dealing with when they captured me. "You'll never make it out of here alive."

Through the darkness of the hall behind him, a small monster appeared from the shadows and latched onto the pirate's neck. His mouth was covered in sharp teeth like a shark latching onto its prey, but it wasn't slick like a shark. It was covered in white and silver fur that was quickly being soaked in the blood of the pirate. The pirate couldn't scream, but he tried to fight and writhed around in pain until enough blood had gushed out of his torn throat. I was curious how Ian would handle the brutality of teeth, tearing flesh apart. It was gruesome, but he watched it happen with a blank face and only mild alarm. I sensed his worry mostly stemmed from what would happen after the wolf finished his victim.

I wasn't concerned. I looked into his eyes, and they were familiar to me. Despite his ferocity, I knew it was an extension of his affection for me. "Napa!"

The man's struggle came to an end, and Napa ceased his attack. He released the pirate, and he crashed to the ground. Ian was bracing himself, but I wasn't concerned.

I stayed focused on his golden eyes as they dimmed into brown. His beautiful fur coat thinned out as his body enlarged, and his legs widened into human limbs. The hair on the top of his head began to darken and lengthen past his incoming shoulders. His snout sank into his face and formed a normal nose, but it was wider than mine. His flesh became golden brown, and he was muscular like I remembered my father's warriors to be. He pushed himself up with his newly formed arms and stood on his unfamiliar legs. He nearly stumbled, but he caught himself.

"Napa?" I asked aloud. I wasn't even certain if he remembered how to speak to me. "Is that really you?"

He spat out a puddle of blood and wiped his mouth. He seemed rather embarrassed that he killed a man, but he certainly wasn't remorseful. "Yeah. It is."

It was very odd seeing him as a human. Tasting the pirate's blood must have triggered his transformation. It was also possible that Ian's strange gift helped. I guess we couldn't be sure. "You're not alone, are you?"

"No. I met your mom." He chuckled as he bent down and patted Eya down. "She is certainly scary."

"But I'm effective," the Sea Witch said while standing in the doorway. She wasn't quite how I remembered her. Her skin was a pasty pink like mine, and she was standing on a pair of beautifully long legs. Her fingertips were also rounded. She had nails, but her ferocious claws were no more, and the sharp fins protruding from her arms were also gone. As far as I could tell, my mother looked to be completely human.

Napa found a set of keys in the pirate's garments. He showed me keys before, so I knew he could open my chains with them. I felt foolish for excluding him on my journey. I should have seen him as a resourceful ally. "Napa, I'm—"

He didn't go for my chains. Instead, he knelt down and dove right into my lips. I was stunned, but Napa was assertive and determined to get a real kiss out of me. To my knowledge, he had never kissed a woman, so I was very surprised when he slipped his tongue into my mouth. I wished I could have enjoyed the brief encounter, but I could taste blood, and I could feel Ian's mind rattling inside my skull. With all the death and the panic that surrounded us, he still had time to be jealous. I didn't want him to get the wrong idea about Napa and me, but I didn't even know what to make of Napa anymore.

He pulled away from my lips with a satisfied smirk on his face. At least he got something positive out of it. "Thank you."

"For what?"

He didn't answer, but he did unlock my chains. Once my hands were free, he tossed the keys to my mother. She freed Ian.

"You must be Ian."

"Yes, ma'am." He was trying his best not to look at her. She was beautiful as a blue and menacing sea creature, and she was certainly stunning in her human form. I also hadn't considered the fact that her attire was inappropriate, but I could see that in Ian's mind. Her genitals were mostly covered by her belt and weapons, but her newly formed backside was plump.

Napa also had a similar new hump on his back that was firm, so I assumed Ian had the same form under his garments with similar genitalia hanging outside of his body. Napa wasn't embarrassed at all by his impropriety. Either he was very proud of his renewed human form, or he was simply not capable of having any shame after being a chicken for years.

Napa swooped me up in his arms, and I was impressed with his strength. He seemed to have an easier time with my weight than Ian. I looked over at him, and Ian had a slight frown on his face and furrowed brows. He truly was envious, though he struggled not to be.

"Everyone else that was on this ship is dead," my mother said coldly to him. "I'm going to sink this vessel. I suggest you find whatever evidence they had of my daughter and destroy it in a timely fashion, or you'll sink with it."

The color from his face began to drain. If he had time to vomit, he might have, but he knew the Sea Witch was serious about destroying the ship. "Yes, ma'am."

Ian began searching Eya's body, but Napa and my mother didn't wait for him. We started making our way through the ship and back up the stairs to the top deck. "Be nice to Ian," I told them.

"I thought you wanted to kill him," Napa spouted a bit snippily.

"My father wanted me to, but things have changed."

"Yeah, they've gotten worse."

When we reached the deck, I don't know why I gasped. I had seen death before. I knew the Sea Witch's lair was decorated in the remains of her victims, but I wasn't expecting to see a man pinned to the mast of the ship by a sword plunged through his chest. The Sea Witch removed the sword and twirled it around for show, as the body dropped to the ground. There was another man torn to pieces. His legs were ripped up by what I assumed to be Napa's teeth. The man probably lost mobility in his legs and collapsed on his stomach. There was a trail of blood from where the attack began to where it stopped. The pirate's head was severed from his body in a quick swipe that must have been from the Sea Witch's blade. Where other bodies would have been, there were piles of dark sand caught by the wind and beginning to blow away.

Napa walked over to the edge of the boat. One pirate must have been thrown overboard; his brains were splattered around the ice. "You did all of this?" I asked the Sea Witch.

"I was highly motivated." She tried to shrug it off, but she was proud of her accomplishments. "We should leave before your father becomes suspicious."

Ian came running up the stairs and was quickly stunned by the gruesome display of death. He must have trusted the pirates since he went on such a journey with them, but they did throw him in a cage—at the risk of him freezing to death—just to catch me. Ian's reaction suggested he was caught somewhere between being a decent person and being an honest one. "I checked everything I could think of. All of their digital proof should be erased."

My mother walked over to Ian and snatched his hand up. He was blushing a bit. I couldn't exactly blame him for admiring her form. She certainly didn't look a thousand years too old for him. He was more afraid of her than attracted, and he tried to pull away from her firm grip. "What are you doing?"

"Borrowing some of your magic."

"My what?"

She didn't explain, but she certainly felt something. I saw a bright gleam in her eye as if he charged her. He hissed in discomfort while she giddily raised her free hand and stretched it toward the ice. Within seconds, the ice that hindered our vessel collapsed into a wave of water that pushed up against us. We all stumbled a little bit, besides the Sea Witch, and she kept Ian from falling backward. "You certainly are incredible."

She, thankfully, released his hand. He tried to step away from my mother, but she latched her hands on his face and stared deeply into his eyes. He was extremely concerned. He didn't understand what she had done to him, but he felt her drawing on his power. He had no reason to fear her, though. She was genuinely impressed.

She let go of Ian's face and turned to me. "I give you my blessing, but I like this one too." She pointed to Napa and winked. I believe both of us blushed, but I wanted to die of embarrassment, and he was wearing a smirk like a prize.

"I'll make sure this vessel sinks. Take Ian somewhere safe and meet me back home."

"Brace yourself," Napa said in my ear.

"What for—?" I had my answer once he flung me from his arms and into the air. I gasped for a moment, but I had been through too much to scream or allow myself to be afraid. I took control of my body and dove perfectly into the water, and I flipped back around to breach the surface once again. "We have to hurry!" I could smell the blood in the water. It wouldn't be long before we were surrounded.

Ian jumped into the water next with a graceful dive. I wasn't surprised, given how much time he spent in the water searching for me. I found myself questioning, more and more, about the sort of man he was. He had a healthy amount of fear, but he seemed unfazed by all the death around him. Even his sailing made me question his mentality. If he weren't scared off by what my family had done to him, then how did his brain evolve to make it all bearable? Did he possess too strong a light to be tampered with, or was I too enchanted to realize that he had already gone dark?

Napa jumped from the boat next, flailing his arms and legs clumsily, and splashed when he made an impact. I laughed and shook my head at my dear friend. No matter what form he took, I'd always know him.

"What is he?" Ian asked.

Napa emerged from the water, knocking his long and wet hair back in a way that I'm sure was to either mock or mimic me. He sprayed poor Ian in the face, which I'm sure was a gesture to mark their new rivalry with each other. He even laughed like a child. "I'm a shapeshifter."

He raised a beautiful, glittering green tail that shimmered in the setting sun. I barely believed it; I had to reach out and touch it for myself. Sure enough, it felt just as real as mine. I even pulled on a few scales just to be certain. "Ouch."

"Sorry." He could fly. He could walk. He could swim. I was actually a little jealous of my friend and all of his glorious possibilities. He learned to master anything, even life and death. He proved to be a warrior, and I treated him like a child. When I imagined his human form, I was half expecting to see a boy as young as twelve or fourteen, but his body certainly belonged to a man.

He slowly began to smile mischievously, as if he were guarding a large secret. The smile continued to grow larger until he began laughing out loud. "I can read your thoughts now," he said in my head.

He was a child, and I felt like a fool for ever admiring his adult body! I fumed up my face and wrapped my arms around Ian's waist. "Let's go, Ian. It's not safe to keep you in the water."

I held on tight to Ian and flipped my tail in a mad fury. I did want to save Ian and get him away from the oncoming predators, but I also wanted to show that having a tail didn't mean Napa was suddenly like me. It might have been childish, but I wanted to put him in his place. My brisk pace must have been a bit too much for Ian because he buried his face in my chest to relieve himself of the pressure. I didn't bother slowing down until I felt the bubbles from his screams blast my stomach.

I brought Ian up to the surface to get fresh air and to allow Napa to catch up. He was several miles behind. Ian gasped as he came up for air, inhaling and choking on more water than he did when he was under. "I'm sorry!" I patted him on the back. It would have been unfortunate if I had managed to drown a man who could breathe underwater. "I've put you through a lot, haven't I?"

He struggled to laugh through his coughs. It was adorable that he was willing to push it all aside, but a nagging voice in the back of my head told me that if he were a normal boy, he wouldn't be able to brush off the violence and death so easily. "Is this close enough?"

"Yeah. I can make it back on my own from here."

I noticed the cut on his arm and held my hand above it. "This should help." Healing cuts was very easy for me, but I couldn't deny that Ian made it even easier. He might have had a past that was darker than I liked, but he was still a gift.

"You're incredible." He pulled on his skin to be certain that his cut was gone. "I shouldn't be surprised."

"I'm glad I got to you before those pirates killed you."

"Well, when I heard your song calling out to me, I knew you'd come to save me." He ever so slightly glared. "I thought I wasn't under your spell," he said with the most charming smile.

"Well," I shrugged, "maybe a small one."

He was irresistibly handsome. I placed my hands on him, and my tail wrapped around his body in an instant. A few days ago, I could barely believe I was turning seventeen. Now, his lips made me feel like a woman. He must have cast some sort of maturity spell. Reluctant conversations with the Sea Witch about procreation came to mind, and I questioned if I was ready for a mating ritual. I also questioned if Ian would have the slightest idea what to do.

"I wish I could bring you with me." He glanced back at the shore. There was beach sand, trees, and all sorts of housing structures, but it was dark, and I didn't see any humans roaming about. "I'm certain that is the Florida Keys. I live a few hours from here."

"I usually don't come this close to where so many humans are, but I wanted to make sure you had a lot of land to hide on." I couldn't help myself, and I pecked his lips again. I wanted to do more, but I didn't want to waste more of his time. "Three days from now, my father will try to kill you. You need to be far away from the shore. Don't fly over the ocean. Don't sail. Don't even drink water. Just run."

I had no idea what was wrong with him, but I couldn't sense any fear for his own safety. It might have been our connection to one another, growing with each passing second. "And what about you?"

"My mother and I will try to stop him. It's the only way to protect both of us." What was he doing to me? I didn't want to kill my father, but my devotion to Ian was rapidly growing. "I'll come and find you when it's all over. My mother will help me get legs, and you can help me break a curse that's haunted my mother."

I stroked his cheek. He was trembling from the cold. I had to let him go soon, or he was going to get sick. It was nice that his health was on my mind. I must have been optimistic that he wouldn't be obliterated on my birthday.

"I don't understand magic and spells," he admitted. "I don't understand what I am."

I laughed at him for not knowing the answer to such a simple truth. "You're mine, and I'm yours. That's all you need to know."

That boost of confidence inspired a burst of passion out of Ian and me, but before we could indulge in each other once again, I felt a sizable ripple. "We should head back, Luna."

I released Ian from my tail. My desire for him hadn't waned, but it was a little too awkward with Napa eyeing us down. "I'll be ready in a minute, Napa."

And he didn't get the hint, even though he could read our minds. "Please," I insisted, in a very threatening way.

His body was very mature, but his face did have a younger appearance. He couldn't have been any older than Ian, and he certainly confirmed my suspicions when he drifted off like a passively aggressive child. I could practically feel him huffing and puffing in my head.

"Were you together before I showed up?"

"No." I only hoped he would be as dismissive when it came to his black-haired woman of former interest. "He's in love with me, and he's a dear friend of mine."

"A dear friend with a tail."

I shook my head. Being with Napa wasn't unfathomable. It might have been a strong possibility if I weren't so infatuated with Ian. "My mother said that Fate was drawing us together. That's why we feel so strongly for one another."

He cocked his brow and jerked his head back. "Really?"

"Do you doubt our connection?"

"I don't doubt anything, not anymore." He began moving in for another kiss, but I dunked myself and popped back up a couple of feet away. If I didn't pull away, I was never going to make it home to the Sea Witch, and he was going to freeze to death.

"Be safe, Ian."

"You too."

For the first time in a long time, I felt like I'd have a future. Light from the stars illuminated my love, and it glittered a path to happiness up to the shore of his homeland. I was curious about how the homes looked. I wanted to see how my collections were used in an ordinary human's life. Maybe I could sing to Ian as we danced inside a home of our own.

Napa hadn't truly given me any privacy. He was about a hundred feet underwater, and that was a close enough range to pry inside my mind, especially when I didn't bother to protect myself from jealous suitors. "What was that?"

"Napa, I don't want to talk about Ian."

"Fine." He folded his arms and smiled as if he had won. "Let's talk about our kiss."

"Is that how you took my DNA?" I was genuinely amazed that it was so simple.

"Yes, but you know that's not what I meant."

He was right. I was stalling, but I couldn't do anything other than shrug. "I don't know what you want me to say. You're a beautiful-looking man. I never thought you'd be anything like this. I've never comprehended you as someone compatible with me."

"And what do you think of me now that you've seen the real me?" He knew full well that his face and body were positive attributes. Ian had a beautiful body, but it was lean. I had no idea if he would be worth anything in a fight as a human, but Napa's appearance certainly gave me the impression that he could hold his own. He had higher cheekbones like Ian, but his face wasn't as chiseled. His rounder face was why I assumed he was probably closer to my age, but I knew he had lost track of how many years he had been trapped.

"I see a loyal companion that would do anything for me, and he happens to be very handsome."

He beamed with pride and brightened up his pretty brown skin. He had such a beautiful smile, and his twinkling eyes nearly disappeared. He took my compliment as permission and nearly charged me. I moved backward, and he paused. "But you're in love with Ian?"

"Don't make this harder than what it is. You're my best friend, but I don't even know if I can fight against what I feel for Ian."

"Then you're cursed!" He insisted. "You're not in love."

"Stop it!" He was the one who introduced me to the concept of true love. I couldn't ignore it just because I didn't want Napa. "You think because you have a tail that you're somehow equipped to handle my world? You're not."

"I killed those men for you!" I didn't understand why a human like Napa held no remorse for killing those pirates, but I had it wrong. He lived his life as an animal for years. You kill to survive. It was about protecting your territory, and he felt as though he had made a respectful claim over me.

"I thank you for your loyalty, but I didn't ask you or my mother to kill anyone for me. I don't want to live a life of violence if it will make my magic go dark."

Napa pressed his hand against his face and groaned. I wasn't a fool. I could understand his disappointment, but I never promised that we'd be anything more than companions. "I can't do this right now."

"Do what, Napa?"

"Dote on you as if I were still just an animal!" There were many times I was grateful that he couldn't hear my thoughts. I did take advantage of his feelings from time to time, but I did truly care for him. "I think I'm gonna go on land and enjoy my life as a man."

I wish I could have controlled my reaction, but my eyes widened in shock. Then, I switched to fury. "Are you trying to make me jealous?"

He misinterpreted my emotions and smirked, thinking he had the desired effect. "No. I was trying to make you happy, but that doesn't mean anything to you. Ian has only brought pain into your life, and he may be the end of you. I can't bear to watch you be destroyed."

"Napa!" I tried to latch onto his arm, but he flipped his tail in my face and hurried off. I might have been envious of his many forms and freedoms, but I certainly wasn't jealous of his human body intertwining with another. I was merely offended that he would taint our friendship with the intention of making me jealous.

I didn't have the time to chase after Napa and give him some glimmer of hope about us, just to make him feel better. He'd come around, eventually. Despite his outburst, I still held his heart. Love couldn't be cast aside, and he'd fight for me. He didn't invest so much time just to swim away when things got tough.

The Sea Witch was probably wondering what delayed me. She had already begun to cast a spell without me. I could feel it as I approached our cavern. Her magic was quivering throughout the water. It was very unusual. It was angry and bitter—as usual—but it was…in pain?

There was another force mixed in. My hand tingled, and I recalled the touch of death from the airplane. It was spreading in my mother's magic and trying to choke her essence from it. "She's not alone!"

I was such a fool to let my sister leave with her life. I was hoping she would have been too embarrassed to report that her youngest sister had bested her in battle, but I should have known that she hated me enough to risk her life and pride. As long as I lived, she could never inherit his kingdom.

The cavern was in darker waters where sunlight barely breached us. Most of the lights came from the Sea Witch's magic, but that was inside. The closer I came to home, the brighter it became. It was a hot and bright whiteness, like the effects of staring at the sun too long. I wouldn't have even known that I was in the ocean if I didn't feel the water on my skin, but even that assurance was being replaced by the intensity of their power. I had entered what appeared to be another realm where only two lovers and their estranged daughter existed. We were in a void, and the two of them were free to fight without the rest of the universe peering in on them.

They hadn't even noticed that I had arrived. My father was just as fearsome as I remembered, but he had aged. His hair was grayish blue when I was very small, but it had been whitening since my mother died. Now, every strand was white. His skin was a few shades darker than mine, and it became splotchy on his hands and face. I hardly remembered him having any wrinkles, but it was apparent around his eyes. His age was finally catching up to him.

He was still powerful. The Sea Witch fought him off with her dual swords, but every time she clashed her weapons against his trident, her arms shook. When he retaliated, her best option was to use her superior agility to dodge. He was brutish and slow compared to her, but she was physically inferior. There was no making up for that.

She tried to make a move with her left sword, and he blocked it. She tried with the right, and he blocked her again. He pulled his trident back to thrust it forward, but she twirled around my father and stabbed him in the shoulder. I took it as a victory, but he didn't even pause to embrace the pain. Instead, he turned around and punched her directly in the nose.

The blunt force temporarily paralyzed her, and she drifted about twenty feet away. My father took that moment to pull my mother's sword from his body, and he hurled it at her as fast as he could.

"No!" I had fought with my mother every day. I knew that sword. I remembered the way that it vibrated against my weapon when we clashed with each other. I had sharpened it for her. I felt its smooth surface and the ferociousness of its sharp edge. I could not allow it to destroy my mother!

The Sea Witch didn't have enough time to dodge or catch it. Her body flexed and braced itself for impact. But when it pressed against her chest, it exploded into black dust.

"You've been teaching the little witch." My father laughed and looked up at me. "That's good. The more powerful my heir is, the better. That boy should be easier to kill now."

"You're a fool." The Sea Witch began to center her magic in her hands. It illuminated her insides as if her skin were translucent. The streams of light matched her glowing blue eyes. "That boy is an amplifier. He makes her magic stronger. She could produce powerful heirs—more glorious than we can ever hope to imagine—and you want to destroy that over your pride?"

"That is interesting news." He was genuinely intrigued, and I became hopeful that we could all put our differences aside. My father cared mostly about power. If he could see that Ian wasn't a worthless human, my sins could easily be forgiven.

"It's true, Father. He's made my magic stronger." I was only going to show him a small sample in my hand, but I accidentally lit up as I did before. It was a bit embarrassing that I couldn't control my emotions, but I finally thought it was safe to express the joy Ian brought into my life. "Father, I love him."

"You do?" He was pleased, but he wasn't ready to lay down his weapon with the Sea Witch ready to blast him to smithereens. The trident flashed brightly, and a crack of thunder echoed throughout the void. "This should change everything then."

"Mother," I pleaded. "Withdraw your attack."

She clenched her fists and began to shake. She only meant to scold his idiocy, not give him a reason to negotiate for peace. She was beaming with hatred, and the thought of turning away from her feud led her to a bloodcurdling scream.

My father was quick to raise his trident. When their two forces clashed, it swept a tidal wave of power that rippled out for miles. Even with my increase in magic, my bones shook, and I felt as if my entire body would come undone. I didn't want to transform, but my body wouldn't be able to withstand their force if I didn't.

"Mother, please!"

Her war cry shriek was ear-piercing, but I knew her well enough to recognize the pain mixed in with her rage. Her eyes were always steady and focused on whatever task she had set before her, but I saw a gleam of anguish that haunted her every time she looked at me. Every day, she relived the same horror. "He killed my children!"

"But I'm still here!" I shouted through our mental link.

Her arms were shaking. She didn't have the power to overcome him. She was going to get herself killed if she didn't call off her attack.

I swam beside her. My father braced himself, in case I joined in on the battle against him. He gripped the trident tighter, and another burst of power was released. She winced but held strong. Her skin was bruising and blackening. She knew that she was drawing on too much of her power. There'd be nothing left of her soon.

"We can make a truce—"

"We can't trust him."

"We have to try—"

"I'd rather die!"

I couldn't let my father's magic destroy her, so I joined my mother in her crusade. For the first time in the battle, I heard my father grunting, and we began to beat his power back. I had never done something so strenuous with my magic, and I wasn't prepared to fight for very long. My arms were rushing with too much force, but if I let up a tiny bit, my body would be smashed apart by his might. One of us had to end the fight.

"I know that you can never forgive him, but I ask that you forgive yourself." She was more than her rage, and she was more than her pain. Her devotion to revenge dominated the clear truth.

She was a mother who failed her children. "Allow yourself to find happiness. Live for me!"

I saw her eyes soften, and she began to pull back. I looked at my father and pleaded with my eyes for him to stop. We all withdrew our powers at the same time.

The Sea Witch held her arms against her chest. She had busted veins that left swollen clusters of blood in her arms. My arms were sore and tender when I twitched my fingers, so I could only imagine the pain she must have been in.

I couldn't believe my father was so strong. He was barely fatigued. The Sea Witch was putting up a marvelous resistance, but if he wanted her dead, she should have been dead. We both should have been.

"If we are going to have a truce, then we need to come to an understanding." I came to the center point between the two of them. "For starters, the blood oath needs to be removed."

"You told her about the oath?" he asked, surprised. "No wonder why the girl doesn't want to kill me. She knows what you would do to Atlantis once I die."

"And she won't feel obligated to destroy Atlantis if you remove the oath."

He chuckled to himself and removed one of his gauntlets. Sure enough, he possessed the same crescent mark on his wrist. "A blood oath can't be removed. It can only be fulfilled."

"There's no hope for peace," the Sea Witch warned. "I know what I must do."

"No!" I snapped. "I don't believe there's no hope. With Ian, we can overcome it. We have the magic of true love. It's for a reason."

"And what do you want out of this truce?" my father asked. "Do you want to be forgiven and return home?"

"No. I want you to stop killing humans, sending messages, and hunting Ian. I'm going to get legs and live on the surface world with him. That's what I want, and I want my mother to follow."

"She's tried that before." He smirked quite maliciously. "It didn't end well." I had the impression that the two of them hadn't seen each other since she was forced out of the palace, but that didn't seem to be the case at all. There was a much richer history that I wished I understood.

"She didn't have me before."

He placed his hand on his hip to demonstrate his impatience. "Is that it? I don't seem to be getting anything out of this deal."

"You get to keep your life. You could at least be grateful for that." I hated how much I must have resembled him, but he had no respect for anyone else. It was best that he saw what he needed to see.

"My little mermaid certainly has changed." His pride in me was like swallowing a meal, only to have a mouthful of quills poisoning and prickling your insides. "You bested your oldest sister in battle, you raised your hand against me, and now, you threaten my life."

I felt as if his compliments were also threats. He wanted me to fear him, but he also admired the fact that I didn't. Honestly, I wasn't sure when I decided the monster in my nightmare wasn't scary. Perhaps it happened naturally once I decided to fight back. "I only wish to be free of you. I'll do whatever I have to."

He raised his trident and floated in front of me—not as an enemy—but as my king and father. I could accept that he would never respect me for the right reasons, but leaving me alone was all the gift I needed. "Do you truly love that human boy?"

I didn't mean to think about Ian and our goodbye kiss, but we were bound together, and it was overwhelming. "With all my heart."

I expected my father to be disgusted by the image of his teenage daughter embracing a human boy, but he smiled. He was genuinely happy for me. "Good. That makes this decision very easy."

A white spark flashed and knocked my heart off its rhythm. A crack of thunder broke my ears, and a high-pitched ringing filled my head. I couldn't hear the Sea Witch screaming in horror from watching the same scenario she witnessed over a thousand years ago. My thoughts were ripped from my mind, and the flood of emotions flowing out of me kept the Sea Witch from getting inside. My eyes were working perfectly well, though. I saw his trident pulsing with hot, white magic. I could only see my father's silhouette and the shape of the trident being pointed straight at me.

I felt my impending death as his magic made a connection with my body. He could have been holding my heart in his hands, prepping to give it a good squeeze. For four years, I kept warning myself that this moment would come, and I still wasn't ready for it. I didn't want to die.

"No!"

I blinked, and another silhouette appeared in front of me. Its arms were stretched outward to act as a shield, and the magic that was about to incinerate my skin clung to it instead. I blinked again, and the image became clearer. She must have been in excruciating pain, but she was smiling.

"Mother?" The pressure behind her came to an end, and the light faded into the darkness I was accustomed to. The only light was radiating from my father's golden trident and my mother's dimming blue eyes.

"Luna…" She held my face, and though her touch was never very gentle, her hands were like stone. Her skin was darkening, and the texture began to mimic granite. She winced as she moved, and her voice in my head was quiet like a spoken whisper.

"Mother, no!" I clutched onto her in desperation and whimpered. I watched my father's sadistic grin grow from my hysterical outburst. I hated him for hurting her, but I despised myself for not knowing how deeply the loss of her would wound me. "You can't leave me."

It was a struggle for her to move, but she pushed me away from her, just far enough to look into my eyes, one last time. "Don't let him turn you into me. Please."

I nodded my head and sobbed in my mother's arms as I watched her eyes turn into gems. All I could wish for, in her final moments, was that she would no longer be haunted by the vision of her children dying in front of her. I hoped that she found some sort of peace in the child she managed to save.

Chapter Twelve

I hugged my mother's body and mourned her in a way I didn't know was even possible. My shoulders shook, and I screamed. I kept reminding myself of how I had failed her. If I had given her my magic or fought by her side, she'd still be with me. If I hadn't separated to save Ian, my father might not have approached her. If I had killed my sister, he wouldn't have known that I was in her care. I must have offended him.

That horrid creature didn't even let me grieve in peace. He was disgusted by my reaction. "Love is weakness unless you master your emotions. Your mother's love for you always made her weak, and now, you are her end."

"Weakness?" I took a deep breath. My magic was rumbling in my stomach. My skin was hot, and my hands were itching. I thought I was terrified of my magic going dark, but when I raised my head and saw the twisted look of satisfaction on my father's face, all I could feel was rage. "You won't think I'm weak when you're begging for your life!"

I rose off my mother's statue and charged my father. My teeth and nails were sharpening. I didn't have a plan. My visceral reaction was to gouge out his eyes with my claws. My plan hit a snag when I bounced off a force field my father created.

"Before you go blue, you might want to consider that I hold your mother's life in my hands.

My hearing was significantly better, even though I hadn't completed my transformation. There was definitely something cracking behind me. I checked my mother's statue and found a small crack in the center of her chest. "You can reverse the spell?"

"Of course. You're bright enough to know that if I wanted your mother dead, she'd be dead."

I gasped when the crack began to spread up to her collarbone and deepen. There must have been a point where she would certainly die if I didn't make it stop. I forced myself to calm down enough to stop my transformation. "What do you want from me?"

He laughed at my foolish question. "To kill the man you love."

"Why?" He was cruel, but he wasn't stupid. "You know he's an amplifier. He's useful to me. He could be useful to you!" I knew Ian would never agree to serve my father for any reason, but I was desperate enough to suggest anything.

But he narrowed his eyes in on me in disbelief of my naivety. "It's because you love him that he needs to die by your hand." I had never seen my father as an insane king, but there was a mystifying presence gleaming from his eyes. He had an awareness of a greater truth that couldn't have possibly existed. "There's so much more to gain when you have power over your heart. I had to do the same with your mother."

"Don't insult her!" I swam up to him fast, but I restrained myself just in time to stop my raised fist from hitting his face. He fed off my conflicted feelings. He must have taken his barrier down just to show me how much power he had over me. I didn't know it was possible to hold so much hate in my heart, and he was thriving in the space I made for him. "You never loved her. How could you?"

"I loved her enough to push her from living her life as a mere priestess, and I made her a goddess. She truly embraced her power when she met me, and she increased it with each kill. Do you think she would have been brave enough for sacrificial magic—the kind that's kept her young for all these years—if not for me?"

"If you loved her, why did you betray her?"

He scoffed and shook his head exasperatedly. "She's a jealous woman. She's wrong to think that I ever cheated on her. I only moved on after her exile, but the intimacy I experienced with other mermaids or human women meant nothing. I only loved your mother."

"You murdered my siblings. You tried to kill me!"

"And, here you are. You survived. Now, we know who the strongest would have been. You didn't have to fight through an army of siblings like I did." I recalled the Sea Witch telling me that my father had lost seven brothers in the war, but I questioned if it was due to her people or his treachery.

"You're insane. You broke her heart. She wanted us!"

"They made us weak, and I couldn't afford that." I began to wonder if I had misjudged my father. I thought his obsession was focused on me, but I suddenly felt as if I were the only one standing in the way of an aggressive sexual predator. "We weren't much older than you are now. I had much grander plans than playing mommy and daddy to a pack of brats."

"And look what you've done to her."

"You can't judge a story if you don't know the details, and you're missing a thousand years of information." He made a move toward her, but I got in the way. There was no way I was ever going to let him touch her again. He tried to move again, and I blocked him once more. He realized what I was doing and chuckled.

"Since you love your mother so very much, I'll strike you a bargain. Fulfill the task, and I will release you both from my wrath."

"I can't trust you."

"That's why we're going to make a blood oath."

I was unable to drown, but I certainly lost the ability to breathe as my world collapsed around me. "No. I can't." The image of the Sea Witch's old body still frightened me. "I've seen what that kind of magic has done to her. I can't let that happen to me."

He shrugged. "Then she'll die. Is that what you want?" He kept her alive for a millennium. To throw her life away now was psychotic. I wanted to call him out on his lies, but he was too insane to ignore. "She's kept you safe for all these years. She just risked her life to save yours. You owe her."

He was picking away at my heart. I wanted to be selfish. It was best for everyone if I did. "She would want me to be happy."

"Can you be happy knowing that you killed her?" He slithered around me like a sea serpent. No matter how much I struggled mentally, his words crushed me into submission. "You should have fought against me to the bitter end. Calling a truce was a mistake. If you had listened to your mother, you'd know that."

I knew that she wanted her revenge—perhaps more than she wanted me—but she would advise against any sort of agreement with my father. She would want me to find another way, but I didn't have enough time to think. "What do you want me to do?"

"If you kill Ian before you turn seventeen, I'll release your mother from the spell."

I closed my eyes and soaked in the reality of his request. Ian was my only tether to happiness and light, but the Sea Witch warned me that we could possibly bring chaos. Making this bargain with my father would ensure it. "Ian is on the surface world. I don't know the transmutation spell to make legs."

"I can take care of it."

I wanted to refuse, but I could hear the cracks in my mother's body expanding. "Give me a moment to prepare."

I entered the Sea Witch's lair. I possessed enough foresight to know that it was for the final time. Each corpse embedded in her wall must have told a story that she would have been proud of. My sisters could have easily made her wall, and I was willing to risk my true love for her.

Was there already something wrong with me? Was it my thirst for power? If I lived with Ian, I'd live among humans who had no concept of the supernatural. I'd have to live as one of them. The surface world seemed like a thrill, but I could grow tireless of trinkets. What sort of power could the mundane offer me? Ian would amplify my magic, but I didn't know if that meant anything without living as a witch.

I grabbed my disk and the dagger. I had made a belt that could hold them both. It also had a compartment to store some of my treasures. Napa said that some of the jewels I had found were valuable, along with some pearls. I also grabbed the amulet that I took from my sister, in case I needed it.

"You look ready to go to war." I turned around furiously once I felt him behind me. He had no right to desecrate her home, but I was in no position to forcibly remove him.

"I need to be ready for anything."

"Good." He removed the dagger from around my waist. I tried to snatch it back, but he was quick for an ancient brute. He grabbed my right wrist with his left hand and turned it upward.

"What are you doing?"

"We need to have a connection with one another and the source that supplies magic to our world."

"Magic is everywhere." What he said went against every belief I had been taught. "There is no central source."

"There is a source that I'm connected to." He took the dagger and began to carve an arch into my wrist. I gritted my teeth and kept my eyes focused on his. I would not give him the satisfaction of my fear. "You'll be connected to it as well."

"Is that all?" I mocked.

"Not even close." It seemed like a simple ritual. He removed his other gauntlet and cut the same symbol into his wrist. I wondered if the crescent symbol had any significance to the power of the moon, but there was nothing important about that night or the moon's position.

"Are you ready for this?" I truly did despise him for asking. He knew that I didn't have much of a choice.

"Do it."

He turned his wrist so our crescent markings overlapped. Nothing odd happened at first. Our blood seeped out of our cuts. If anything, I felt a little cold.

"This is silly…" Our hands began to shake on their own. I bent down to get a closer look at our blood. The wisps of red were threading together. I looked around the cavern as I felt it darken, but the lights hadn't faded. Then, I saw into my father's blackening eyes, and I realized that mine was also being flooded with a coat of dark magic.

"Name your terms, little mermaid." He spoke aloud, and the power in his voice rippled throughout my body, leaving a trace of itself inside of me.

"Before I turn seventeen, I will kill Ian with my own hands." The threads of magic spread underneath my skin and into my veins. It traveled through my blood and to my heart. By the time I made my father's request, it felt like a promise that I wanted to make.

"And when he draws his last breath, your mother will be free from my spell."

"And you will never hurt us again!"

His brows pressed angrily against his black eyes. "And you will become my heir when I'm ready to pass on!"

I always thought that would make me the queen of my people. I could rule them the way that I wanted. I could restore some semblance of morality that existed a millennium ago. But I felt a dark burden crushing my insides. I had to pull away, or my lungs would have collapsed. "What was that?"

The spell came to an abrupt end. I didn't even feel the dark magic that bound us. The black symbol on my wrist was the only evidence of our pact. "You added to our agreement first. Being my heir is an honor."

"For who?"

He was too amused to be offended. He was genuinely thrilled, and I took that as a sign of how colossal my mistake was. "I commend you for being loyal to your mother, but I do not doubt that you're trying to get out of killing your beloved. I can relate to contemplating another way. My less admirable choices weren't always my first whims."

If that were meant to be comforting, it failed in easing my sense of betrayal from killing my brothers and sisters. "I'll find a way to defeat you."

He handed me the dagger and continued to laugh. His chipper mood was certainly disturbing. "Your mother thought she was wise when she added to our deal. She promised to destroy my kingdom as a way to keep me in line. It didn't work out too well for her. She could have fulfilled her blood oath by now. It drives her mad that she can't. The reason why this spell is so effective in deal-making is that it drives the parties involved to complete their bargain."

I pressed my cursed hand to my chest in disbelief. I could still feel great love for Ian. I was determined to save him and my mother. I only needed time. "If that were true, you would have made me do a blood oath four years ago when you first exiled me."

"You weren't strong enough then." He tapped his trident against the floor and brightened it up. "I spared your life…accidentally. This blood oath that you fear is the only reason why you're alive."

Was he being honest with me? The Sea Witch assumed that I was alive because of Fate or my own power. I didn't know there was a darker magic at work. But if dark magic preserved my life, was there ever a chance that I could stay away from the darkness?

"This will all work out for the best." He raised his trident once again and aimed it at my glittering green tail. "You'll see why, sooner or later."

He hurled a blast at me that was so powerful that I felt my tail rip in two. My body was flung back into an arch, and I screamed at the top of my lungs. My scales were scattered along the cavern walls, and I lost all feeling from the waist down. I landed in a pocket of air, and it carried me out of the place I had called home for the past few years and up to the surface. The bubble rose above the water and popped.

When I crashed back into the water, I saw my unresponsive legs drifting like dead fish. My arms were strong enough to lead me back above the water, but there was no way I could swim. I barely felt a tingle in them.

"Napa!" I swallowed my very large pride and called out to my friend. I didn't mean to be overly arrogant, but I doubted he went to shore to bury his feelings for me. However, it was a possibility that I was too far for him to hear.

I raised my hand on the surface and steadied the water with my magic until it froze solid. I stabbed the sheet of ice with the dagger and pulled my body out of the water. It was cold, but it was safer than dangling around like a free meal to predators or frisky dolphins.

I rolled over and sat up to see my legs. I pressed my fingers into my skin. They still tingled, and they hurt. I tried to move my toes as I would move my fin, but it ached, and the tingling spread in a bad way.

I took a deep breath and began to sob, but it was different than any other time I had been upset in the water. I could feel water leaking from my eyes. I shouldn't have been so upset. I was alive. I had a chance to save my mother. I knew what my father said about the blood oath, but I had hope that my love for Ian was stronger than the source of his dark magic.

And if I could find a way to conquer the evil that sought to destroy my life, I could finally be part of Ian's world.

Chapter Thirteen

I didn't have time to sit on my new bottom and leak from my eyes. I kept my eyes focused on my limp legs and struggled to wiggle my toes. My terrible father could have at least aimed for an island or close to the shore, but I was surrounded by water for miles. The ocean was threatening enough as a mermaid. I sure enough didn't want to have a shark bite off my legs.

My legs eventually stopped tingling and throbbing. I pulled my legs into my chest, as I would often do with my fin. It was a thinking position, but I mostly wanted to feel my new toes. They were plump little fingers. I held my right foot in my hand and squeezed it a bit. It was much softer than my fingers. They hadn't toughened up from my years of fighting.

I let my legs go, so I could rub them against each other. They were incredibly smooth. It was hard to comprehend that they were attached to my torso. I kept expecting my tail to reappear. "This is real."

My father was wrong about my curse. I still loved Ian, and I wanted to be with him. If I could get to him, maybe our combined powers could free my mother. If she were safe, I didn't care about the damage of my blood oath. We'd find a way to break it together.

I rolled on my stomach and pushed myself up with my arms. I wanted to stand for the first time, but I was a little puzzled about what I should do next. I raised one of my knees into my chest and pressed my flat foot on the ice. It immediately began wobbling. I wasn't sure if I was doing something wrong. I didn't know what else I was supposed to do!

"Napa!" I should have thought to ask him how to walk when I had the chance, but I couldn't wait. I needed to keep trying.

I took a deep breath and pulled my other leg up. When both of my feet were flat on the ice, I pushed myself up.

I gasped and wailed in excitement. I had done the impossible! It even lasted for five whole seconds until they started trembling, and I fell flat on my chest. Perhaps a sheet of ice wasn't the best place to practice falling on my face, but life had never been kind to me before. Why should it start now that I could live as a human?

That began a series of repeated attempts to walk. Standing took around five tries, and then, I was able to plop my foot forward before crashing on my face. I stumbled and wobbled again and again. My skin was very durable, but my arms, elbows, and knees were beginning to bruise.

It took a full hour of attempts before I realized that pressing the front of my foot to the ground, followed by the heel, was a better method than the whole foot. I was scraped up and even a little bloody on my weaker and lower half, but I was walking. I probably looked like a fool, but that was the price of progress.

I continued to use my magic to lengthen the path of ice. I couldn't go very far without the insides of my legs itching. My feet had begun to ache, but the ice soothed that pain. The freezing wind had dried the water in my hair, and it was hardening and crunching.

"Napa..." He had never heard me sing before, but I had to believe that my voice could find him and that he would recognize me. I kept trying to imagine his brown skin or his perfect black hair. He had high cheekbones and a strong jawline, except for his baby-soft chin. I thought of the odd noises he would make when he laughed as an animal, and when I knew he was blushing at something I had said. I thought of how he pulled my hair with his tiny flounder fangs, in an attempt to save my life, even though I had told him to flee to safety.

I felt as if I had known him for longer than three years. He brought joy into my life and taught me so much. He did far more than bring mere trinkets to fulfill my curiosity. He provided a world for me to hold onto. He gave me hope.

I walked until my legs fell from underneath me, and my right arm made a hard landing on the ice. All my remaining strength was knocked out of me. I didn't know if it was due to the cold, my transformation, or emotional and physical exasperation, but I was down. I hunched myself into a ball and shivered. I was close to blacking out and was concerned if I'd ever wake up. "Napa, I need you."

I felt something soft come into my hand and curl into my fingers. I figured that I might have been hallucinating, but it felt familiar. "Napa?"

"I'm glad I don't disappoint."

I smiled. I was too weak to roll over and confirm, but I certainly recognized his arms when he swept me up. "You came back to me?"

"Well, I told you that love was 'irrational logic.' I couldn't let a silly thing like humiliation, the destruction of my pride, and total heartbreak keep me from my girl."

He walked to the edge of the ice path and jumped into the water. It was good to know that I could still breathe underwater, especially since he failed to ask. The rush of water woke me up, but his body heat gave me more warmth than I had above the surface.

It was strange that I had to rely on Napa's shapeshifted form to get me to the shore. I felt like a fool for being so defensive toward him when he first changed. I was envious. He got everything that he wanted, and my life had only gotten more complicated.

"My life became more complicated as well," he spoke in my mind. "It was easy to be your friend when I couldn't be more…"

I tried not to think of a response at all. I didn't want to lead Napa on and make him believe that if he proved himself to be a fearsome warrior, I would fall in love with him. I should have told him that wasn't the case, but I didn't want to hurt him.

I knew that I would love Ian until I drew my last breath. Certainly, my last breath could have been near, but I had hope that I would find a way to survive.

Napa stayed as a merman until we were close enough to the shore for him to stand on human legs. I think he would have liked to carry me forever, but I practically jumped out of his arms, so I could finally feel what it was like to have sand between my toes.

"I like this." I flexed my feet in the mushy, wet sand. It was smooth and grimy at the same time. When I walked to drier land, the sand was coarse and very fine. I twirled around to see the impressions of my feet. "This is amazing."

"Just wait until you discover shoes."

"Shoes?" I shrieked. "Those are garments that go on your feet. Why would I need such a thing?"

"Because you're a woman. That's how these things go."

I snapped my head at him and glared, though I didn't understand what it meant. I just assumed that it was right to be offended. "Where do we go now? I told Ian to get far away from the shore, and that was hours ago."

"Why does he need to get away? What's going on?"

"When I returned home, the Sea Witch was battling my father. Because of me, she was turned to stone." My voice began to quiver, and my eyes were leaking again. I wiped them quickly, feeling defective. I didn't mean to upset Napa by my outburst, but he had furrowed brows and a frown.

"I made a blood oath with my father. It's a curse." I held out my wrist so he could see the black crescent moon. "If I kill Ian before my birthday in three days, he'll release her, and he can never hurt us again."

"…but you don't want to kill him." He was treading very lightly. Napa was uncertain how supportive he should be and if he would come off as the jealous lover.

"I'm hoping that with our powers combined, I can free my mother without fulfilling the oath."

"What about temporarily killing him? You could drown him and resuscitate him."

"Ian can't be drowned. He's been kissed by a mermaid."

"Well, I'm sure there are other ways." A tiny and twisted smile crept on his face. "Electrocution, suffocation, medication…freezing should be very simple for you."

"I'm glad you have many ideas…" I needed them, so I tried not to be concerned. "I can't kill him if I don't know where he is."

"Between magic and technology, we can probably find him. First, we've got to get some clothes."

"Why?"

"Because we're indecent."

I looked at my mostly naked body. My breasts were covered by netting and shells. I only made garments because I was bored, and variety amused me. It had nothing to do with being indecent. "You don't seem to mind."

His skin began to deeply redden. Was I not supposed to notice that his eyes were on my chest for the past three years? "I've been naked for years, and I don't know how old I am, but I assume I'm a teenager."

"Does that mean you're horny all of the time…like a dolphin?" I only laughed because he was obviously embarrassed.

"I'm not having this conversation with you!" He sped-walked away from me and started heading toward some manmade structures.

"Napa, wait!" I didn't have experience running. He was much faster than me, and by the time I caught up, I was breathing heavily, and my chest felt as if there were a tear inside of it. "What are you doing?"

He had jumped behind a small wall and kicked open a piece of the bigger wall. I recognized that the structure was made of wood, but its roof was softer and had a mix of greens, yellows, and lighter browns. Napa quickly searched and returned with a few garments. He tossed a few to me. "Put this on."

I held up one. There was a hole at the top and two at the bottom. I watched Napa put a similar garment on, except his was larger. He put his leg through the holes and pulled them up. It seemed simple enough, but I began to wobble when I lifted my leg.

"Whoa!" Napa latched onto my arm before I fell over. "I guess your balance is still a little off."

"Thank you." I tried to mimic the way he put his second garment on, but it got caught over my head. Napa yanked it down and nearly pulled off my ears. "Is this really what humans like to wear?" I recognized the image of trees and the sunset on them, but I had no idea what the other symbols in black were. My garments were loose, and his seemed to be too small. His chest was very well-defined through it.

"It's just a souvenir shirt. It's to commemorate your visit." Napa grabbed my wrist and pulled me away. "We should find a place to sleep for a few hours."

I looked back at the water, and it truly dawned on me that I would miss exploring and swimming every day if I lived my life as a human. "What's wrong with sleeping on the beach?"

"We just broke into this place and stole stuff. We should be nowhere near here."

I wasn't aware we had done something wrong, but I certainly knew that I hated it when I worked for a kill, and a scavenger snatched it from me. "Fine. I'll defer to you."

We ran together, even though I wanted to look at the structures that humans made. There were many "souvenir" places with bright and wonderful colors. I recognized a few things, like variations of chairs, jewelry, and other garments, but there was so much I didn't understand. It was all rushing away from me in a giant blur. I only wanted a moment to explore.

Napa kept looking around to make sure that we wouldn't be caught by humans. I still had weapons on me, and I had my magic. I wasn't concerned about escaping, but I also wasn't concerned about pirates. My arrogance didn't help me much in that situation.

We ran into an area of thick green, and we kept on running. My poor feet were being pricked and scratched. I had no idea that they were so vulnerable. No wonder why women liked to wear shoes. To Napa, running barefoot in nature was a part of his childhood. He didn't make a peep, but I moaned and hissed with each unexpected cut or stub. My toes were especially sensitive. Napa became frustrated and threw me on his back.

I thought I was being a burden, but I saw him grinning when I wrapped my arms around his neck, and my breasts were against his back. "You really are a dolphin, aren't you?" I didn't mean to ask in such a sultry tone. I only made his infatuation worse.

"Hey, if you don't want to know what goes on in my head, don't poke in."

"I didn't need to read your mind to know what you're thinking about." That time, I admit, I was more consciously flirtatious. It was actually very fun. I was beginning to see why my sisters enjoyed having power over men.

He didn't run for much longer. He was tired, and I was getting to the point where it was difficult to keep my eyes open. He stopped and sat me down to catch his breath. "Let's sleep here."

I looked around for the famously soft and fluffy structure that he called a "bed," but there was nothing that looked like a cluster of clouds anywhere near us. "On the ground?"

"You sleep in a clam."

I crossed my arms and mumbled, "It's very comfortable."

Napa sat down and pressed his back against a tall and solid plant. "You can sleep on me."

My curiosity got the better of me, and I pressed my fingers against the plant. It was hard. Pieces of it cracked off if I pressed too firmly. I sniffed it, and it was pleasant. It wasn't like anything I had ever experienced, but the smell was actually in the air.

Napa was chuckling. "This is a tree."

I laughed in amazement, but I was truly confused. "This doesn't look anything like a boat."

He pulled my arm and yanked me down beside him. "Go inside my head. It should be easier now. Just learn everything that you can."

I sprang up with excitement. I had been waiting years to completely dive into Napa's mind. I knew from digging into Ian's memories that humans were quite easy to read, but it was impossible to immerse myself without cooperation, and it could have been dangerous for both of us. "You don't mind me seeing everything?"

He shook his head with what little energy he had. "Learn to read, to write. I can't dance, so Ian will have to show you that…"

I only hesitated because I was concerned about Napa's feelings. I didn't want to know how much I had sinned against him, and I certainly didn't want to take the risk that there was anything more to my feelings than friendship.

But I needed to know about the world. I couldn't afford to be distracted by every tree. "Close your eyes and relax."

That wasn't a difficult command. I placed my head on his chest and locked our fingers together. It soothed him and opened his mind up to me.

The story of his life didn't come to me in the proper sequence of time. His time trapped as an animal was still very difficult to read. I only saw glimpses of myself through his eyes, and I was as radiant and glorious as the sun. His world rose each time we met and fell each time we parted. Each encounter was centered around the belief that he would be able to kiss me one day. And when he did, an entire new chapter was opened. He saw the possibilities beyond the horizon, and that hadn't changed, even with Ian reemerging into my life.

I dug a little deeper and found Napa, much smaller, with his people. He liked to run through the forest and climb through the trees. He had a group of friends who followed his every lead, which would have been hard for me to imagine. He was so awkward around me. I didn't expect he'd be admired in his childhood.

He lived with his mother and two older brothers in a log cabin. His mother never spoke of his father, but Napa would often sneak away in the woods to hunt with him. Napa was naturally strong and agile. His father taught him to hunt with a bow, and his accuracy surpassed that of the adults in his tribe. He had a kind heart, but hunting put him in a different mindset. I was surprised when he rescued me from the pirates, but Napa had always been a superior predator. No wonder why he was so anxious to prove himself. As a man, he could.

I saw the infamous chicken incident. The poor thing was only seven when his powers, accidentally, activated. When he returned home as a boy, his mother was frightened and asked that he never transform again. He made a promise to her that he never intended to keep.

His father knew about his son's abilities. He encouraged him to keep acquiring more forms to become more powerful. He was well on his way to mastering his gift until he hunted and killed a silver wolf. He knew that it was sacred to his people, and they believed spirits lived within them. He didn't take it seriously, but his people found out what he had done. They practically ran him off the reservation. He transformed into a wolf to escape, but he was never able to change back, nor could he locate his father.

He was only ten years old.

I fell asleep while I was snooping in his mind. When I woke up a few hours later, Napa was snoring so profoundly that it could have been his divine purpose. I let him sleep a little while longer and stood up. Yes, I still had legs. No, my curiosity hadn't been satisfied. However, I had a better understanding of what I was seeing. Vocabulary was beginning to align with pictures and explanations.

I was wearing a T-shirt. It had a palm tree and a sunset on it. The black symbols were words, and it said, "Florida Dreams." I gripped the shirt with a newfound excitement. I wanted to find a shirt that fit well on my body, and I really wanted a pair of shoes. I touched my hair. I needed a brush. I needed a shower! I had grains of sand that had snuck up into uncomfortable positions.

Napa's snoring came to an abrupt stop. "Why are you giggling?"

"Because I'm happy!" I was finally beginning to understand the possibilities I could experience as a human. "I want to try a steak and French fries! Oh, can you turn into a cow?"

He scoffed. "What for?"

"I don't know. I want to see one in person. I want to drink milk—chocolate milk—with cookies." I didn't know how I could crave food I had never tasted, but the mind was a powerful thing.

"Ok. We can do that—"

"We should go on a rollercoaster!" Thoughts and desires born from Napa's memories rapidly bombarded me, and I didn't know how to slow down my sensational mind.

"I've never been on one."

"I know," I bent down and clutched onto his hands, "but you watched videos on the internet with your brothers. You said you wanted to go on vacation, but you never went anywhere, because you were poor."

"Thanks for pointing that out…"

"We can go together, as soon as we save my mother." I had to succeed. I had only lived about seventeen years, and there was an entire world of discovery. My mother and father had seen the surface world. I deserved the same chance. "We can use the internet to find Ian."

"Maybe." He took my hand and stood me up with him. It was a surprise seeing him as a human for the first time, but it was even stranger after seeing his childhood. We came from different circumstances, but we had more in common than I thought. "First things first, we have to get some money and some clothes. We don't want to look like hobos."

I gasped and pulled on his arm. "I know what that is!"

He had himself a good laugh, though it was short. "Come on."

I was more cautious about where I placed my feet. I didn't want to appear weak to Napa, and he was incredibly more impressive in my eyes. He probably had calluses all over his feet from his adventures in the Canadian wilderness. "How did you get down here?"

"I was a bird, and I had an instinct to fly south. Besides, there were too many hunters up north, and I didn't want to be a victim of irony. I figured I was much safer as a seagull than a deer or a cow."

I was surprised that no one found us while we were sleeping. We were out of the trees and among civilization in half a mile. We were getting some intense stares from the humans. Everyone was very old or young. They were crisp and pristine vacationing professionals, and we looked like…hobos. Crazy hobos, because I still had a weapon—a chakram—attached to my hip.

It didn't help that I stared right back at them. Merpeople's skin varied in shades, but I had never seen so many gorgeous colors on flesh before. I was completely stunned by the beauty of a woman who walked by me in a bikini top and shorts, with skin as smooth and dark as a black pearl. She was confident as she strutted in her long legs, and she was practically as tall as Napa. "There are so many beautiful bodies here."

"Don't talk like a crazy person so loud."

Another woman walked by, and her pleated skirt caught the wind and flowed out like the sails on a ship. I reached out to touch it, but Napa grabbed my arm and pulled me back to his side. "Hey, don't do crazy things either."

"How am I supposed to know that touching people is inappropriate?"

"If I let you touch that poor woman, you would have found out."

I wouldn't let Napa get me down. It was a beautiful morning; the sun was shining down on my radiant human body, and I could freely walk down the street. "I can't wait to live like this every day."

"Do you have anything useful in your pouches to trade for money?"

"I'm certainly not parting with my chakram. It was a gift from my mother, but I do have a pendant that can turn the wearer invisible."

He blinked hard in shock before laughing. "I don't know anyone in the market for that type of thing."

A child walked by holding a red balloon. I wanted to feel the smooth and rubbery texture. I was curious if it felt like a whale's stomach, but Napa grabbed my hand and locked his fingers with mine. I sighed. He was being no fun. "I have some of the jewels you gave me, but I don't know if I want to part with those either."

"I'm flattered, but I brought you lots of treasures. If you hang onto jewelry, it'll make your new boyfriend upset."

"What about these?" I reached into one of the pockets and pulled out a handful of pink pearls, and I still had more inside.

"Holy cow!" He squeezed my hand and jumped. If he thought I was making us look like crazy hobos, he was certainly trying to outdo me. "This could be worth tens of thousands of dollars. Probably more!"

"Really?" I was familiar with the currency of the dollar, but it was hard to believe. "I find them everywhere. You've seen me wear them in my hair before."

"Yeah, I guess I never thought about being rich when I couldn't enjoy money." I didn't bother to read Napa's mind, but I figured he was probably relieved that he had enough money to take me on a rollercoaster. "This is amazing."

We found a pawn shop, but the owner was a little bald man who was far too ambitious. He offered us five hundred dollars for seven pearls. Napa was so desperate that he was going to give in. I saw into the merchant's mind, so I didn't even reject his offer. I pulled Napa out without so much as a goodbye. He was no credit to the human race.

We tried a jewelry store next that had many diamonds and anxious women with their boyfriends, but they wouldn't even let us inside the building without shoes. I was going to force my way past the security guard, but Napa pulled me away.

The last place we tried was a little, eclectic trinket shop by the shore. There were mostly children inside poking around, but I was no better. There were pretty necklaces taken from butterfly wings and encased in glass. They ranged from blue, pink, purple, gold, and so on. I imagined that if I got married to Ian, I could wear necklaces like that as a statement piece to begin an interesting conversation. Thinking of that possibility made me excited about what other trinkets I could put inside our home, and what sort of furniture we would pick out to make a room speak to who we were. We'd have to find out more about each other before we could know, but I assumed he'd advise against being a hoarder.

"Can I help you?" asked a human girl. She was a little smaller than me and seemed concerned by our attire.

Napa took my hands away from the butterfly rack. "Yes. We want to know if the owner would be willing to buy some pearls from us."

"Pearls?" she perked up. "You didn't steal them, did you?"

"Of course not," I smiled. "I'm a mermaid. I found them while I was swimming in the Caribbean. There are tons of them out there."

She rolled her eyes and laughed. "I'm gonna get my dad. Tell him whatever story you want, but I'd love a string of pearls for my prom. Give him a good deal." She walked behind the counter and into a back room.

"Mermaid?" Napa scolded through his clenched teeth.

"It's better than her suspecting we stole them. Besides, no one will believe her."

A man came from out the back. He was between mine and Napa's height, and he had a bit of a gut, but his arms were a little toned. His face was scruffy with the beginnings of a beard, and his hair was frosted gray. He had kind eyes, but there was an obvious tiredness in them. "My daughter said you were trying to sell some pearls. That's not something I normally do. I don't know what you're expecting."

"We'll take what you have." I set a couple of pearls on the glass countertop. "We're in a hurry to sell these. There's someplace we need to be."

His eyes lit up as if he had a burst of magic to enhance them. He had a little eyeglass that he pulled out of his pocket to help observe them. He allowed a small gasp to escape him, but he kept on with his tests. The man picked them up and weighed them to the best of his judgment. He rubbed the pearls together to feel how they reacted against one another. Then, he even put them in his mouth to feel the gritty texture of their imperfections. "Sweet Jesus…" The shop owner took my pretty pink gem out of his mouth and set it back on the counter. "These are real."

"We didn't steal these," Napa quickly insisted. "These are hers. She's lived her life on the sea. Now, we're just trying to get away from her dad. He's a bad man, and she's trying to start a new life."

I braced myself for how he would take advantage of us. Humans were beginning to disappoint me. Napa was a good guy, but he was hardly human. Ian had goodness within him, but there was a side of him I hadn't seen, including an ex-fiancé. Napa was a killer, and Ian sailed with pirates. Maybe humans were just weak monsters too afraid to acknowledge their nature.

I listened in on his thoughts, and his head was filling with opportunities. He thought of retiring, he thought of paying off his bills, and then, he thought of his daughter begging him for the perfect dress for a silly dance. "I have five thousand here, at the most. I can't give you what you want for them."

Napa frowned and reached for the pearls, but I grabbed his hand and set it down at his side. "That's fine." I reached into my pouch and placed about ten more on the glass. They weren't all pink. Some were off-white with pink undertones. They varied in size, but they were all dazzlingly lit by the lights under the case. "You can take them all."

"Are you sure?" he whispered like a prayer.

The doorway to the backroom was open, and his daughter had dropped a can full of liquid on the floor from shock. Her reaction trumped Napa's bucked eyes. "I'm positive."

A jolt of joy burst from the store owner's mouth. He had tears in his eyes, and he laughed hysterically and boisterously. He was overwhelmed when I first saw him, and now, his head could have floated off his shoulders. "I'll be right back."

As soon as he walked through the doorway, Napa quietly flailed about. "I thought you didn't want to get ripped off. Why'd you sell them for so cheap?"

I turned to the back room and saw the owner talking to his daughter. I knew he was about to tell her good news, and I smiled. "He seems like he's a good father, and I've never met one before. I wanted him to be able to make his daughter happy."

She screamed, jumped into his arms, and he rocked his beloved daughter back and forth. They were both crying, but I didn't sense any sadness. When I went inside their heads, it was hard to hear any thoughts. They were overtaken with happiness. It had a little bit to do with selling the pearls for much more than he could give me, but it had everything to do with buying time to be with their family. I had seen the loving embrace of a parent through the mind of Ian, but experiencing it—and aiding in the intensity of their happiness— created a warm wind that swept throughout my body. I was seeing what I wanted my world to be like, and I was reminded of what I was fighting for.

"Ah…" My wrist began to ache exactly where my cursed marking was. I rubbed on it, and the pain quickly faded. However, the image of my mother's stone statue waiting for me outside our home was burned into my mind. The sound of her body cracking became a faint whisper in my ear, like wind tossing the waves on a clear and starry night. I gently shook my head to get rid of the sound, but the tiny burden persisted as background noise that could be ignored, but would not fade.

"You okay?" Napa asked curiously.

"I'm fine." My heart was shaking deeply inside my chest. I wondered if something was wrong with my body because it was becoming increasingly difficult to catch my breath. I wondered if the Sea Witch could breathe or if she was aware at all while trapped in my father's spell. Was she suffering because I was too naïve and weak to do what needed to be done, against a man who meant to separate us forever? "I just need to save my mother."

"And we will." Napa was an optimist and rubbed my back to be supportive, but I wasn't satisfied. I wanted more time with her. I needed it, like a craving that wouldn't rest until I had partaken.

The owner came back to us with an envelope full of cash. I looked at Napa, and he looked back at me nervously. I knew he was ten when he was turned into an animal, but I had certainly never counted money. We were at an awkward standstill, and he conceded. It was a bit embarrassing that he had to make stacks of money to be certain, but I wouldn't have done any better.

"Is there anything else I can do for you?"

My head snapped directly toward a bin of flip-flops. My feet were filthy, and they hurt. "Can we get a pair of shoes?"

"Actually, could we take a shower?" Napa finally finished and put the cash back in the envelope. "Use a computer?"

"I'd almost be willing to give you my house if you asked." And he meant it. He was genuinely indebted to us.

He had his daughter mind the shop while he escorted us into his lovely home above the store. The walls were painted yellow, and there were photographs everywhere of him, his daughter, wife, and two boys. They ranged from the time of the children's infancy to the present. It was a place full of memories, and I didn't see any pain. There were no smoke cauldrons to conjure up illusions of betrayals or bones embedded in the walls. It was all perfectly mundane, and it was the most beautiful thing I had ever seen.

"Is there something wrong?" the human asked.

"No." I hadn't realized that I was crying until he mentioned it. I quickly dried my eyes and smiled. "Everything is perfect."

Napa tugged on my arm and pulled me away from our host. "I'm gonna let you shower first." I think he was being cautious, in case I had met a human more curious about my body than he was. I wasn't worried about it. I could take care of myself, but it was admirable of Napa to care for me.

I had seen Napa's bathroom in his memories, but it was tiny, and the tiles were busted. The tub wasn't white, and I wasn't sure if it was supposed to be. These humans kept their home tidy. It was extremely bright, but the smell was strange and didn't seem very natural. I opened a window and took in the fresh air of the spring. There was a garden of flowers under my window. I think I was smelling them. It was a relief not to smell the saltiness of the ocean…or blood in the water.

I turned the silver knob and jumped when the water shot out of the showerhead. It was like a rainfall, but it was warm. It was a simple pleasure for humans, but it wildly amused me. I stripped bare and jumped in.

There were bottles of different-smelling soaps. I could read the shampoo bottle and understood what it did. I squeezed half the bottle into my hair and massaged my head. The slimy goo multiplied into a curious foam substance. I wasn't careful enough, and I yelled when the foam demon caught me off guard and slipped into my eyes.

"You okay?" Napa barged inside with a few garments in his hand. He covered his eyes. For what reason, I'm not sure. He knew that I'd be naked.

"I got shampoo in my eyes. It's nothing to be alarmed about."

"I brought you some clothes." He sat them down, and he did it without looking at me. He was even redder than the last time. "You got water everywhere. You're supposed to block the water with the curtain."

I turned my head. There was a clear fabric hanging from a metal railing around the tub. When I pulled it, the bouncing drops of water were blocked. "Oh!"

Napa cowered out of the bathroom in a hurry, and I got to enjoy my shower for a little bit longer. I even put more shampoo in my hair and washed it all again!

I got a glimpse of my cursed mark and was reminded that I didn't have time to waste enjoying the simple pleasures of humanity. There would be plenty of time for that later.

My skin was smoking and red. I stepped out on the squishy carpet and dried myself off with a towel. One garment was for my breasts. It was a struggle trying to snap it on behind me, but I eventually mastered the maniacal contraption. Another garment was for my genitals, which I didn't understand. Mine were inside my body. I only put them on so I wouldn't be indecent. Over that, I had a pair of white shorts that were nearly the length of my fingertips and a bright yellow shirt with no sleeves.

When I came out of the bathroom, Napa was holding some sort of tablet in his hands with words and pictures on it. I guessed that it was some form of computer, but I didn't recall anything specific from his memories. I took a seat next to him on the couch. He seemed upset. "Is everything alright?"

"Ian doesn't have a presence online, but his family owns a tech company about two hours from here. Mr. Dobbs called us a taxi. It should be here in about ten minutes."

"How will you be ready in ten minutes?" I didn't mean to be childish, but I bounced on the couch. It was very comfortable. "I was in the shower for much longer than that."

"I know."

I jerked my neck back. If I didn't know any better, I would have thought he was annoyed with my long shower. Napa patted my leg with a hard grin on his face, and he made his way to the bathroom.

"I made you some food." I jumped to my feet and followed Mr. Dobbs' voice into the kitchen. There was a plate sitting on the table with fries and a sandwich. It was strange having a meal prepared by the miracle of fire.

"I appreciate it." I snatched up a fry first. It was crispy on the outside, but softer in my mouth. I attacked the sandwich next, and it was totally unexpected. The bread was soft, the tomatoes were juicy, but the lettuce was crisp and fresh. But the star was the salty layer of crunchy meat dancing on my tongue. "Wow! Is this bacon?" It was famous in Napa's memories. If he could turn into a pig, I made no promises on whether I would eat him in the future.

"Yes. It is a BLT…" He cleared his throat. "I fry it in butter. I know it's not good for you, but if you've got to die, you might as well live." They were wise words to live by. I could be reckless on occasion, but there was plenty that I never got to do in the water.

I devoured my lunch, and I didn't feel like I was being appropriate with my manners. "I thank you for your hospitality."

"Don't mention it." He took my plate and put it in the sink. He paused there for a moment. He had to muster enough courage to bring it up. "My daughter said you were a mermaid."

I was a little surprised that he even considered it. "Do you believe in stories like that?"

"No, but I believed your friend's story when he said you're abused by your father and trying to get away." I tried to avoid eye contact with Mr. Dobbs. I knew how my father treated me wasn't my fault, but I couldn't push away the guilt sitting in the bottom of my gut. "You've got a certain look in your eye. It never quite goes away."

I was uncomfortable knowing that he recognized such a weakness in my eyes. I had learned to heal from my wounds. How could I miss such an obvious one? "You broke the cycle, though. Your daughter seems to love you."

He nodded slowly, but his eyes were looking toward the past. "It always scared me when I was a young man. When you're raised in a violent household, you find yourself asking if you're capable of breeding that type of violence yourself. Is it in your blood? And if it is, can you escape it?"

I was afraid to ask. "And what did you discover?"

"Of course, it is. It's in everyone's, but we get to make our own choices. I chose to be happy. It wasn't easy. Sometimes, being miserable is the simplest path. Blaming my old man would have been understood and accepted. But…I wanted to love."

I think he laughed at how ridiculous it seemed, but he was fully confident. "You can't hold onto love and hate at the same time. They require both arms. And when you embrace either, they embrace back."

I was far from the point in time where children would even be discussed, but it was nice to think that they wouldn't be inducted into the war between my two parents. He even gave me a little hope for myself. Maybe there truly was another way to live after I saved my mother.

The bathroom door opened, and Napa came out fully dressed. He managed to find another tight shirt. "How did you do that?"

He threw his hands up. "I'm a guy." There was a horn blowing outside. It must have been the taxi. Napa's impeccable timing was beginning to startle me.

"Thank you, Mr. Dobbs." Napa shook his hand. Mr. Dobbs reached for my hand, but I stepped away. I was grateful, but it was still hard to trust anyone. I think I only truly trusted Napa, and it would take time for everyone else.

He didn't allow himself to be offended. He even offered me a small smile, as if he understood. "Good luck, Luna."

I gave him a nod and pulled onto Napa's arm. If I couldn't find a way to stop my father, Mr. Dobbs, and his family could have been pulled into my mess. I had to make sure that didn't happen. He escaped the dysfunction of an abusive home, and I didn't want to be responsible for pulling him back in.

I had to do my absolute best. "Let's go."

Chapter Fourteen

A green van carried us across the lower state of Florida. I rested on Napa's chest and watched the other cars. There were so many other vans filled with families. Children in the backseat bickered and hit each other with toys, little babies were nestled safely in gargantuan car seats, and busy moms and dads just wanted to make it to their destination alive and sane. I wondered if I'd be sitting next to Ian on a vacation ride. We could go as friends, and Napa could be with us. We could try out one of those rollercoasters.

A little over two hours later, we arrived at our destination. Ian talked about showing me tall buildings, and it was certainly high. It was forty stories of concrete, steel, and glass windows. Even Napa looked intimidated, and he had certainly flown higher. "This is where Ian lives?"

"No. This is where his mega-rich uncle conducts business. We're hoping that someone may know where he is." I didn't sense that the people wandering around were like Mr. Dobbs. They were professional and cutthroat. They would have been fine warriors for my father's army if they were trained to fight with their briefcases and satchels.

There were guards inside the building and scoping out the sidewalks. One of them noticed us and used their radio to call someone. He said something about a weapon, and I realized that humans didn't carry protection. I found that utterly insane. "They'll never let me in with my weapons unless I use force."

"I'm sure that you shouldn't do that."

Well, I certainly wasn't going to enter a strange territory with no weapon. I was going into that building, and no one was going to stop me.

"Luna, stop!"

The only reason why I didn't forcibly remove Napa's arm and break the bones of the guards was that a skinny girl with black hair came out of the building. It was surreal seeing her in real life. When I saw objects from Napa's mind, it was like watching a picture and experiencing a splash of euphoria when it burst into reality. None of it was real until I could touch it and smell it, and when I did, I could barely contain myself.

I wasn't experiencing the same thing with this girl. It was eerie. I didn't understand what she was to Ian when I peeked inside his head. Now? I did, and I sort of despised her. "Napa, I know that girl. She was engaged to Ian before she broke up with him."

"You're in love with a guy who's engaged?" I punched him in the arm for being such a ridiculously loud blabbermouth. The poor baby had to rub his arm to soothe the pain.

The woman walked down the stairs leading up to the building, and she glanced at us. To Napa, I'm certain that it only felt like a second, but our eyes locked. She didn't know me, but I sensed something odd about her. I was reminded of my first encounter with the Sea Witch and how the light was sucked from the world without it dimming at all. I couldn't let her go before satisfying my curiosity. "Hey! What's your name?"

She had finished her first section of stairs, and she only had two more to go. She could have ignored me, but I wouldn't have taken that well. I also didn't appreciate the way she rudely addressed me. "Do I know you?"

"No, but I'm looking for someone. His name is Ian, and I'm certain you know him."

"And how do you know...?" Her dark eyes flashed with a sense of wonder and disbelief. "You're his anime fetish."

"I'm not his fetish." I tried to swagger down the steps to meet her. I held the railing in the center to keep my balance and held my nose up higher to her. "I'm his true love."

"No..." A worry wrinkle appeared on her forehead, but that faded when hysterical laughter spewed from her mouth. "No! I can't believe this. Ian really is crazy, and he found a crazy person to indulge his delusions."

I began to realize something about her. After spending some time around normal humans, I knew what they felt like. Magic was very apparent to me, and most humans didn't have access. They were weak and hollow. She was like an oasis that was difficult to find, but it certainly existed. "You're a witch."

"Sticks and stones, baby."

"I'm not trying to insult you. I'm stating a fact. You are a witch." I stepped closer to the girl so I could look into her eyes. She was pretending to be bewildered, but there was just enough awareness in them for me to know a great storm raged on inside of her. There was great darkness within her, and it only made me more suspicious about Ian's life.

"My mother warned me that women would be after Ian for his powers. Is that why you're in his life? Do you want to make an all-powerful coven? You need his sperm—"

"Shut up!" She covered her face with her hands. She didn't mean to scream, but I had frustrated her. "I'm not having this conversation with you."

"He doesn't know. Does he?" She didn't have to answer for me to know. Her confession was so clear in her head that it might have been written on her forehead. I could appreciate that she felt guilty about putting Ian through the lie of being loved and appreciated for who he was as a person, but guilt wasn't enough. He cared for the girl. This level of betrayal would crush him.

"I'd prefer if he doesn't find out." She was threatening more than begging. "He wants to reconcile."

"That's a lie."

"He called me." She crossed her arms and smirked. "He said he wanted to meet at his place."

"What a coincidence. I'm trying to find him. You can take me to him." I wasn't asking. It was more like a promise to break her legs if she didn't comply.

"You're trying to steal my amplifier from me, an amplifier that I happen to also love. What makes you think that I'll go down without a fight?"

She was a scrappy girl, but I was a warrior. I could slit her throat with my chakram before she could take another breath. I can't say I didn't think about it. The thought of breaking her in two stirred me up in a way that only battle could. "Oh, you can fight me. It won't be much of one."

Napa jumped between the two of us and pushed her out of my way. He tried to push me, but I wouldn't allow him to show me up. His brows were furrowed when he looked at me, but he shouldn't have been concerned. Fighting was just part of my nature. "We need his help," he told her.

She rolled her eyes and pressed a hard smile on her face. "I don't care."

I made a move to strike her down, but Napa stepped in front of me again. "What if we give you some form of payment?"

She hesitated, and her jaw tightened. "Money means very little to me."

"Power does, right?" A spark of brilliance shot through his brain. If he were a bird, he would have been flapping his wings. "Luna has a pendant that can make the wearer turn invisible. Take us to Ian, and it's yours."

She tried not to be intrigued, but through her pursed lips, I could see that she was breaking. "Is that true?"

I didn't think I had a real use for it, but I still glared at Napa for mentioning such a thing. I could have made her talk. Now that she wanted the pendant, I didn't have a choice but to slap it in her hand. "If you can't use it, that's not my problem."

She held it up to the light and watched the sun reflect off it. I knew that she couldn't have figured it out so quickly, but she could at least recognize the opportunity. "I'll take you to Ian, but that doesn't mean it's over between us."

"By the way, I'm Napa." He offered a friendly handshake, but I knew that boy. He was bashful because she was very attractive.

She was a horrible woman, though. She wasn't even polite enough to shake his hand. She just stared at it as if it were diseased. "I'm Nessa."

"Is that short for Vanessa?"

"No." She hated me for the same reason I was defensive toward her, but she was unnecessarily annoyed by Napa. "Let's go."

Maybe she didn't enjoy having his attention. He didn't make it very obvious, but for a brief moment, she shone in his eyes. She might have been a lying witch, but she was a pretty girl. Her hair was the same color as Napa's, but she kept it in a messy bun. I suspected that it probably stretched down to her lower back as his did. Her skin was also similar to his complexion, but it was lighter. He was closer to a chestnut, and she was more like an almond. She didn't have much meat on her bones, but she was muscular. Her chin was manlier than Napa's. She even had a cleft.

It was curious that Nessa didn't park her car in the lot of the building she visited. We had to follow her through a park. There were many different corporations around the area, so the greenery was well tended to. Joggers were running on paths, and enthusiastic pet owners were taking their dogs for walks. A teenager on a pair of rollerblades nearly ran into Nessa, but he nearly fell when she glared at him. She might have been intimidating to me if I hadn't grown up in the ocean.

"Momma!" My feet began dragging, and I came to a full stop. The sound of a little girl's voice shot a cold chill down to the base of my spine, and a wind whirled around inside my chest.

Nessa kept on walking, but Napa stopped for me. "Are you okay?"

There was a little girl in a frilly pink dress—practically too tiny to walk—running into the arms of her mother. Their noses collided in a tender kiss, and they both exploded into a joyous reaction. I couldn't hear their entire conversation, but I read their lips. "I love you."

The sunny scene at the park changed to a blurry image of the Sea Witch smiling down at me, distorted by a yellow liquid. There was a hard layer keeping me from her—like a shell—but I could hear her singing to me. I wanted to reach out and touch her, but I wasn't strong enough. I wanted to be born!

For more than a thousand years, my father kept us separated from one another. I couldn't let him win anymore. I was aching inside to have her. I felt as though I would die if he couldn't free her from the stone. It was becoming harder to breathe.

"Luna?" Napa waved his hand in front of my face and brought me back to the park.

"Yeah, I just want to save my mom."

"We will. I know Ian will want to help." He rubbed my arms and offered a kind smile. "If he loves you like I do, he'd be willing to do anything for you." It was nice of Napa to reassure me, but who would want to die to save a sea witch? A pang of fear burrowed its way inside of me, and I didn't know how to make it go away.

We ran to catch up with Nessa. She parked in an open and free community space. That was also curious, but I didn't care enough to clarify what her methods were. She'd be out of Ian's life soon enough.

She did have a cool car, though. Napa slid from the back of the convertible and spun into the backseat. I mimicked his movements and plopped in beside him. Nessa rolled her eyes and quietly scolded us under her breath.

I wasn't thrilled about having to ride in a car again, but it turned out to be a pleasant experience. The top of the car was down, so we had a lot of hair flying between Napa and me, though his was in a ponytail. I even raised my hands and yelled when we hit a higher speed. It might have been the closest I would ever be to a rollercoaster, so it was good to enjoy it.

Nessa didn't approve, and she retaliated by raising the top. I wasn't going to make demands in her car, but I took a mental note. I was making a list of all the ways she offended me. Nessa was uncomfortable with the new tension she created and engaged in small talk. "So…how's the ocean?"

"It's wet," I said sharply. "How's being a witch?"

"It's dark." I saw her eyes look up at me through the mirror. I think she was judging me as some sort of hypocrite.

"I don't use dark magic."

"That's cute!" She laughed, and it alarmed me a little bit. "Sweetheart, I don't know what you are, but there is something twisted inside of you. I've been practicing the black arts my whole life, and I've never felt the pull that you have. If you love Ian, stay away from him."

"I can't do that. He's my true love."

"True love?" She adjusted her mirror to better gauge Napa's reaction. That coward hid his face in the road. "Love is knowing someone, building experiences with them, and standing the test of time. If you're truly his fin fetish, that means your family is responsible for making him an orphan. Do you think resentment just goes away? It'll grow inside him and destroy everything you are together."

"At least he knows what I am!" I wasn't about to be lectured by a cowardly witch whore.

"If he knew what you were, he'd run."

I didn't mean to let my rage escape me, but when I saw her fox eyes practically glowing from her attempt to hurt me, all I wanted to do was hit back!

The rearview mirror shattered and exploded throughout the car. The two of them hollered, and the car swerved outside of its lane. There was a car next to us that began honking insanely. It also swerved and managed to avoid us, but the young man inside was furious enough to flash profane signals. Nessa turned to me, gasping for air to recover from her scare. If she were looking for an apology, it wasn't going to happen. I took pleasure in the cut across her pretty cheek.

"Let's stop talking…" Napa's voice quivered, but he found enough courage to scold me with his eyes.

"Fine." I faced the side of the road. I had nothing I wanted to discuss with that wicked witch anyway. I felt sick to my stomach sitting behind her. We couldn't trust her. She was going to get in the way of saving my mother, and the moment I confirmed that, I was going to snap her neck.

Nessa took us to a neighborhood that was crowded with many homes nearly touching each other. Napa's backyard was a forest. These people had a couple of palm trees and a patch of grass. The homes were bright, colorful, angular, and new.

Nessa parked on the street behind a black convertible that matched hers, and I failed to see it as a coincidence. "He's here. This is his car."

I was curious to go inside Ian's home and learn more about him. I was relieved he lived in a neighborhood with other families. It gave an impression of stability and that he was thinking about the future. Hopefully, Nessa wasn't the only reason he bought that house. "I told him to run. He's in danger."

"If that's true, he probably wanted to make sure I was safe. I bet that's why he asked me to meet him here." I don't think she was being purposely hurtful…that time, but she was becoming a problem. She ran up to the door, and all I could think about was whether I was going to make her death quick or painfully slow. A mix of both wouldn't be bad.

"Luna, what's wrong?" It was annoying how Napa kept asking me that.

"I just want to save my mom."

"Ok, but…" He reminded me more of that little flounder scrambling to get away from the sharks, rather than the wolf that tore men apart. "You're starting to scare me a little bit."

"I'm fine—"

"No. You're not." I tried to open the door to get out, but he latched onto my arm. He was stern and steady, and his fingers were like teeth gripping my flesh. The wolf was still in there. "Tell me what we're here to do."

"I'm here to save my mother."

"And you're not going to hurt Ian, are you?"

"He's my true love." I did notice that my words felt hollow. I heard the sound, I felt my lips move, but it didn't seem like me. "I'd never hurt him."

"I hope that's true. I don't know what this curse is doing to you, but you're acting weird. I know you can fight, but you've never been into violence. You've only used your magic to protect. Don't do anything you can't take back."

Nothing was wrong with my ears, but I somehow missed what he was saying to me. I felt as though I was trapped behind two glass walls. On one side, Napa was making perfect sense. He was only preserving my desire to stay pure from dark magic. That's what I needed him for, to remind me. But when I turned to the other glass, there was a cloud of black smoke swirling around and banging against its prison. There was a tiny crack in the center of it, and the closer I got to it, the more rapidly it spread.

"I'm here to save my mother."

I didn't mean to draw magic into my arm. I didn't even realize what I had done until he hollered, and the smoke rose from his sizzling hand. "What is wrong with you?" He shook his hand and gritted his teeth. I didn't mean to cause him pain, but I can't say I didn't enjoy it.

"I'm going to save my mother." I jumped out of the car and ran for the open door. Napa wasn't going to stop me!

"Luna?" Ian's arms were wrapped around Nessa. She was watching for my reaction, expecting me to be jealous. That was impossible. When I walked through the door, there was no one else in his world, so I wasn't about to make room for her. "What are you doing here?"

He let go of his ex, and I jumped into his arms. He spun me around a few times, and we laughed in relief. Napa was insane. I wasn't going to harm Ian. I could still feel the bond between us, and it would only grow in time. We would get to know each other and withstand those tests that Nessa mentioned. We belonged together.

"Why are you with Nessa?" He ushered in the sudden awkwardness that should have existed between an ex and a new love. I held all the power now, and her bug eyes were begging me not to out her dirty secret.

"Your little mermaid spotted me. She told me you were in danger, and I brought them here."

"You believe she's a mermaid?" he asked in disbelief.

"Oh, she's something…" She clapped her hands together and looked around. She was truly embarrassed. She really thought he was going to fall all over her as if he didn't remember her accusing him of being mentally insane. "She seems a little young for you."

"I'm nearly seventeen!" I'm not sure why Ian threw his head back and moaned while Nessa glared over at him to project shame.

"We're barely two years apart. Don't judge me."

"Oh, you're judged, but falling for a sixteen-year-old is certainly the least of your offenses."

"What about your offenses?" I asked. I'm not sure why Nessa turned to me with betrayal beaming from her eyes. I held no loyalties to her.

"What is she talking about, Nessa?" He already had a twinge of anger and hurt in his voice.

I crossed my arms and waited for her to destroy everything they ever had together.

"Well…it's complicated…"

"Luna!" Nessa was very lucky that Napa cautiously came inside the house. He was still clutching his stinging hand. His entire palm was bright red. "Luna, are you alright?"

"I'm fine, Napa." I glanced at the mark on my wrist. I couldn't believe that little moon was making me go mad. "I'm really sorry about your hand." I started walking toward Napa, so I could heal my only friend in the world. My hands were reaching out for his.

"Did you and your mom stop your dad?"

I drew my hands away, and my feet paused. Ian didn't know the circumstances of the curse, but it was almost insulting for him to ask. "No. He put her under a spell."

"Can it be lifted?"

The hairs on the back of my neck were standing up. I was so livid that my body began to tremble. I balled my fingers into fists to relieve my tension, but I couldn't shake it. "It can."

"Uh, what's wrong with your fish?" Nessa asked Ian.

I was back at the wall, tracing my finger along the cracks. I wanted it to be free, and I needed it inside of me to do what needed to be done. I found the center point and tapped.

"Napa, get him out of here." The light inside of my stomach—that came to life around Ian—began to churn. I felt ill, like I was about to vomit. I loved him. I was certain I did, but...

I tapped the glass again.

"Luna, just think!" Napa begged. "You don't have to do this violently—"

"Do what violently?" Ian asked fearfully.

He wasn't a warrior like the ones I had become accustomed to. How could he survive with me? How could he be strong enough to help me save my mother? If he truly loved me, the least he could do was die for my cause.

With one final tap, the wall exploded and flooded me with the necessary power that I needed to survive: no remorse, no shame, and a sharp focus on fulfilling the pact I made with my father.

"Run!"

Chapter Fifteen

There must have been something wrong with my face because they all had to take a gander before they were terrified enough to process the severity of the situation. I turned around, aimed my back to the door, and dared any of them to make a move for it.

Ian and Nessa knew the place very well and ran off to the back. Napa didn't rush away with his tail between his legs until I gave him a nice smile.

It was a nice place, though. It was an open space, had hardwood floors, a pool table, and a newer kitchen with granite countertops. Of course, it was a terrible reminder that my mother was encased in rock until I slaughtered the owner.

I got to the back of the house and saw them beating against a shield. I still had a long way to go with my barriers, but it was good enough for the three of them. It was a pity that none of them were strong enough to get through to the sliding glass door or bust through the windows. No one was going to escape. "Did you really think it would be that easy?"

"Did you?" Nessa latched onto Ian's hand and began to drain him. By the goofy, open-mouth gaze on his face, I confirmed that he didn't know Nessa was a witch. She must have pulled too much and too quickly because he hollered and nearly doubled over.

But Nessa certainly got the charge she wanted. Her pupils dilated until her eyes became like drops of oil in the ocean. "Buh-bye, fish."

I wasn't expecting any bit of a challenge, so it was a shock when Nessa's power knocked me straight through the wall and into the den, where I collided with the pool table. My force pushed it up against the wall, and it exploded behind me.

I was a little stunned. I sat on the floor blinking for a few seconds. My friend and my true love had made a stand against me with a witch who openly practiced dark magic. Had I pushed them too far? Was my behavior unacceptable? Did they have to turn on me?

No. I had to save my mother, and I would peel the flesh from their bones as delicately as she would if it would free her from my father's curse.

The three of them ran up the stairs, practically tripping on one another. Ian stood out as the weakest among them. He wouldn't last long. He even took the time to gaze at me when I stood at the bottom of the steps. "You don't have to do this, Luna."

"Keep running. You make it fun this way." I was finally beginning to understand my father's fascination with the hunt. It had never exhilarated me before, but there was a unique thrill tingling inside my chest as they ran for their lives, not knowing that their hearts were already in my hands. They had no idea that nowhere was safe. Just because I wasn't in the water didn't mean I couldn't sense where they were. I could hear the creaks in the wood and the stomping of their feet. I stayed on the first floor and followed their dragging corpses.

I shot off a blast of magic on the ceiling. It wasn't enough to kill anyone, but it did blow a hole through the floor that Ian was standing on. The fall didn't kill him, but he certainly hurt his back against the heavy dining room table. He couldn't even twitch his way out.

"Ian!" I didn't expect Nessa to be so emotional and frightened for the man she was using as a battery.

"I'm warning you, Luna!" Napa yelled from above. "I won't let you do this."

"And how do you intend on stopping—?" I looked up to the hole in the wall and caught a glimpse of a silver wolf diving down and to my arm. I screamed, just because I wasn't expecting to feel any pain. I also wasn't expecting my friend to betray me for his rival. "You dare to stand in my way?"

I punched him in the face, but he refused to let me go. As I watched my blood ooze out of my arm, and into his mouth and floor, I was reminded of his earliest ambition. He wanted to break his curse and require the merman form. Was he ever truly my friend, or was he just using me? He would be helping me if he truly loved me. He knew what my mother meant to me.

"You'll pay for this!" I gathered magic into my hand to force Napa off me, but the little monster's firm grip loosened as his body rapidly shrank to an animal small enough to crawl up my shredded arm, my shoulder, and my back. I saw a glimpse of a bushy brown tail in the corner of my eye. When I turned my head to find him, I was blinded by the swipe of a black paw.

I was on the floor screaming. It took me a moment to know if my vision was lost; I had so much blood in my eyes. He might have tried to avoid clawing my face off, but he still gashed open my cheek. I didn't know how resourceful Napa could be. I was impressed.

A black bear was towering over me on his two feet, and my prey was nowhere to be seen. I could still hear the sound of panting and clumsy footsteps on the floors as they made their way back up the stairs. "Looks like Nessa figured out the pendant. She's a decent witch. There's more potential in these humans than I originally thought."

"Luna," Napa urged with his thoughts, "this is the curse. This isn't you."

"And who is this fighting me?" I was leery about bringing darkness into my life, and he was proving to be no different than my father. He was just another man trying to hurt me. "Is this my 'friend' standing in my way? You'd rather hurt me and protect your rival than save my mother's life?"

"You don't seem too interested in bringing him back after you kill him."

"I haven't really thought beyond his death…or yours." I raised my hand and generated a force powerful enough to knock Napa off his feet. His fur shook and retracted until his human skin was visible. By the time his back hit the brick wall across from me, he had become his human self. He was down and out.

I heard Nessa and Ian run upstairs. It didn't work out so well the first time for them, but I indulged their fantasy of hope. Everyone needed to believe in a chance of survival. When I touched the wooden railing that led upstairs, I was reminded of Napa's suggestion. "I could try freezing Ian to death. I think that would work."

As I exhaled a breath, I felt the cold in my lungs already beginning to spread. My visible breath spread on the walls, and a trail of frost followed up the rail. Each step that I walked on froze over. By the time I turned the corner, the upstairs was a tundra.

I glanced around the hallway. They could have been invisible, but I was certain they were hiding in one of the rooms. I took my chances and walked through the master bedroom. It had some darker colors, but it was elegant in its design. It was certainly spacious, and the bed had plenty of room for two. It disgusted me to think of Ian and Nessa writhing around under the sheets, but her scent was embedded in the walls. I bet she still had a drawer packed to the brim with clothes. I'm sure she would have loved to let Ian rescue her from the cold by letting him warm her body with their indecency. I was looking forward to her death more and more.

There was a bathroom connected to his room and a large walk-in closet to hide in. Napa would often play a hiding game as a child. He'd hide in closets and adjust his body when his brothers reached inside. His siblings would rarely find him.

But I didn't believe they would bother hiding in those rooms. Nessa would want to be close to the door, so my back would be to her when I began to search. She'd want a way out for Ian.

I turned to the corner of the room. There was a leather chair that slightly moved, and there was certainly enough space in between it and the wall for two people to hide. They were doing their best not to make a peep, but Ian didn't have any shoes on, and he was wearing a pair of shorts. If he continued our standoff, he'd die anyway. I dropped the temperature until I heard their shivers and saw their breath released in puffs of smoke.

"You might as well let me see you when you die, Nessa." She and Ian reappeared before my eyes, and I laughed at their blue lips. "I'm a little surprised the lovers couldn't keep themselves warm."

"Ian, run."

"I can't leave you."

"I can handle her." Her voice was a sharp whisper, weakened from the cold.

I could tell by looking into Ian's eyes that he was overwhelmed, but he didn't seem very hurt. He was fiercely gazing into my eyes, telling me that he didn't believe I'd go through with destroying him. He was practically daring me to prove him wrong as he headed toward the door. "This isn't you, Luna."

I felt a quake inside my chest, and it quivered my entire body. I could still feel our connection scratching at the back of my throat and mixing my insides together. He was tangling me up in a terrible way. I didn't want to feel any more pain, but I knew that I wouldn't stop. I couldn't be stopped. "I'd prefer if you're last anyway."

He shook his head slowly, still trying to convince himself that there was enough love between us. "Luna, don't—"

"Run."

I admired him for wanting to stay and protect Nessa, despite lying to him about what she was. However, Ian did the only thing he could. He ran away like a coward.

"He's right, you know." She pointed to the crescent mark on my wrist. "That mark you keep looking at is a curse. Isn't it? You're not this way." If she were trying to convince me, she was doing an awful job. She didn't sound very enthusiastic about me not being like her.

"What way? A warrior?" I unlatched my chakram and twirled it for dramatic effect. A flicker of reality bounced off my diamond blade and reflected inside her eye. I had no idea what tragic events hardened her, but she was beginning to understand that she was nothing compared to me. "I've been fighting my entire life. This is the way of my people. It's my way."

She raised her hands and summoned her magic, but it certainly wasn't as strong without her human booster. "I won't let you hurt Ian."

"Really?" I laughed. The wispy spots of purple light in her hands were barely going to result in a tickle. "What if I gave you a chance to survive? I could let you walk right now."

She took a breath of relief and nearly cried. "You'd lift the barrier and let me go?" Her magic dissipated. Self-preservation was not a foreign concept to me, but I was accustomed to doing what was right for my pack. Now, my pack was my mother and me. It disgusted me that Nessa could be so selfish, but it also satisfied me to know that she didn't truly love Ian. It gave her less meaning.

"You're not my priority. I couldn't care less about you." I kicked the chair out of the way so I could get close enough to feel her neck. Her whimpering brought me joy. Nessa thought very little of me until she knew I was capable of killing her. Was that truly the only way to garner respect in the world? Murder made my parents great and powerful, and I would respect Nessa more if she put up a better fight. Maybe violence was the only way. It was the only absolute in my life.

Nessa was quivering so much; she was beginning to shake me. Her pretty skin had begun to discolor. It wasn't a very difficult choice, but she certainly took a lot of time for a girl freezing to death. Her tears barely rolled down her cheeks before freezing against her skin. "I know you think I'm a horrible person. Maybe I am, but I do love him."

I must say, I was surprised by the rise of courage in her eyes. She even had the audacity to push my hand away from her neck. "I'm not gonna let you hurt him."

"I don't require your permission." I gripped my chakram tightly, but I hesitated to swipe it across her throat. Instead, Nessa's head was knocked into the wall with a left hook. She wasn't strong enough to fight and bounced right onto the floor. She tried to push herself up, but the cold air in her lungs had zapped too much of her strength. I could have decapitated her. She was my biggest obstacle. I remember thinking about it, and her eyes widening as my wrist flinched.

Still, I decided to walk away. It would have been better for her to die knowing she failed. I would return to her once the darkness had totally consumed my heart. It would have been more satisfying afterward.

"Luna, don't do this!" She begged. "You'll regret this."

"How can I regret such an interesting game?" I waved my hand in front of the door and created another barrier. If she were frozen solid by the time I returned to cut her head off, I'd learn to live with my decision.

Interestingly enough, Ian decided to go up instead of futilely running for the typical exits. I was intrigued enough to walk across the hall and follow the once-hidden staircase to the final level.

Napa had been inside an attic before. They were mostly junk storage. At a glance, it was neatly organized, but there were certainly a lot of boxes. Ian was waiting behind a couple of stacked crates. It wasn't as cold as his bedroom, but I could still see his breath peeking out from his protective wall. "It is a little strange that you're hiding in an attic."

"I'm not hiding." He rolled off the crates and turned to face me with some sort of weapon in his hand. It was long and made from metal and wood. By the time I realized that a harpoon was aimed right at my chest, I was flung against the wall and pinned down.

I coughed, and a mouthful of blood spewed across the floor. I looked at the spear sitting inside my body, right under my right breast. It had broken through one of my ribs, and it was difficult to breathe. My chest was burning, and every slight movement sparked an explosion of pain.

I looked up, and Ian was standing in front of me with a spear gun in his hand. I thought he was a curious explorer, madly in love with me. To say I was thrown for a total and complete loop would have been a vast understatement. "You said you weren't hunting us."

"I said I was searching for you. I never meant that I wasn't hunting your psychotic father." He raised the gun to my head, and his steely eyes were very resolved in what he had to do. It was hurtful but impressive.

"This is certainly an interesting turn of events." I chuckled, though it pained me. Maybe he truly could be part of my world. He could hunt. He could kill. There wasn't much more to it than that. "This isn't enough to stop me."

"I'm sure the second spear will do."

I could certainly respect him for fighting. I wanted my mother to live—more than I wanted to survive—but I was still willing to fight for me. My transformed state wasn't as easy to access with a human body. I should have been able to slip into it as soon as my life was jeopardized, but I felt it was buried underneath the fragile state that my father had created. It would require much energy to break it, and I wasn't sure if I should use it for anything other than healing myself and destroying Ian. "You had best kill me now."

His radically focused glass eyes morphed into pools of uncertainty. "I don't want to kill you, and I know you don't want to kill me. You could have done it by now."

"You're wrong." Desperation sprang from me, and a burst of bright colors sparked into existence and spread across his floors and walls. I was too naïve to know a fire when I first saw one, but now that I had seen the devastation through the eyes of Napa, I was ready to burn him alive. "I do want to kill you."

He must have had some valuable items in his crates. He was horrified when the fire spread to them. Ian threw his gun on the ground and grabbed my shoulders. "Stop this!" Each tug of his fingers resulted in the tearing of my insides. I hollered out, but he wouldn't stop. "Your friend, Napa, is in this house, too. Nessa has nothing to do with all this!"

I wasn't expecting him to beg. He had the upper hand until he dropped that gun. He was such a fool! I couldn't stop. Sparing my life meant his death, but he did it anyway. Our love couldn't have been that strong. We were both bloodied messes, due to wounds we gave to each other. We weren't at all what I had seen through his mind four years ago. I didn't want what we had become.

I held my head back to protect my eyes from leaking, but the tears flooded my face regardless. The ache in my chest deepened, and it was more than my injuries. The light inside of me wanted to be free. I understood that he loved me, and I would always love him, but he was destroying me. The darkness was pulling every speck of my existence away from our light. If I didn't destroy him, I was going to rip in half.

And my mother would still be dead.

"It's a curse." I exploded with emotion and blubbered out. I held up my wrist so he could see for himself. "If I don't kill you, my mother will die. I don't know if there's time to find another way, and it's driving me to hurt you. I can't stop it…"

"Okay, okay. Just…" He looked at the spear and panicked, as if he had just realized what he had done. He paced around the room for a few seconds, but he didn't have much time to think. His instincts led him to hurt me. It was essential that he found a way to remain calm. "Put out the fire, Luna."

"I can't." I tried to focus on the flames, but I didn't have the will. It was wild and dangerous, like the freedom I longed for. The curse was calling me to be reckless and ruthless. I wanted to destroy and rage, even though his love made me feel beautiful and bright inside. It was chaos, just like my mother warned. "I'm so sorry…"

Ian took a deep breath and braced himself instead of warning me. He gripped onto my arms and yanked me off the harpoon. It prompted an agonizing scream, and I clutched onto Ian's arms to alleviate some of that pressure. I didn't mean to pull on his source of magic, but my instinct to survive kicked in. I felt my broken rib snap back into place, and the pressure on my chest was released. I breathed normally, and the hot, open gash on my face began to close as my skin pulled together and sealed itself.

"Can you bring me back from the dead?" My face was still stained with blood, but Ian was mystified by my capabilities. He caressed my newly formed skin, and I trembled in his grasp. It was terrible that I found myself wishing it wasn't so difficult to kill him. I wanted to forget the tender kisses we shared on the beach, or the exposure of love he granted when I saved him from my father. I didn't want any of it!

"I…" My tears fell like heavy pearls. "I don't know." I closed my eyes and tried to sort out what was real between us, and what I felt I had to do. The darkness corrupting my mind wasn't so obvious. Things that I had never appreciated about my mother were amplified. She sheltered me, strengthened me, and she protected my heart. She encouraged me to love. Part of me knew how furious she would be about the deal I made with my father. She would want me to be happy with Ian, but I didn't know if I could let her die.

"Hey…" I was so full of shame. I tried to look away, but Ian raised my head and held me in his eyes. I was reminded of the first time I beheld their beauty when he didn't know me, but he put my needs before his own safety. He took his leap of faith, and though his parents were killed, I was able to save him. "I trust you."

"You shouldn't." Something was wrong with my body. My mother never quite explained her transformation into that monster, but I feared I would soon find out. As I thought of sparing him, my heart began to quiver. The curse was twisting my insides. I wouldn't have a thousand years to find a way to beat it. "You should have killed me. It's too late for us—"

"You're the only reason I'm alive anyway." He took my hand and placed it on his chest. It was alarming how fast it beat against my hand. The pale blue complexion faded from his skin. Splotches of red were in his cheeks, neck, and ears. The warm air was in my lungs, so I knew it wouldn't be long before he was roasted from the inside. How he calmed himself was a mystery. "I owe you my life. I will give it back to you, if it'll save your mom."

I shook my head and whimpered, even though my fingers were tensing up for the kill. "You don't owe me anything."

"Oh, but I do." He laughed at the irrational clarity that dominated his mind, perhaps since the moment he first set eyes on me. "I already decided to give my life to you. You don't need to take it."

Ian's endorsement of his death began to solidify my resolve. I knew exactly how I wanted to destroy him, and my hands slid up his chest and rested on his neck and shoulders. My eyes glanced over to his tender lips and back at his steady eyes. "I thought we could live our lives together."

"We still can…if you want it bad enough."

I saw the flames coming up from behind us. I had no time and no more options. I stood on my toes and pulled him close. The way he collided into me—like a tropical storm forming above the ocean—morphed me into a force I couldn't control. Despite the life I wanted or the undeniable power he flooded into my body, I couldn't fight the curse. I felt his passion in every fingertip, and it shot out as a bolt of lightning from his chest to mine. I really did take his heart when I gave him my breath. I felt his life force as our lips intertwined. It was tainted with its own darkness, born from obvious reasons and hardships unseen. It was prevalent, but not stronger than the hope he had in us.

I would like to say that I felt guilty for sucking that hope from his body, but the truth is, there was nothing in this world more satisfying than fulfilling the blood oath that I made. The power that flowed through me, as I drew every ounce of oxygen from his body, was absolutely intoxicating.

I let his body drop on the floor, and the thud released a shockwave of air that blew the fire out. It was a merciful death and the least I could do after he boosted my magic again. I shook my arm as it tingled. The black marking on my arm faded, but the crescent symbol embedded on my skin as a scar. I dropped to my knees when the tingle rushed through my veins. It was painful and dangerously pleasurable. When it reached my heart, I gasped for air that tasted different. The world wasn't sweet. It was savory and mine to devour.

"I darkened my magic…" I was horrified, but I laughed. It didn't feel as awful as I expected, and I certainly hadn't deformed. Perhaps it would take more killing to push me further into becoming a monster, or I could have been different than my mother. She said I had greater potential than even herself. My oath was fulfilled. She should have been freed from my father's spell. I was eager to continue my training and explore the darker side of myself.

I glanced at the corpse beside me. I wondered if my father knew how much stronger and more ambitious I would feel after Ian's death. In a sick way, he must have cared. He always believed in pushing me, even if that meant leaving me broken. I couldn't deny that I was on a path to be more powerful, but I was crushed.

"Ian…" I had opened a gateway that corrupted me, but my mind was no longer twisted to fit my oath. The absent shame for hurting my friend had returned and magnified. And once I realized I had suffocated my future, I collapsed on his chest and wailed.

"What have I done?" His body was still warm, but he had no pulse. The light in my chest had dimmed, and I was hollow. The new darkness within me was mine. I made it, and I'd have to own it. I didn't know if I could fight against it without someone to love. "Please, come back to me."

I sat up and held his face. I didn't know if I believed in a higher power, but I prayed that he would open his eyes. I needed to see them again. I wanted to make one more memory of his sea-glass eyes. "Ian!"

Four years ago, almost to the day, I hovered over Ian. I sang his mother's song, and it came to me once again. It was distorted through my pain, but I wanted to repeat the past. I wanted to see the potential of his heart. He was my true love, and what we had was mystic.

"You're still with me…" I suddenly remembered what my mother told me about death. Ian died violently, and he had an abundance of energy. His heart had stopped, but the energy that fueled his life was left behind. I still had a chance to save him.

"Ian…" I placed my hands against his chest and concentrated. "I do want it badly enough." I knew his magic intimately. It flowed through my body and magnified my own power. Ian was a wonder and a gift to my life. He was kind and compassionate, but he was a fighter. He wouldn't leave me without a fight.

I closed my eyes and began to pull on the energy. I could see how the lives of merpeople fueled the youth of my parents for a millennium. My skin and eyes began to glow as I took in the extra power. I was frightened that darker ambitions would trap it within my body and add to my power. I'd probably have to face those fears for the rest of my life, but I was determined to have Ian stand by my side to combat those temptations.

I opened his mouth and breathed my breath into his body, and I fueled that breath with his own power and my will. I refused to sacrifice my happiness or my love for a man who abused the heart of my mother. I refused to let him hurt me anymore, and I, sure enough, wouldn't destroy myself for his sick crusade.

I was ready to embrace love with my arms wide open, and a remarkable miracle happened once I did: it embraced me back. "Ian?"

His eyelids fluttered, and I saw that flash of blue. They were pale in color—compared to mine—but they were extraordinarily intense and lively. He held my entire world in them. "Luna, are you okay?"

"Yes." I smiled and continued to cry, but at least they were joyous tears. I held his face and pecked his lips. I couldn't believe that he bothered to ask if I was alright after I killed him. "The curse is gone. I'm me again."

"I knew you'd find a way." He sat up and took me into his arms. I wasn't used to accepting many hugs, but I was willing to get used to them. I loved the feeling of his heart pressing into my chest, his arms wrapped tightly around my body, and the sound of his breath in my ear. His light brightened and filled my chest again, and I began to laugh.

"I'm so happy you're alive!"

"Well, I am too."

He had done more for me than I could ever repay. My mother was not only free from the spell, but my father's wrath would never come against her again. He could never abuse us. We were truly free.

Chapter Sixteen

I hurried downstairs to Ian's bedroom and released Nessa from my prison. She used her magic to summon a fire, but she must not have been very good at it. It was tiny and constantly flickering, but it was probably the only reason why she was alive.

Napa was alright. Ian woke him up with some smelling salts. I apologized a dozen times in the span of thirty seconds. I had to give him credit for being much tougher than I thought, and for having the courage to stand against me.

After it was established that everyone was going to live, Ian wanted to take some time to talk to Nessa. They went to his bedroom and closed the door. Napa gave me a bag of chips to eat, and I took them to the top of the stairs, where I could sit and listen to their conversation. Napa followed.

"You do realize that eavesdropping is rude, right?"

"Ian wants to spend the rest of his life with me. If he wants to have private conversations, he wouldn't have fallen in love with a mind-reading mermaid."

"You didn't give him much of a choice." He chuckled before becoming incredibly serious. "You didn't give me one either."

I took a deep breath and sighed. Napa was a handsome man with a beautiful body. He certainly knew me better than Ian, but I had only known him as a friend. It was difficult to see him in another way or to change the sort of love that I felt for him. It certainly wasn't impossible to want him romantically. If he had waited to kiss me without blood in his mouth, I probably would have enjoyed it.

I didn't want to complicate my life when I knew that Ian could make me perfectly happy. "I already made my choice, Napa."

"No, you assume that you made a choice. You've experienced a creepy and magical connection. You didn't actually choose to fall in love with Ian."

"No, but I've chosen to accept it." I could see the hurt in Napa's eyes, along with a fierce and fiery determination to fight for me. I wouldn't have been intimidated before, but he did turn into a bear and slap me. I was concerned about what he could do to Ian. "My hope is that you can also learn to accept it. I don't want this to come between our friendship."

"Nothing ever will." He forced a small and miserable smile on his face. "Pass the bag."

My eyes widened, and I crushed it, feeling embarrassed. "I ate them all."

"The entire bag?" He snatched it from me and looked inside. He was horrified.

"Was I not supposed to?" The chips were salty and smoky, and they tingled my tongue. I thought I would only want a couple, but I couldn't stop. Besides, half of the bag was filled with air.

"You'd be dead if it weren't for me!" Nessa screamed from inside the bedroom.

"That doesn't excuse what you've done!"

"Your mermaid tried to kill you!"

"This is between us. Leave her out of this." Ian was furious that she would invoke me as an excuse. Their argument continued, but they both lowered their voices.

"Sounds like they're really upset."

"I feel bad for Nessa."

I cocked my brow. "Really?" I didn't think my blatant dislike of her stemmed from mere jealousy. I also hated that she deceived Ian, and she questioned his sanity. I didn't know if she was capable of understanding the depth of how hurtful her actions were to him.

"She can't be all bad. You saw the way she fought to protect Ian." He had a point, but I wondered if Napa would possess such clarity and maturity if Nessa looked differently. Pretty things distracted him.

The door opened, and Nessa barged out. She was surprised to see us sitting on the steps—mortified, actually—but she held her head up high. "Congratulations. You've won."

I did start to feel sympathy for her once I realized her shining eyes were struggling to fight off tears. "It wasn't a competition."

"You're right. I never stood a chance."

Ian leaned against the frame of the door. I sensed he was emotionally drained. "Don't leave, Nessa. There's a storm, and you suck at driving in the rain. I want you to be safe."

"Fine. I'll make myself useful and clean up the place." She snapped her head at me. "I didn't forget that someone trashed it as they tried to kill us."

We made way for her to go downstairs. I wanted to make sure Ian was alright, so I motioned Napa with my eyes to follow after Nessa. "I guess I will go help her."

He left us alone, and Ian threw his head back and groaned. I followed him into the room, and he fell on his back and bounced on his bed. His mind kept repeating how tired he was, which I found strange. He just woke up from being dead.

"Do you think you were a little hard on Nessa?"

"She only found me because I can amplify her magic. I know she loves me, but everyone in my life thinks I'm crazy, or they know I'm not and took advantage of me anyway. She was the only person on my side, but that was a lie. She was using me, too." His memories revealed a story of a man who was holding onto the past and an impossible love, but maybe I didn't read it correctly. He wouldn't feel so betrayed if there were no love between them. It made me question how ready he was to move on.

"Your abilities do make you appealing. My mother encouraged our relationship as soon as she found out. When a witch has children, her power is shared. She could have created new magic with you. You're incredibly special."

I eased onto the bed next to him and took his hand, but the fury in his eyes never subsided. "I don't care. She betrayed me."

"What about us? I tried to kill you."

"You were cursed."

"Well…" His bitterness sent a sweeping chill against my nerves. I was afraid to make my confession. "I set the terms of my blood oath. My father didn't give me many options, but I agreed to kill you."

He sat up and stared at me blankly, but his jaw was tight. He wasn't thinking about anything, but his mind felt hot. His thumb began to rub on my hand, and his mind was soothed. "I don't want to begin to imagine the life you've lived or what your father put you through. I've got some real messed-up people in my own family, and there are things I've been pushed to do that I'm not proud of."

"Like what—?"

"There will be time to discuss those things later. Right now, I want to forget about everything from before. I just want to be with you."

I was grateful he was so willing to forget, but it made me uneasy how dismissive he was of his past. "I should see if my mother is okay. She should be awake by now."

"Wait until the storm clears."

I got up and looked out of the window. Nessa was outside loading a box into her car. I assumed she was gathering some of her memories since they weren't getting back together. She was cursing profusely and soaked to the bone. It had just started a few minutes ago, but it was raining hard enough to hear water crashing against the sidewalk and street. "You know that I live in the ocean, right? What's a little rain gonna do?"

"I don't want to be rude, but you look a little tired."

I touched my face. It was too early to sleep, but I was exhausted. I certainly didn't want to look that way! "Napa and I haven't really rested."

"Take a nap." I noticed he wasn't getting up to let me have the bed.

"All you want me to do is sleep?"

"Yeah." If I had insulted him, he would have laughed it off. He did get off the bed, so he could hold my hand in his and place the other on my hip. I began to recognize the gesture, and I placed my hand on his shoulder. I was so nervous; it felt like a school of fish was alive and well in my belly. I didn't want to step on his feet. I looked down and followed his movements exactly, but he tapped my chin to gaze into my eyes. "We don't have to rush anything. Hopefully, we'll have a lifetime to get to know each other. I'm willing to take my time, be romantic, teach you how to dance…"

He unexpectedly dipped my body back. I gasped and giggled. Ian was rather pleased with himself. My legs flexed up, and he scooped me in his arms and spun around. I wondered if dance was loved by all humans or if it was special because Ian was finally by my side.

"I'm afraid that if I wake up, I'll find out this is just a dream."

"This isn't a fairytale, Luna, and it's certainly not make-believe. This bond between us has to be real. The world out there, that's the dream. We can make it whatever we want."

He sat me down, but the world still felt like it was spinning. I held onto his arms to steady myself. "Do you truly believe the two of us can make it? I know that we're connected, but there's so much we don't know about one another."

"You're mine, and I'm yours. As long as we remember that, the rest should fall in place." I could feel that Ian was a greater and darker mystery than I would have hoped for, but I wasn't pure anymore. If I could see how he handled his darkness, I could better handle mine.

"I'm trusting you with my heart."

"I think I've earned it. I did let you kill me." It was nice that he could laugh about it.

"And I thank you for that." Nessa rejected the idea that I could genuinely love Ian, but my instincts were telling me he was capable of strengthening the bond we felt. I wanted to spend each day with him and test our limits. How much more difficult could our trials be than me feeling the irresistible urge to kill him? I couldn't wait until tomorrow, and the day after, and so on. We would continuously prove to one another how devoted we were, and nothing from either of our worlds would tear us apart. They would all see, soon enough, what the power of true love could accomplish.

I decided to take Ian up on his suggestion to sleep. His bed formed around my body, and his sheets were warm and smooth. I kicked my legs just to feel them slide against the cloth. Even that tiny gesture thrilled me.

I looked above me and saw Ian's amused smile. "I guess you're still pretty excited about the human world, huh?"

"I learned a lot from Napa…" I shot right up in excitement. "May I go inside your mind?"

"Haven't you been doing that enough?" he chuckled nervously.

"I can do more than read your mind. When you're vulnerable, I can see your memories. If you allow me to, I can see your entire life. Imagine how much I could learn!"

I thought going further into his mind would be beneficial to both of us, but I quickly realized that I had committed an egregious intrusion. "I'm completely uncomfortable with that. Don't ever do that to me."

He didn't raise his voice, but his tone certainly felt like rage. "I don't understand. If we want to spend our lives together, why can't I know everything about you?"

"We have to build that type of trust."

He broke me a little. "You don't trust me?"

"That's not what I meant, Luna. Of course, I trust you. How can you ask me that?" I could sort of understand his frustration. He did put his life in my hands. But it boggled my mind why I couldn't be shown the same courtesy with his memories.

"I would show you mine if I could." I didn't know what else to say, and he wasn't speaking. I wanted to respect his wishes, so I resisted the temptation of going inside his mind. I turned from him and rested my head on a pillow.

In the morning, we would find my mother and begin our happy new beginning as a family that could fully love one another. When I opened my eyes again, I would see the world as a free woman. It would take time to grasp the customs of the human world, but I would do my best to accommodate Ian. I genuinely believed he was worth it.

"Ian, wake up."

I woke up to the sound of Nessa's voice around four. Ian had fallen asleep in a chair next to me. I guess Napa didn't want to leave the two of us alone and made himself comfortable on the floor. He was waking up as well.

"There's something wrong..." Napa jumped to his feet to check up on me. "I've still got some of my animal instincts working, and they're telling me to run."

"You're not wrong." Nessa's voice quivered. I was uncomfortable with such a strong woman being terrified. "The governor got on TV and declared a state of emergency. There's a hurricane headed our way."

"No." Ian wiped his eyes to wake himself up. "That's impossible. It's too early in the summer."

"That's not even the weirdest part. It started forming around the Bahamas."

He was puzzled, but as he thought deeper, he shook his head and became more baffled. "That can't be right."

"It's headed straight for Palm Beach. We have to evacuate."

I sat up slowly and watched them discuss the impossible conditions of the weather, but it all sounded like ringing in my ears. The intensity of magic was blocking my sight and ability to hear. I sensed a fury swirling around us, and it bled from the seams that held our universe together. I didn't know my father was powerful enough to force his hateful reach so far. "My father must know you're still alive."

"But he can't hurt you anymore," Napa said. "That's part of your blood oath."

"I'm not the one he's after." I locked eyes with Ian, and he knew. Oddly enough, he didn't seem afraid.

"This is insane." Nessa pulled on his arm. "Ian, we have to go. It's not safe."

"I'm the reason why it's coming. If I run, people will die."

Poor Nessa. When she looked at me, she saw an anchor wrapped around the heart of the man she loved. She lacked the strength to remove me, and he lacked the will to help her. It was maddening for her. "I fought to save you, but I'm not suicidal."

"You should go. I want you to be safe." Ian kissed her hand. The disparity in affection between the two of them was obvious, and it was the last injustice Nessa could bear.

She pulled her hand away. Nessa was furious with him, but she clearly despised me. "You've brought him nothing but death. He will die again—because of you—but he'll be happy. This is what 'true love' gets you."

She ended her rant with an eye gaze at Napa. I questioned what sort of conversations they had while they were alone. He seemed to understand her unspoken warning.

"Nessa—"

"Enjoy your death." I believe she slew her heart at that moment. It was the only way she could leave Ian to die idiotically with me, but I was glad she found the strength to do it. I didn't need another death on my conscience.

"If I kill myself, will that stop it?" I doubted the sincerity of Ian's question. I felt an indignant anger stewing inside of him.

"It's not about you. This is about me." My father received what he wanted, in a way. I corrupted my magic, but he probably expected me to devolve into a murdering psychopath like my mother did after her first kill. Without true love fighting for me, I might have fulfilled his complete wish. "I have to face him. Maybe I can stop him before the hurricane reaches the shore."

"How are you gonna do that?" Napa asked. "You're not strong enough to stop him."

"He can't hurt me. He'll be defenseless."

Ian laughed and threw his hands up. "Considering there's a hurricane headed our way, I'd say he has his ways."

"Where's your mom?" Napa was made a believer in her scary power. He wasn't the only one who would feel a lot safer if she were fighting with me.

"I have no idea. I don't know if there's time to find her." She had more means to find me than vice versa. I had to trust she would get to me. Maybe it took time for her stone body to become flesh and bones.

"Then, you have to use me." Ian wasn't asking or suggesting.

"You should join Nessa and run away from here."

"Or...I can stay and help you kill the man who murdered my parents." Ian had a small grin on his face. If he had any good sense, he would have been terrified of facing my father again. Instead, I sensed an excitement building inside of him.

"Revenge isn't worth your life."

"I don't plan on dying...again. I don't understand this power I have, but I've got a pretty good understanding of what you can do." Ian pointed at me, and though he didn't physically touch me, I felt as though I was shoved in my heart. I clearly owed him my father's death. "I can't walk away from this."

If Ian's life was on the line, being merciful wasn't an option. I couldn't rely on my mother to take the brunt of the responsibility. I had to be ready to kill my father. "Napa—"

"I wouldn't dream of leaving your side." I shouldn't have bothered asking. Napa was loyal to a fault, and Ian earned his respect for proving his loyalty to me. When it came to this battle, they'd be partners. "We can do this together."

"Okay." I took a deep breath. I was petrified of what killing my father would mean for my magic. The new darkness inside of me thirsted for it, and I wasn't sure how to sort out necessity and desire when they intertwined so well. "Let's get ready to battle."

I was right about Nessa having a drawer. I borrowed a pair of black leggings that had sheer slits going up the side of the legs, along with a black tank top. I had a hard time trying to kill Ian in a pair of flip-flops, so I was lucky to find a pair of running shoes in the closet. They were a little snug on my new feet, but much better for a fight.

I didn't destroy all of Ian's weapons. He had a gun and rounds of ammunition stored in a safe downstairs. The attic was probably where he stored his unusual weapons, and some of them were safe. He had a special metal chest that contained a large speargun, made up of six other spearguns, and rigged together. There was a central trigger on the end that pulled a string around the triggers of each gun. Ian nestled it in his arms like a father proud of his child.

"Thank you for not shooting me with that."

"Well, you're lucky that I love you."

Ian was full of surprises, but Napa found something familiar to my mind. He used to hunt with a simple wooden bow, but Ian had a black one made from carbon. Napa kept raising the bow and pulling on the string to test it out.

"I was told it was a good hunting bow, but I've never used it. I never had the time to learn."

"I don't need any lessons," Napa assured. "This should work. If not, I can always turn into a bear and maul King Fish's face off."

It was insane that the two of them were ready to go to war for me. They had an idea what my father's power was like, but they weren't even afraid. If they were, I was impressed with how well they overcame their fear.

"How do you plan on confronting your father?" Napa asked. "Is there a way to draw him on land?"

"He's already here. I can feel him." The magic from his trident was practically choking me. I bet he swam for us as soon as he realized Ian was alive. I doubted whatever power I tapped into for the blood oath would simply let me go. We were still connected. "He's close by."

The lights in the attic suddenly flicked off. There was still some light from the bleak daylight looming through the window, but it felt like a horrible omen. "That's not creepy…" Napa mumbled.

"We should go." Ian looked at me. "If the wind is knocking out powerlines, the storm is only getting worse."

"Then we should head to the ocean." Outside, the world was reacting very differently than us. Many people were packing up their things and leaving. Most had already gone through the night. The people next door to us were nailing boards on their windows. That was probably the smartest approach now. The streets were already beginning to flood. People wouldn't be able to drive for long. There was no way the city would be able to properly evacuate.

The wind was so strong that it destroyed my umbrella as soon as I stepped outside. I let the wind take it and ran to the passenger side of Ian's car. Ian and Napa threw their weapons into the trunk before jumping in. We were all soaked to the bone, and we were only outside for ten seconds. I thought I wouldn't mind the rain, but the sky was abusing us. Also, squishy shoes felt weird.

"Tomorrow is your birthday," Napa refused to sit back in his seat. His face was between me and Ian. "I hope we live long enough to be concerned about getting you a gift."

"Oh, we'll live." I just couldn't promise what I'd be by the next sunrise. My father wasn't going to give up on his named heir so easily. He was going to force that mantle on my shoulders, even if he had to pin it on my back with the trident.

We were headed in the opposite direction from all other cars, and the traffic was bumper-to-bumper. Clearly, the humans didn't have enough time to prepare for a mystical hurricane. Some of the major roads were restricted to direct traffic away from mandatory evacuation areas. Ian took as many backroads as he could, but it was difficult to drive in flooded areas. His car was fashionable, not practical. I tried to direct Ian as he made adjustments. It wasn't an exact science. I just knew that we had to get as close to the ocean as we could.

"He's not far…" My father was pulling on me. He wanted me to find him. He was still angry, but his emotions were more complicated than that. The closer we got, the less anxious I felt. I didn't feel his warrior spirit or thirst for battle, but he was desperate to see me.

Police officers were trying to direct us to turn around, but Ian ignored their signals. He even plowed through a wooden barrier, and they had far more important things to do than chase after suicidal teenagers. We were the only people crazy enough to ignore the sirens and their call to death.

A tingling sensation went down the back of my neck and through my spine. My stomach felt as though it would burst, and I took a deep breath. "Stop."

Ian pumped the brakes. We were on a side street in front of a small bar with big glass windows. There were no lights on inside, but there was a big figure moving around at the bar. I couldn't be certain with my eyes, but the power of the trident made me positive. "He's in there."

"Your father is in a bar?" Ian scoffed. After all these years, it was probably a strange place for him to avenge his parents.

I checked again. The hairs on my arms weren't all standing up for no reason. I nodded, and Ian nearly jumped out of the car. I had to pull him back into his seat. "Wait here for me."

"Are you sure?" Napa asked because Ian certainly didn't want permission.

Ian's eyes were intensely begging me to let him go in and avenge his father. He had a passion for revenge that was just as real as our love for each other, except this was earned. I did not feel like I was being kind, but I also knew that I didn't have a choice. "I'm positive."

I handed Ian the dagger. I knew his guns were very powerful, but the dagger also possessed some magic. If he could find a way to tap into his own power, he could be a real force. I didn't know if it was possible, but it made me feel better. "Stay safe."

I wanted to kiss him. He even inched his neck toward me, but Napa was right behind us. He was begging me in his mind not to do it, so I maneuvered my way to his cheek. To make it fair, I gave Napa a friendly kiss as well.

I jumped out of the car and ran inside the building. My instincts served me well, though my eyes were in disbelief. The space had lots of light wood and fake palm trees inside. My father was casually behind the bar, and he had human legs. He was wearing slick, dark green—maybe leather—pants, and armor on his chest. That was unusual. Even when he left for a kill, he didn't bring armor. He was more arrogant than wise, and he certainly wouldn't have cared about human decency.

His trident leaned against the wall while he played with bottles and glasses. My best chance would have been to steal it for myself, but he was quick for an old man. "Since when did you become a bartender?"

"I've lived a long time. I couldn't complete my life without knowing how to make a few signature drinks." Napa had very little knowledge of alcohol, besides the fact that his mother and uncles liked to drink. I had no idea what liquid he mixed with pineapple and cherry juice to produce a pink and foamy beverage, but he pushed a glass my way. "This was your mother's favorite."

I glanced around the bar. It was seated for thirty or so people, but no one was in my sight. I couldn't smell anything besides the booze, and I couldn't hear what was going on outside, besides the rain pounding the roof, or the wind trying to bend the world of man to its knees. I had a gut feeling that we weren't entirely alone, though. "The humans frown upon giving alcohol to girls my age."

"Suit yourself." My father took the glass and gulped it down. Then, he grabbed the clear bottle and downed that as well.

"You don't seem to be well, Father." He had dark rims around his eyes, and he had broken out in a sweat. If he were drunk, he might have been too slow to stop me from grabbing the trident. It was my best chance.

"That's because I've faced the facts. I'm becoming irrelevant. My task is almost completed; therefore, you'll soon ascend to be my heir."

"I don't want to be your heir!" His obsession was maddening. I failed him at every possible turn, and I planned to continue disappointing him, but he would persist and pursue me until one of us was dead. "I want to run away with Ian."

For a terrifying reason, my father wasn't angered. He giddily chuckled and took another swig from his bottle. "And you are free to live with your human—if you prove he's worth killing for."

I stepped back far enough to make sure the car was fine. The only threat in the area appeared to be the storm, but my heart quivered. Something was coming.

"I had it all wrong," he happily admitted. "I thought forcing you to kill your true love would turn your magic dark, but it barely penetrated you. But your mother was willing to do anything to make sure I was safe from war, including making a blood oath."

"What does that have to do with anything?" I kept inching away from him. I wanted that trident, but I could sense Ian had more to fear than the storm.

When I had gotten too far, my father jumped over the bar. I stepped toward the trident, but he grabbed my arms. "She killed her teacher to get the trident, and each death that followed made her thirst for it. It was her love for me that made her a murderer, and it was my love for her that pushed her to become one. Love fuels darkness." I didn't understand the mystifying awareness he possessed in his eyes before, but I recognized it after seeing Napa's memories. His people were very spiritual and were connected to the world of the supernatural. My father had a belief, and it extended far beyond worshiping Death. Either he had gone mad a very long time ago, or he had been following the wishes of something with a darker heart than his.

"You created this hurricane because you want me to kill you before it kills Ian?" Considering what he just did to my mother, I didn't require such theatrics to want him dead.

"No." He let me go to strut around dramatically. "My death would make an impact, but how much? I've abused you your entire life. I may be your father, but I think I'd barely make a dent. It's got to be bigger than that. How many men would it take? Ten? Twenty?"

His back was toward me, and I was closer to the trident. I had to act!

"A few of your sisters?"

I nearly tripped at the thought of him sacrificing my sisters. They might have been weaker than me, but they shared his bloodlust. If he cared about anyone, I thought it would be them. "What have you done?"

He chuckled so quietly that I could barely hear him above the rainfall. His shoulders slightly shook, and he turned to face me with a benevolent grin. It was the closest I had seen my father to being loving. He was excited to gift something extraordinary to his child. "I'm beginning my invasion, and when I draw my last breath, it will be yours."

His eyes were fanatical. My father genuinely believed he was helping me become strong. How was I supposed to reason with a madman who possessed such clarity?

I made a run for the trident and pushed myself up on the bar. I wasn't nearly as quick or coordinated as I needed to be. Before my feet could hit the ground, it flew past me and into his hand. "This will be yours soon enough."

His trident lit up like a beacon, and there were crashes and screams. I ran to the window and saw men fall from above and land on their feet. I recognized the tribal scars on their backs of mirrored fins, scales, and ocean ripples. They were my father's warriors, marked for battle. Across the street, more Atlanteans came from a building. I saw one of my sisters among them.

Napa and Ian were both alarmed by the sight of Atlanteans armed. There were very few people on the street, so they stood out.

One of the warriors noticed them and began walking over to the car. Ian and Napa climbed out through the passenger side to get away and then ran around to the back to get their weapons. I didn't think they had enough time to arm themselves. I pushed on the door, but a small light flashed brightly enough to temporarily blind me, and I was knocked off my feet.

I heard my father chuckling, and I knew it was his doing. "Release me."

"Soon. I want to let our people wreak a little havoc before you kill them."

I heard a loud noise—like a sequence of thunder ripping holes through the universe—and rushed back to the window. Ian had to use the gun to protect himself. The Atlantean warrior fell, but two others were close to the building, and they were enraged by their slain brethren. Ian continued shooting, but they were fast and learned to dodge his weapon. He kept firing at one while the other ran on top of the car and jumped clear over them. The Atlantean drew his sword, but Napa grabbed his arms inches before Ian could be decapitated from behind. The two of them began a power struggle, but it was clear that Napa was physically outmatched.

Ian had wounded the other Atlantean with a shot to the gut, but it didn't stop him. He grabbed Ian by the neck and lifted him off his feet. Ian desperately pulled the trigger, but he had emptied his clip. Napa couldn't save Ian. He was tossed further away by the Atlantean's superior strength.

I tried to focus on the Atlantean attacking Ian, but my father's barrier disrupted my magic. "How are you this powerful? You're not even a sea witch!"

"There are far greater dimensions of power than you can possibly fathom. Your mother will guide you, and you'll be her aide."

Out of desperation, Ian threw the gun at the Atlantean's nose. It hindered him enough to drop Ian to his feet and stumble backward. Ian removed the dagger from the back of his belt and swiped it across the warrior's throat. The Atlantean shielded his bleeding neck and left himself wide open for Ian to stab his chest quickly—three times. I guess Ian wanted to be certain that he got his heart, and he must have.

Ian was unfazed by his kill, but I had become a bit numb. He rushed to Napa's aid by jumping on the other Atlantean's back and slitting his throat much deeper than he had for the other warrior. As he carved through his skin and severed his arteries and trachea, I thought I witnessed the tiniest smile on Ian's face. When he kicked the Atlantean—one of my people—in the back and knocked him on the ground to wheeze and bleed out, it was clear.

I thought that because I felt his love for me, he would always tether me to being good. I, suddenly, wasn't so sure. My father might have been right about love. It was Ian's love for his parents that fueled his hatred for my father. The blood on his hands might have washed away in the rain, but he'd always be a killer, and he didn't seem to mind.

"I'm not going to kill anyone." It was the only way to make sure that I didn't fulfill my father's wishes.

"So, you'll let those men kill on your behalf? You'll let them taint their souls and leave yours intact?" He chuckled. "It didn't work out too well for your mother, did it?"

I took a deep breath to pacify my rage. I felt warm, and I knew that I was close to losing control. I didn't want to give him the satisfaction of burning him alive. "I can stop the hurricane. I'm stronger than you—"

"You can't even break this barrier. How will you stop a hurricane?"

Ian and Napa ran to the door to let me out, but it wouldn't budge. My father came right behind me to stare at the boy he traumatized. Ian's crazed, raging eyes brought a smile to my father's face. That angered him all the more. He raised his hand to break the glass open, but it violently repelled him and Napa into the middle of the street.

There were still Atlanteans in the area, though most of them had run off to find other humans to kill. I heard women screaming. I had no idea how many men my father deployed and hid. I estimated there were about ten that came from that block. Three were dead, but two more were coming for the boys. "There's no shame in killing in self-defense."

"Do you think your lover is killing out of self-defense?" Ian and Napa got up and retrieved their weapons from the trunk. Napa was faster to arm himself with the bow and arrow. His precision in his memories was unmatched, but the wind was a hindrance. Instead of hitting vital points, he only slowed them down long enough for Ian to grab his absurdly large spear gun.

I watched Ian as he pulled the trigger. He smiled as a circle of spears flew out and dug into one of the warrior's chests. The force knocked him on his back, and he was certainly dead. Ian took the time to celebrate by pumping a fist into his chest. In normal circumstances, I wouldn't have thought there was anything wrong with that, but I had my father buzzing in my ear.

"Your lover fights for revenge, not justice. Your companion kills because it's natural. Men like them would never meet the requirements I needed to be met."

The other warrior came at Napa with a sword, and he dodged out of the way and pulled on his arm. The clothes on his body fell to the ground as he transformed into a small squirrel, quick enough to run off his shoulder and jump off his back before he had time to figure out what was going on. Napa's tiny body scurried down the street, and the Atlantean started to chase him. It was an impossible task. We were fast, but we certainly weren't used to running. Besides, Napa made a quick turnaround once he had enough space to charge.

His tiny limbs expanded, and his neck elongated. His hands became hooves, and bone began to protrude from his head. The majestic creature plummeted straight through the Atlantean that was expecting to catch a cuddly rodent, not be impaled by a powerful buck.

It wasn't an unfamiliar sight to watch Napa struggle to remove his antlers from the Atlantean carcass. I had to pull my claw weapon from the guts of creatures, but I was unnerved. Napa had to revert to his human form to free himself. He merely wiped the blood off his forehead and carried on casually.

"Killing always leaves a mark on your soul," my father warned. "It doesn't matter the reason. It's worse for hearts like yours: filled to the brim with compassion. You get it from your mother. When you take on darkness, you resist it. Your guilt overwhelms you until you finally break. And when you're finally broken, you're ready to ascend."

He threw his head back and sighed in relief. "It's taken one thousand years to make your mother ready, but it will happen today."

The boys were still trying to get me out. Napa was standing by the door, and Ian was reloading his gun. They wouldn't be safe if they waited out in the open for me, and Ian wasn't going to leave if my father was still breathing. More Atlanteans would come for them. I was running out of options.

"You have no power over us." I twirled my chakram and turned to face my father.

"You're right. I have no power at all."

I aimed for his neck to end the fight quickly, but he blocked me with his trident. I aimed for his hands, but he quickly pulled away. I was reminded that he couldn't strike against me, and it made me more confident to attack. I didn't have to worry about the horrible strike of an oppressive father. The best he could do was dodge and run, and he couldn't do that forever. He even pulled some tables and chairs between us, but that only made him look more pathetic. Trapping me in that bar with him was bound to be the very last mistake he ever made.

"Why are you even fighting? What are you trying to prove?" I thought he was open to an attack to the face, but his trident glowed and repelled me through several tables and into the bar. My back cracked as I got back on my feet. I had cut my head on some glass. I had been through worse, but I certainly wasn't expecting it.

"I'm highly motivated not to hurt you. That doesn't mean I can't shield myself."

I tried to laugh at my pain as I moved my hips and arched my back. It was throbbing, but I had been through worse. "Good to know."

I caught a glimpse of a furry animal in the corner of my eye and looked out of the window again. There was another Atlantean body full of spears, but my eldest sister had found the boys. Ian was on the ground, and Napa had transformed into a silver wolf to fight her. Napa had proven a capable fighter, but she was faster than the men he had outmaneuvered.

"Lower the shield," I warned through my seething teeth.

"If you want to overcome my power, you have to take it."

It was near the top of the list of things I didn't want to happen, but Ian and Napa dying were even higher. I let out a scream and ran, as fast as my new legs would carry me, to my father and the trident. I gripped it with my left hand and raised my right to strike him down, but a pulse of power shot out of it. I felt my grip loosen, and my body flung upward. I had to let go of the chakram and pull myself through the force and back down on my feet.

My father was smiling at our duel, but I was disgusted. The trident was an heirloom, passed down through my mother's people. It didn't belong to him. It was rightfully my mother's, and I couldn't allow him to have it any longer!

He was weakening. His hands were firmly gripped around the trident, but they began to singe. His gauntlets burned in an instant, and the ashes flew away in our gust of power. The crescent symbols on his wrist became visible, but they also began to fade. "It's time, my daughter."

"No!" I shook my head. "I'll never—" I arched back and hollered as a new surge of power swept through my soul. My vision blotted out, but I refused to black out and let go of the trident. The magic—the dark source that he worshiped—was gripping around my heart. It was difficult to breathe or to think. All I could do was hold on. I wouldn't allow my father to keep me from saving my friends!

I saw a burst of purple light, and I heard the crash of an explosion as if lightning struck between my father and me. I didn't realize I was thrown from the bar until I heard the whimpering of a wolf in pain.

I took a deep breath, and my vision returned to me. My face was against the asphalt, and Napa's bloody wolf was in the street. I quickly sat up and saw my sister holding a sword against Ian's throat. He was holding his bloody gut, and I knew by her twisted smirk that it was my sister's doing. I knew the trident was in my hand when I heard the bottom of it scrape against the road as I stood. "Let them go."

"Not until you give me father's trident."

"You're too weak to use it."

She grunted and held the blade closer to his neck. "You're in no position to argue with me." More warriors were beginning to surround me—six in total—but I didn't see my father among them. Either he was still inside the building, or he was expelled to the other corner.

"What have you done?" The block was full of empty business buildings, but there were a few slain humans. There was a young couple with two kids with their faces near a storm drain. They must have been pulled from their car. A police officer must have tried to help. His body wasn't too far from theirs. "These people didn't deserve this."

My magic began bubbling up inside of me. I wasn't trying to concentrate and hurt her, but I was infuriated that she would resort to such horrors. Even worse, she offended me with her blatant disrespect. Could she not see the difference between her weakness and my greatness?

"My king told us to go to war. We went to war." But there were very few of them. Even in the midst of the humans hiding and running during the hurricane, it wouldn't be enough. There would be more humans like Ian. My father must have known that.

I was trying to remember any sweet childhood memory that might have kept me from killing her, but all I could recall was her jealousy. The weight of her life became so much smaller when scaled against her foolishness. "He brought you here to die."

Her blade nicked Ian's neck, and a small stream of blood began to pour from his body. "I'll give you until the count of three."

"Don't need it." I tossed the trident to my dear sister, and her thirst for power blinded her to the fact that she was unworthy to wield such a weapon. Everything happened very slowly from then. She released Ian to ready herself, and he crawled away on his hands and knees. He collapsed on his bloody hand from the pain of the wound she caused. My hand was already hot from my rage. Without even needing a thought, I raised my hand and shot a beam of power into my sister's chest.

When the trident hit the palm of her hand, it sent a shockwave across her unstable body. The fool didn't even realize she was dead. A smile was forming on her face as her fingers closed to grip the trident. But that pressure sent another shockwave across her body, and the particles that held her together dispersed. The trident fell to the ground, and my sister was ripped out of existence. She didn't even have magic to leave behind.

"I'm not weak like my father." I turned to the remaining warriors huddled together. They were doing their best not to project fear, but I could smell it. It was an awful lot like the foul smell of death, except it was sweet. "I don't need the trident to control magic. My strength comes from my mother, the Sea Witch!"

As soon as I raised my hand, they dropped to their knees. "We pledge ourselves to you!"

"Spare us, Queen!"

"We beg of you!"

"Beg?" My father emerged from the corner, flinging my chakram into one of their back's. They rose to fight him, but he was king for a reason. He plowed his fist into one of their faces, blowing out their eye socket. He removed that warrior's weapon and used it to decapitate him. I had to hand it to my father; he certainly was an expert at murder. The way his blade and body melded into each one of his victims reminded me of finding the right rhythm to a dance. He was easily the last man standing.

I knew that he couldn't hurt me, but I instinctively reached for the trident, and it flew into my hand. That genuinely pleased my father, and he smirked. "It looks like you're ready to be my heir. The trident is yours."

Something had changed in me. I was overflowing with magic. As I walked by Ian and Napa, I released some of it into their bodies, and their wounds mended. Whatever I had inherited from my father was genuinely incredible. The blood oath opened the gateway, but I was certain my father had—at some point in time—crossed completely over. He had met this dark force, face-to-face.

"I feel its power. I feel the power that connected us together—whatever it is—but I don't feel you. I don't sense the magic you stole from my mother and my siblings. I don't even feel your heartbeat."

He laughed, and his shoulders jolted. He had smiled more in one day than he had in my entire life. I failed to see what was so humorous to him, especially once he removed his plate of armor to show me the gaping hole in his chest. "Your mother took my magic when she stole my heart. It's poetic, don't you think?"

I wouldn't have believed it if I hadn't seen it with my own eyes. I was too curious not to approach him. Instead of blood, it was coated in black goo. There was no exit wound in his back, and it didn't look like there was ever an end to the hole inside him. I didn't even see his organs. He was totally hollow. I almost reached inside of him, but I couldn't bring myself to do it. "How are you alive?"

"I'm not, but I couldn't move on until you had taken my mantle."

I blinked very quickly to fight off a rush of tears that sprang to my eyes. I refused to be sad for him! I didn't even want to mourn my sister. They both deserved to die.

"Are those for me?" Even in the end, he made a mockery of my heart. "Don't insult your lover. I did kill his parents."

Ian and Napa were both waiting for me, but it was evident how difficult it was for Ian. He was looking right through me and at my father. "Stop the hurricane."

"I can't." I hated that I amused him so, but he had a sincere smile with a dash of relief. It was as if he had been waiting all night for us to arrive at that moment. "I'm not the one who made it."

My world began radically shrinking with his confession. I knew what he meant, but I couldn't wrap my mind around it. She genuinely cared for me and wanted Ian to mate with me. "That doesn't make any sense. Why would my mother—?"

"To distract you. After my death, she only had one more commitment to fulfill. She trapped Atlantis in her own barrier. She couldn't allow you to stop her. They were the only ones that escaped."

I looked at the dead Atlanteans. Their bodies were becoming hard white husks, and the same transformation began happening to my father. It started with his legs and rose from there. It was the beginning of his literal end. I should have been celebrating, but I couldn't stop myself from crying. "Why didn't you ask for my help to stop her?"

"Because my life is over, and your inheritance was never about our people. It was about power." He held my face. "Because of you, I realized the only way to release that power was to let your mother fulfill her oath."

I pulled away and punched my father in his face. The impact cracked all of my knuckles, and he only moved his head, but it was mildly satisfying. I wished I could have done more. "If I am truly like her, she'll return to how she was before you ruined her. She'll be kind and compassionate. She'll be—"

"Broken." There was a song in his voice, though he never sang. His body completely solidified into a soft white crust with a sliver of a smile on his lips. I had watched a tyrant fall, and he left the world in total peace. I didn't understand what I needed out of his death. Maybe there was nothing I could have done to pacify the neglect and manipulation. I'd always carry his scars and the weight of what he had made me.

"Is it over?" Ian came to my side and took my hand. It was sweet of him to hide his happiness.

"He's gone." The wind picked up, and his body softened and bubbled up into foam clumps. In seconds, the strong winds blew my father and the warriors out of my life forever. I should have felt free, but I was more terrified than I had ever been in my life.

"I have to get to the ocean." I picked up my chakram and took off running as fast as my human legs would carry me. Ian and Napa followed me through alleys and backyards of family homes. I could feel that we were close. I could smell salt and the scorched sky from the lightning bolts dancing in the atmosphere.

When we got to the shores of the beach, the aggressive waves were there to greet our feet. A dawning sun should have filled the sky with rustic and warm oranges, exploding through the clouds in pale pastels. Instead, the sky was a murky blue, and the darkest cluster of gray was fast approaching. The waves were rushing like a mob of people fighting to beat each other to freedom. I had no personal fears from the storm, but I could hear Napa whimpering.

"What about the hurricane?" Ian's voice quivered.

I wasn't sure if I was stronger than my mother, but she had mastered her powers. I simply had no idea what to do. If I opened myself up to the darkness my father served, I think it would have shown me. It would have given me the strength without putting Ian's life at risk. But…the consequences of doing that—of using such dark magic—would be too great. "I can't stop it."

"We have to try." Sweet Ian grabbed my arms and pleaded with his gorgeous eyes. He truly would risk his life to save others. I wasn't sure how to sort that out with the lives he had taken. I needed time, but I could already feel my father's spell breaking down in my body.

I slipped out of his arms and bent down to Napa. His fur should have been soft and fuzzy, but it was wet and matted. He took liberty with his form and licked me in the face. I laughed because licking my mouth as a wolf was still more pleasant than the bloody kiss. "Take care of Ian. Get him somewhere safe." I knew that I could trust him. Napa never disappointed me.

I couldn't bear to say goodbye to Ian, but he wouldn't let me slip away. "Where are you going?"

I glanced at his hand on mine. If I allowed myself to have a moment with him, he would have distracted me with hopes for our future. My love for him hadn't dampened in the slightest. Considering the amount of violence that we brought into each other's lives, I questioned the sanity of our union. It scared me how much I needed him. "If I live, I'll be on that island I took you to. Do you understand?"

"Luna, whatever you're doing—"

"I'm sorry, I have to go." I took a chance and used a small bit of my magic to knock him back on the ground. He was well enough to jump to his feet, and I retaliated by pushing out more of my magic and willing it into a small dome, around the two men I loved.

Ian immediately pressed his hand against the invisible barrier, but he would never be able to make it budge. I couldn't blame Ian for beating against it, once it dawned on him that I was leaving them both behind.

Napa cried out in howls and begged me to free them. They didn't want me to face what I had to alone, but I think they were also frightened of the oncoming onslaught. I wasn't concerned, though. I might not have known how to stop the hurricane, but my barrier was a lot safer than his car or hiding in a building. They would live through the crisis.

"I know that this will be terrifying, but you will be safe." I was honestly more worried about whether or not they'd be able to stomach me after my mother's magic destroyed the city.

"And what about you?" Napa asked.

Ian's eyes were fixated on mine. His gaze had a way of cutting through any posturing and straight to the truth. It must have been a trait developed from surrounding himself with liars. "I have to do this."

"Luna, don't go."

I immediately walked away. I refused to allow him to steal the strength I mustered up to do what needed to be done. If I didn't find a way to save my mother from herself, there was no hope for any of us.

Chapter Seventeen

My legs were considerably weaker than my tail. I couldn't understand how Ian became such an expert diver and swimmer. The waves tossed me in circles, disrupting my orientation, and this was happening while my bones were shifting. I kicked off my shoes and ripped my leggings and underwear with my hands to alleviate some of the pressure. My legs fused, and the bones in my legs tore out of their sockets and reformed together to make my tail. The pain was brief when my father cast the spell, but it was incredibly intense. Reverting back only happened a bit slower, but the pain was more radical. I hoped that the boys couldn't hear me screaming underwater.

A flash of light rippled through my legs, and a shimmer of green collided downward into my newly formed fin. It twitched, and I instantly felt stronger. It wasn't just my strength to swim. I could feel my stronger form again.

The temperature of the water was schizophrenic as the sediments from the shallow areas mixed with the water closer to the surface. Even with the strength of my mermaid tail, I wasn't strong enough to swim through the raging storm, fueled with the full force of my mother's restored magic. I didn't have time to consider if I would be too tempted by my stronger form. My desperation to reach my mother was enough motivation to spark the transformation. The added power surging through my muscles allowed me to easily dive deeper and cut through the chaos like a torpedo.

To say I didn't feel different would have been a lie. If I had the time to focus on anything other than stopping my mother, I would have realized how natural it felt to be a sea witch. It was ironic. When

I was small, I wanted to look more like my mother because I believed it would connect us. I wished for all the wrong things with the wrong woman. And when I triggered my first transformation, I rejected my prayer, because I was too ignorant to know any better.

I hoped that when the Sea Witch laid eyes on me, our connection would be strong enough to pull her from the darkness. She was in my bones, my blood, and her magic was inside of me. She was in my eyes, my skin, and my radiantly shining silver hair. I wasn't afraid to be like her, now that I knew there was always good inside. I couldn't allow her to fade into the abyss. We had been through too much!

When I was exiled and alone, all I wanted to do was get back home to where I would be safe. I wanted a chance to survive. The Sea Witch offered me that, and she gave me a family. I was hoping that I could one day repay her kindness. I never expected her to reconcile with my father—he had done far too much—but I wanted us all to have a chance to regain some sense of family. I wished there was still time to find a way to be happy.

I focused on a fantasy to fuel me forward. Ian and I were married in a little home by the beach. We greeted my mother at the door, embraced her with a hug and a kiss, and it felt normal to be affectionate with one another. After stepping inside, she noticed a framed picture of an ultrasound sitting on the fireplace. She'd smile and touch my swollen belly. My mother would laugh and comment on how she couldn't wait to spoil our little girl. That would spark a tiny pang of jealousy. I'd be reminded of all the things I never got to have or experience as a child, but I'd also be grateful that my mother was given a second chance. In her glistening eyes, I'd see such relief in the fact that we escaped a horrible nightmare, and I wouldn't need to read her mind to know what she was thinking. I'd feel her, just as I felt our future inside of me.

It was such a beautiful lie. It didn't fade from my mind until I felt a massive wave of death ripple throughout my body.

It was eerie returning to the familiar waters of my home. The pit of my stomach sank to my tail when I realized the barrier was down. The silence was so overwhelming, I could hear the blood flowing through my own body. I couldn't feel anyone's mind. I didn't even feel vibrations from anyone other than me. It was darker than I remembered. The blue crystals that built our walls were broken and scattered against the ocean floor. They were scorched and scratched from some kind of fruitless battle. I had no stomach to continue, and I had barely breached my home.

Then, the atmosphere changed. I felt the energy of the dead huddled together and screaming throughout my body. I could feel that it was too late, but I had to be certain. I had to witness the genocide with my own eyes.

I jerked back and covered my screaming mouth when I saw the first corpse. It was withered away—practically a skeleton—with glossy black gunk for skin. It still had eyes, but they were yellow and glowing. It didn't have any thoughts or life, but it moaned in agony. It didn't have any arms, and its tail was crumpled and sticking to the floor. It writhed around, screaming in hoarse whispers until it solidified into a mound of dirt and bones. It wasn't the only one. Everyone I had ever known in my kingdom was gone.

It seemed pointless to cry in the middle of the ocean, but I couldn't help myself. I could feel the only mind there, distraught with grief. I followed the trail of bodies to my father's throne. She was there with her face buried in the marble chair and shaking as if her shame were freezing her to death. She wouldn't even look at me.

"Mother…" It was difficult to look past what she had done. There were corpses surrounding the throne, huddled and fused. My sisters were among them somewhere, but they were indistinguishable from one another. We used to all stand out together in an array of beautiful colors ranging from golds, blues, and reds. We shared similar traits, but our hair and tails were as diverse as an ecosystem of coral reefs thriving with life. Their hair had whitened and fallen out. Their tresses were scattered about like the touch of a spider's web, barely thin enough to see.

I couldn't see the abuse and the petty atrocities I suffered under their care. The horrors of their death wiped away the bitterness reserved in my heart, and I was left feeling the vacuum of their loss. The world was empty now, and it killed me that I didn't even realize they held such a profound place in it. I didn't understand why their loss devastated me so. Perhaps I realized that their behavior wasn't entirely their fault. When you're born inside of a nightmare, the monster is your default nature. If they had found a reason to love— just like I did—they could have awakened into a new world with me.

"Mother…" I couldn't even afford to be angry if I wanted to save her. "…please, look at me."

She pushed her head further into the throne until the marble began to split. I sensed that her strength was alarmingly glorious, and I feared what would happen to me in an unstable outburst. "You shouldn't have come, Luna."

After everything we had been through, how could she expect me to abandon her? "Mother, please!"

She hesitantly did as I asked. The crack in her chest never healed, but she didn't bleed. It was almost like a natural deformity, except for a purple light peeking from within it. Beyond the ominous glow, I sensed a major shift in her spirit. I could feel that she was lighter—perhaps even more beautifully brighter than myself—but I saw that in her radiating eyes, she was broken. "I killed your family."

"It wasn't you!" I dropped the trident and swam to grab her face. I wouldn't let her hide from me. I needed her to look into my eyes and know that I was willing to fight for us. I couldn't afford to face another heartbreak, especially from someone I genuinely loved. "You have to forgive yourself. Please."

My mother saw right past my willingness to forgive and clung to the travesties she committed against me. Her lips trembled, and she whimpered in my arms. "Humans are dying right now. I killed my family and my friends…" The light in her chest began to glow brighter. My curiosity was greater than my fear, so I peeked inside her. I didn't see any muscle, tissue, fat, or even the blood that we used to share. She was hollowing out like my father.

"You did it all for love," I quickly reminded her with a desperate smile. "You have to remember that you can love."

"That makes it all worse." I didn't know how to make her self-hatred subside. I was honestly furious with her, even though I knew mysterious forces pushed us into our predicament. The curse pressed me to kill Ian in a day. I couldn't imagine what was in her head after a thousand years of manipulation.

"Don't do that." Believing in love was the only reason our paths crossed. If she cared for me at all, she shouldn't have ruined my belief. If I didn't subscribe to the doctrine of fate-changing love, my purpose in this world would wither into one of those awful husks. "Love makes us better. It can save anyone."

"It didn't save me…" It was difficult to see her as my mother in that moment. She retreated into a young girl from a thousand years ago. That girl trusted a boy, and she learned entirely too late that he was wrong for her. I never wanted to be that girl, but I did question if I was capable of being just as blind and naïve.

My mother moaned and tried to turn her body from me once more. The purple light continued to spread, and I sensed her presence thinning out. I didn't have time for her to doubt herself.

"Don't let go," I begged with everything I had. If she could only resist the darkness a little bit longer, we could be free. I could marry Ian in a few years and give her a couple of grandchildren. She could finally hold a child in her arms. There were so many possibilities. All she had to do was choose to hold onto me. "Don't you dare leave me again!"

The Sea Witch continued to weep as she held my face. In it, I'm certain she saw herself before the mistakes. She was young, beautiful, and foolishly optimistic. She didn't see a monster with blue skin and glowing eyes. She was just an ordinary girl, searching for love, in a world that didn't love her back. We understood each other's fears, and we knew the trauma of suffering through neglect and abuse. But we had spent enough time together to know that there was hope. The inspiration to live—the spark of magic I had been searching for—was strong enough between us. "I'm here, Mother. I'm here, and I'm not letting go."

She managed to smile as she admired the features we both shared, but my heart continued to ache as I watched her eyes settle on the harsh reality. The Sea Witch had lived too long and had done too much. She would never dare to have faith again, because she had already learned the truth of who she was. "I don't deserve you. I never did."

"Mother, no!" She pushed me away with a bit of her natural strength, but mostly with a gust of her magic. There was smoke rising out of the light, and it blotted out everything surrounding her. Our family's trident was also swept up in its wake.

I considered braving through the darkness to pull my mother out, but I sensed she had changed again. The lighter spirit had ruptured in the blast. All I could sense was a ravenous hunger from the smog. If it weren't satisfied after consuming the power of the Sea Witch, I quaked in horrendous fear of what it would do to me.

I'm ashamed to say that I didn't stop when her magic finished pushing me out of the throne room. I continued to swim away from the smoke that engulfed my home. It fed off the energy of my mother's victims, and I didn't want to be next.

I was too late. It might have been by a day or by a thousand years—I don't know—but I knew that I never wanted to see her again. My mother was gone, and I had no idea what horrible force would be wearing her face—our face—when I saw it again.

Chapter Eighteen

I crawled up on the shore of the tiny island I brought Ian to. The pain of growing legs and changing back was so vivid; it wasn't difficult to replicate the transmutation. The wonder of having legs had been sucked out of me, though. I collapsed on the beach and cried on the sand for hours. I was starving, but I couldn't find the mental strength to get up and hunt for food. I probably wouldn't pick up a berry if it dropped in front of my face.

A cold nightfall came, and a gloomy morning sky followed afterward. I think I fell asleep at some point. There were gaps of time missing from staring out at the dark ocean. I was always aware of the danger of my world, but I was legitimately frightened to go back.

Whatever the Sea Witch became was waiting for me. I could feel her pulling on my magic as strongly as the day I met her. Did that mean there was a familiar part of her that I could reach? And if there was a piece of her that remembered our bond, did that make her more dangerous? I couldn't remove my father's rants from my mind. Was love just a curse?

I thought I was too drained—mentally and physically—to shed any more tears. Then, suddenly, they burst from me like a wave exploding against a cliffside. When I touched the crescent moon embedded in my flesh, I shook and wailed like a dying animal trapped in man's world and suffocating. My father played a long game with my mother's soul, and he came out with a victory. I couldn't help but feel that his plans for me extended far beyond his death.

I thought all my other birthdays were horrible. Clearly, I hadn't lived long enough. Four years ago, I was abandoned by my father. Why was I surprised that the Sea Witch would do the same?

I wanted the boys to find me, but I knew it would take time. I was confident that my barrier protected the boys from the storm. Many boats would have been destroyed, but Napa wouldn't allow me to be alone. He would grow a tail and chase me to the ends of the world, and Ian would follow. I just had to be patient…

…but I was afraid I had already lost them. I was so determined to get to my mother that I didn't realize how cruel I had been. Once again, I trapped Ian within my grasp, while he was helpless to save anyone. I would have never forgiven him for committing such a crime against me, and I had betrayed him twice.

Maybe Napa and Ian weren't coming for me. Maybe that was for the best. It was better that I was alone. I couldn't be hurt by the ones I loved, and I couldn't hurt others for them.

The sun rose to its highest point and began to lower. The scorching sun had browned my skin by a few shades, but my cheeks were hot from a slight burn. I had found the strength to sit up with my knees pressed under my chin, but that was all. I didn't want to leave in case I was wrong about what I wanted. I needed to know if it was possible to revive my heart, and I was certain that the faces of the men I loved would be the key to its resurrection.

But even if I could be reborn, was it better to slay the heart of a beast before it could roam free? Did I deserve a chance to redeem my family? I didn't honestly think so.

In the distance, I saw a glimmer of white and gray. As it got closer, I was overwhelmed with guilt from my past and fear of my future. Was it possible to overcome what I had done and what I had been through? Happiness was such a fragile thing, and my insecurities were strengthened through the years of struggle. How could I overcome myself after creating such impossible odds?

But when I saw a seagull soaring through the sky and heading in my direction, I burst into tears. I trusted that Napa would find a way to survive, but I was so relieved to see him landing from the sky with his wings extended out like a guardian angel.

He landed his human feet on the beach, and I ran into his arms. "You came back for me."

"Of course, we did." I could hear from his shaky voice that he was flustered. He was also blushing. "Did you not want us to?"

I started to speak, but I wanted my answer to be honest, and I just wasn't sure. "It's good to see you both."

He took my hand and pulled me toward the water. Ian had steered a boat close enough for me to see his smiling face, but he wasn't getting any closer. "I brought you a birthday gift. And there's food on the boat. Come on."

I flinched when my feet hit the waves, but Napa jumped into the water without hesitation. I was embarrassed that I wasn't a very good swimmer as a human, and I had mentally surrendered the domain to my mother. I couldn't explain that to Napa. Even if I described to him what I had witnessed, he couldn't feel the darkness as it swept through my home and sucked the energy from everyone I had ever known. Napa couldn't hear it calling out to him like a steady hum in the background. I shouldn't have recognized my mother's singing voice, but I could feel her song rattling my bones. No matter how far I swam, the darkness was never going to let me go.

I tried to control my fear as I came into the water. Ian was watching, and I didn't want to appear weak in front of him. My body was trembling so much that it was difficult to paddle my arms and legs. I dunked my head in the water to hide my tears from the boys, but that only intensified my terror. The water was much darker than I remembered, and the humming increased in volume. With each agonizing stroke, the notes grew louder until I could feel her breath tingling my ear. I had to hurry. I couldn't let her take me!

I leaped out of the water like a clumsy fish flopping along. Napa offered his hand and helped me onto the diving platform. I clutched onto his chest while I gazed into the peaceful sea. I alarmed him with my sudden clinginess, but he wasn't complaining. "You okay?"

"Of course." I forced myself to calm down. It was silent in my head. Perhaps my fears were making me paranoid. I couldn't let the boys see that my imagination was bleeding into reality. I had to be strong.

Ian was also standing on the platform. He wanted to sweep me off my feet in an epic kiss, but I went in for a hug instead. I could tell that I made things extremely awkward between us, but it was impossible to feel anything other than horror and guilt.

I let him believe my indifference was due to my indecency, which I couldn't have cared less about. The boys must have had one heck of a time surviving the hurricane, buying a boat, and sailing to an uncharted island in the middle of the Atlantic Ocean, but they still found time to buy me a pretty dress. After a long shower, I emerged from the bathroom wearing the shimmering silver dress that went down to my knees. I assumed Ian bought it, but they were both gawking at me like I had given them something. It was very strange for them both to be so in love with me, while I was considering spending the rest of my existence alone.

"You look beautiful!" Of course, Napa was the first one to break the ice. I think he lost his sense of shame somewhere between being a chicken and a teenager.

"Thanks." I tried to avoid their eyes, but I made contact with Ian. "What happened to your home?"

The two of them exchanged glances that equated to some kind of unspoken manual, but beyond their infatuation with me, they were traumatized. "When the storm broke, Napa turned into a merman. We tried to follow you, but we didn't know where to look. We figured the best way to find you was to come here. I had faith that you'd find a way to the island. After all, you're a survivor."

"That's not what I asked." I took a step closer to Ian and grabbed his hands. I wanted to respect his privacy, but I could hear his mind screaming. Winds and rain must have ripped the world until the eye offered a false sense of relief. I imagined them prepping themselves for the continuation of abuse, struggling not to shake and scream before it continued. But once it did, they were free to be terrified.

When the hurricane passed over them, and my barrier broke, they must have turned around to face the damage. Even if they felt they had no time, they swam hundreds of miles and sailed to me. I didn't accept that the two curious young men didn't take the time to look it up on a phone or a television. Everyone in the whole world must have known about the devastation caused by my mother's madness, except for me.

They agreed not to speak about it, but Napa couldn't resist a good glare from me. He broke down after a heavy sigh. "It was more than a hurricane. There were tornadoes and—"

"It's your birthday," Ian insisted with a quivering voice. Even his hands were trembling. "I don't want to talk about it."

"Ian—"

"A lot has happened," he snapped at me and, instantly, regretted it. His eyes were always rocksteady, but he had been shaken. I sensed he blamed me—to a degree—but I think he mostly had guilt weighing on his mind. I was too intimidated by the burden to go inside and see. "There's obviously a lot to say, but I just want to focus on something good right now."

Ian kissed me on the cheek and went outside to the deck, but he had grabbed a lighter off the counter before he went out. I figured I should give him a minute. Our priorities were too different anyway.

How could I stand to be with a man I had crushed so many times? I feared that Nessa was right. Even if he chose to focus on his infatuation with me, how could he overcome his bitterness?

"We need to go back to Ian's house and burn the rags Nessa used to clean up my blood."

"Oh, she threw those away. She was very adamant about having a biohazard lying around." My brows furrowed, and Napa became flustered. "Not that I think you're especially a biohazard, but—"

"Napa…" Nessa didn't strike me as a kind person who would volunteer for anything she didn't have to do. I thought she was desperate to separate herself from Ian and me, but it didn't sit right at the time. "Are you sure she didn't steal the rags with my blood?"

"Why would she do that?"

"For spells!"

His face was blank, for half a second, before he nodded in firm agreement. "She did it. She's a very ambitious girl." He spoke as if he admired her. When I had the time to care, I would have to interrogate Napa and find out if something went on while Ian and I were sleeping.

"We have to find Nessa and stop her before she does anything with my blood." I feared that it would provoke the darkness ashore, and I didn't want to be responsible for causing Nessa more pain.

"Tomorrow."

"No, we have to—"

He did the only thing he knew to shut me up. He kissed me. It was quick, so I was a little surprised by how long I felt his warm touch afterward. It definitely topped the list of our kissing experiences, but I didn't feel a brightness in my chest, or a tingle in my fingers, or anything else Ian made me feel. I'm sure he could physically please me—if I allowed him—but Napa didn't need to be a merman to know that I wasn't breaking my heart's current commitment. My eyes revealed his place in my world. "I'll give you two a minute."

I didn't have the energy to constantly fight the two of them over my birthday, so I went outside to the deck and played along with their trivial game. Ian was sitting in front of a white cake lit with seventeen candles. It was sweet, but normalizing what we had been through, or dismissing it, wasn't what I wanted to do. I didn't want to play pretend, but it was difficult to break his heart.

I sat down across from Ian, and he instantly burst into smiles. "This reminds me of a movie. I'll have to show it to you, one day."

"One day…" It was such a simple phrase that was meant to hold such incredible promise. He couldn't have known all of what my "one day" meant, and who I longed to spend it with. My idiotic illusion of a grandmother congratulating her children drifted beyond the horizon and into a realm that I could no longer see. I tried to smile with Ian, but my lips involuntarily quivered. I was ruining such a pretty sunset with my tears.

"Luna, please don't cry." It was a brave thing to say, but he turned his head to hide his reddening eyes.

"But everything is wrong!" I was never willing to abandon my mother if it meant her life would be ruined, but that's exactly what I did. "My mother is lost to me. She was overtaken by some dark force that my father served, and he shackled me to it. I'm afraid to use my powers. I don't want it to find me, but I don't know if I can escape it."

I felt like a tyrant for mourning her loss after what she had done to his home. "You must hate me."

"I could never hate you, Luna." His tone didn't inspire confidence in our relationship, and I didn't want pity to hold us together.

"You must hate me. I would hate me…" I didn't want to cry over my cake, so I got up and walked over to the railing. So many were dead because I couldn't anchor the Sea Witch, and there would only be more bloodshed. I think what truly broke my mother was that I witnessed the horrors she had done, and she knew that she had disappointed and hurt me. I didn't want Ian to break me in a similar manner. I couldn't take him discovering that I was a monster, and it was only a matter of time before my terrifying nature was revealed. I was, after all, a sea witch.

"I'm sorry. I know you loved her." I felt his strong chest against my back and his lips on my shoulder. There was still too much I didn't know about his past, and he had a darkness within his heart that could have easily multiplied in my own. I desperately yearned for the strength to walk away and leave Ian forever, but I trembled in his arms.

It never became more apparent how messed up we were for each other until that embrace. Why was he choosing to look past the damage my family had done? His heart could not easily forgive others. Ian taught me, with a spear gun, that he was not content with being a victim. He was a warrior, and he certainly had enemies. Why wasn't I among them, and who did he desire to destroy? "What if we're not good for each other?"

"I refuse to accept that."

I could feel his heart beating through my chest. Our breaths synced together, and my fingers tingled as if I were stroking a storm cloud. I felt his power charging my body, and my eyes brightened. Even though I was petrified of using my magic, he stirred my thirst for fulfilling our potential. I wasn't sure if I could resist the temptation to quench my desires, and if I indulged—just a little bit— I knew that I would never be satisfied. "What if we're not good for the rest of the world?"

He gently guided my body to turn toward him, and he held my face. He felt so good against my skin. Perhaps he meant to seduce me, but he couldn't have known how dangerous his affections for me were, and my will to resist him was quickly slipping away. "You are my world. Everything else is just a dream."

And with that, I gave myself permission to fall into the madness of Fate's desires. I threw my arms around his neck, and he dove into my lips. No matter the cost, I knew we were connected. It frightened me—more than anything—how devoted we were becoming to one another, but it also thrilled me. I had finally found what I wanted to live for. How many I was willing to kill on his behalf was yet to be determined. I loved him, and I was willing to take on Ian's hopes and scars to prove it.

I spent the rest of my sunset in his arms, swaying to a rhythm trapped between the two of us. Were we made for good or chaos? Destruction or creation? I had no idea. But I was certain about one thing: I was willing to find out.

God help you all.

Continue Luna's Journey

THE
SEA WITCH
CURSED WATER SERIES
CHRISTINA L. BARR

Enjoy these companion titles from the *Cursed Universe*:

For more titles, visit http://www.ninjadustpublishing.com.

Don't forget to follow us on these social media platforms:
Facebook: https://www.facebook.com/ninjadustpublishing
Twitter: https://twitter.com/ninjadustpub
Instagram: https://www.instagram.com/christinalbarr/
Youtube: https://www.youtube.com/user/NinjaDustOfficial

www.ingramcontent.com/pod-product-compliance
Lightning Source LLC
Chambersburg PA
CBHW050342030726

47503CB00008B/2568

* 9 7 8 0 6 9 2 9 4 5 3 4 6 *